LOST CONTACT

edited by
Max Booth III & Lori Michelle

PMMP

Perpetual Motion Machine Publishing
Cibolo, Texas

Lost Contact
Copyright © Perpetual Motion Machine Publishing 2021
All Rights Reserved

ISBN: 978-1-943720-64-4

PERPETUAL MOTION MACHINE PUBLISHING

www.PerpetualPublishing.com

Cover Art by George Cotronis
Interior Illustrations by Luke Spooner
Interior Layout by Lori Michelle

STORIES

IN THE WIND

Michael Paul Gonzalez

THE SUN WAS GONE. The Wyoming wind sliced through Chico's shirt like it was an open window to his heart. He bent closer to the ground to look at the jacket pinned under one end of a seesaw. A satin Denver Broncos jacket, one elbow frayed and threadbare. It looked like Nando's jacket, because it was. The two small plastic legs jutting from the pocket looked like Nando's favorite action figure, because it was. The one Chico got him for his birthday, that he carried to help him feel safe.

The way the gravel on the playground was disturbed could be from anything, kids playing earlier in the day, after-school programs. But it was long after dark and Nando's favorite jacket was on the ground. It wasn't supposed to be here. Maybe he got hot. Sometimes he got hot, even in winter.

The way the collar was torn.

The blood on the sleeve.

The blood on the sleeve.

What was that. What *was* that? Nando wasn't supposed to have come here. He just wanted to play with their walkie-talkies. Chico had his. Someone else had Nando's.

Leave the jacket. Leave it because he'll come back for it. Leave it because it's his favorite. His prized figure was in there. What the hell was his codename, Grizzly? Kodiak? Some kind of bear. Heavy weapons specialist. Nando was only eight. He used to cry that Chico couldn't walk him to school because he'd been bullied a couple of times. It had been Chico's idea to get him the figure as a kind of secret bodyguard. It had done wonders for Nando's confidence. Maybe too much.

Are you here? Are you ready? A man's voice, deep and rough like sandpaper, heavily distorted by the small speaker on the radio.

The sound shot an electric jolt of fear down his spine. His thumb locked, hovering over the button to respond. He stared at his walkie-talkie, trying to decide if the smartest thing to do was answer or stay quiet. His brother's life might depend on it. *His* life might depend on it.

When he realized Nando had disappeared, he thought, *I'm dead.* When Mom finds out. When Dad hears about this. And he felt like he deserved it. Mom wouldn't be off work until midnight, and Dad wouldn't be home for another week. It didn't happen often, and Chico took his responsibilities seriously. Why had he ignored Nando tonight? To watch movies? Nando wanted to play, insisted on using their new walkie-talkies while they played with army guys while they played with nerf guns, that hyper-sugar-fueled mania where he demanded every kind of attention, wanting to play three things simultaneously, refusing to sit still.

Chico had tried to hide out, parked in his room in front of the tiny hand-me-down TV, the one they'd gotten the same day they got the radios. Dad came home from what he called a government field trip and set a cardboard box next to a giant white trash bag, asking "who wants the box and who wants the bag?" Someone had retired or moved bases or gotten arrested or something, and Dad grabbed a couple of things. Nando saw comic artwork through the white plastic and that was enough. He chose the bag, a mountain of classic comic books. Chico got the box, thinking it would be more comics or action figures, but it was a TV. Thirteen inches, color, two-dial VHF/UHF, glorious.

Nando wasn't mad, because he always got the hand-me-downs. Dad had a cool jacket. He'd give it to Chico, Chico would eventually grow bored with it, and then it would become Nando's jacket. Then, as always, there was a "both-of-you" present for getting a glowing report of good behavior from Mom. The walkie-talkies. Military grade. Huge and heavy and built for adventure. Nando made Chico swear an oath in front of their parents that they'd play with them at least once a week. That was three weeks ago, and Chico had had enough.

Now, standing here in the middle of the darkened school playground, clutching a radio in one hand, staring at his brother's coat, waiting for a reply that wasn't coming, he wished he'd said yes. Wished he'd gone running around the backyard. How hard would it have been to just give Nando orders over the walkie-talkie every five minutes?

He was watching Friday Night Video Fights on MTV while Nando chirped in a few times over the radio. Eventually Nando got annoyed that he could hear Chico's voice in the house more than he could hear it over the speaker. Nando wanted to try them outside. Chico said it was cold. Nando said he was going outside to test the range. He bet these walkie-talkies would work all the way from school, or maybe farther. He said he was taking backup and not to worry, wiggling Grizzly or Kodiak or whatever the action figure was in Chico's face. Chico nodded, not even making eye contact, he muttered something about staying in the backyard. He'd placated the first few broadcasts, giving one-word answers. Not realizing the reason Nando was only saying things every few minutes was that he was trying to get farther and farther from home to test the range.

Chico had no idea when the radio had gone silent. He yelled out to see if Nando was hungry for dinner, got ready to make the usual latchkey mac n' cheese that was his specialty. When Nando wouldn't answer, Chico stalked around the backyard looking for him to no avail, eventually remembering the walkie-talkie.

"Nando?"

Silence.

"Hawk?" That was his codename, he insisted, and sometimes the only thing he'd answer to. "Hawk, where are you? Chow time!"

Nothing. Chico's heart sank.

Come and see. Come and find him. He thought you'd hear him from the school . . .

Chico skidded to a halt. The Voice was heavy and deep like a demon's. Hard like Kyle's dad down the street, like there was a layer of something explosive underneath that you had to be careful not to set off. Maybe this was crossed signals. Maybe he was getting a conversation or picking up a cordless phone or something. That happened sometimes.

The elementary school was a mile away. "Nando. This is serious now. Tell me which way you went. You gotta come home now. You were supposed to stay at the house. If I find you at the school, I'm gonna kick your butt all the way home."

Where's home? Tell us, maybe we'll bring him to you.

Chico started to jog to the neighbor's house, but all the lights were out. Every house nearby, every adult he could think to try, they all seemed to be out.

Come and see, now, while you can. Don't stop for help. Don't tell anyone. You don't have much time.

Someone was out there, someone who knew where Nando had been. Chico fast-walked toward the school. Nando was a creature of habit. Anything outside the universe of their block had to be traversed through the same routes. He always stuck to Green River Road when he walked to school because the traffic up on Dell Range scared him at night. There were two houses with dogs on the way, maybe he'd stopped there. His friend Kevin was a couple of blocks from the school. Maybe he'd gone there and they were playing games, and he just turned off his radio and forgot. Maybe—

He won't be here long. He waurhg—

The radio descended into garbled static. Chico couldn't make out the words. He ran faster. He'd gotten to the school and found the jacket. He waited for Nando to poke his head out and admit he was playing a terrible joke.

The night was silent and he was alone. His knees shook and his jaw trembled. He couldn't feel his fingers.

The sound of heavy metal popped across the air, a van door unlocking and sliding open.

Chico squatted, scanning his surroundings for movement. He was at least fifty yards from the street, plenty of ground between him and anyone that might be out there. He didn't see any headlights. Hadn't heard a van pull up.

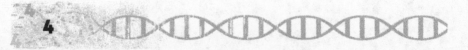

IN THE WIND

He wished he'd grabbed a warmer coat. He wished this walkie-talkie worked like a phone, that he could call people like he saw the rich people on Airwolf or the A-Team do. Was *A-Team* on tonight? Nando loved Mr. T. That would have kept him inside and entertained for an hour.

"I'm here. Nando, I'm here, where are you?" Chico hissed through clenched teeth, hoping if something bad was in the dark it couldn't hear him. He needed to move. Every minute that ticked by was another minute Nando drifted further from home.

Swingset chains blew in the hard wind, clinking against metal poles. The classroom windows were all dark. There were dim lights in the hallway, but it always looked this way late at night. Maybe another kid would come by to play. It happened sometimes. Maybe the janitor was in the school. He was creepy as hell, like seven feet tall and always smelled like sweat. When he'd gone here, a bunch of kids accused the janitor of being a vampire. Somehow, that morphed into him being a murderer. Then the school put him on leave, or maybe he quit.

What if it was true? What if that light on in the hallway meant the janitor had found Nando, dragged him into the school, into the boiler room to . . . Chico had no idea. What if he was in there, standing over Nando's body, waiting to taunt Chico over the walkie-talkie? Why wasn't he saying anything now?

"I'm here. Where is he?"

No answer. A whistle cut through the night, the same kind the playground monitors used. A short, sharp blast to let you know someone was in trouble. Someone had been seen. Chico remembered stories people told them from before they moved in, some dude named Robert Jahnke—or was it Richard?—who shot his dad in the driveway. Killed him. That was three years ago. He set up in his garage with a rifle, blew a whistle to get his dad's attention, and then *bang*. But he was in jail. Couldn't be that guy. Why would that guy want to shoot Nando? Why would anybody want to hurt Nando at all?

"I'm here. What do you want?"

What do you want?

"Please don't hurt my brother."

Chico whipped his head around, trying to scan the street, the playground. Where had that noise come from? There were houses across the street, way down at the end of the baseball diamond. Could he run down there, get someone's attention? If someone had gotten Nando, would he be next?

His walkie-talkie crackled. Chico lifted it, pressing it close to his ear. The wind was loud enough that he could barely hear the speaker. Rustling, banging, breathing. Someone walking. But where?

You need to come find him.

"Let me talk to him. Can I talk to him? He's just a little kid, come on . . ."

Talk to us. You'll hear him soon enough. You'll hear him every time you close your eyes at night. You'll wonder what you could have done.

Chico squeezed the button to reply, but he couldn't break the signal. Why wouldn't they shut up? He turned the volume down on the radio, not wanting to give away his position. He saw a woman in the top floor window of the house on the corner, the one that was only three hundred feet away, three hundred feet that felt like three hundred miles. She was on the phone, mindlessly twisting the cord around her hand as she talked and gesticulated, probably unaware that leaving her lights on and the curtains open meant people could see in and she couldn't see out.

That was the first lesson Dad taught them about when they had to stay home alone. Curtains always closed. Doors always locked. That's how you stay safe. Inside. Doors locked. If he screamed loud enough, would she hear? Would she be able to see him out here in the dark?

Chico's thoughts drifted into all his past wrongs, the times he'd told Nando to shut up or ignored him or hurt him when he'd done nothing. Tripping him once as he ran laps around the living room, just because he was annoyed. Tweaking a wrestling hold because he knew it would hurt him just enough. The time he'd accidentally dropped him while carrying him on his shoulders. If he could just find Nando, he'd make up for all of it.

The whistle blew again. From his vantage point behind the seesaw, only a sliver of the teacher's parking lot near the end of the L-shaped building was visible. A small flashlight flickered, swiping across the playground. It wasn't coming anywhere near Chico. Maybe it was a teacher taking one last look around before leaving for the night. Maybe it was the police. Had someone seen Chico walking around the playground and called the cops? He started to stand, then looked at the jacket on the ground. Take it? Would anyone believe him that his brother had been kidnapped?

Footsteps on gravel. The light was low, sweeping. Chico couldn't see who held it. He didn't know if they could see him.

Another whistle, from behind. Chico turned and saw a shadow walking from around the corner of the school, boots heavy on concrete, then crunching onto gravel. Both lights had stopped moving. They were sweeping around the playground, looking for someone. Looking for him.

You said you were here. Did you lie to us?

Chico smothered the radio under his armpit, keeping low, but it was too late. The light painted his arm from one side, then the other found him as well. Footsteps crunched across gravel. They'd locked onto him. He dropped the walkie-talkie and ran, or tried to run, making a beeline for the end of the playground where that woman was on the phone, still. He screamed, hoping she'd see him. He couldn't hear anyone approaching from behind over the sound of the wind and his heart thundering in his ears. He just needed to get out from the dark of the playground and under the streetlight. She'd hear him soon, she had to. She could call the police and they could find Nando.

He hoped he had the advantage, that maybe because he'd come to this school, he'd know the fastest way out of the playground and they wouldn't, that he could disappear into the familiar surroundings. But he'd forgotten so many things—how hard it was to run on gravel, especially down the slight hill to the corner, and most especially he'd forgotten about the large logs that separated the softball area from the rest of the playground. Giant telephone poles that ran the length of the field, completely invisible in the dark. The front of his foot made contact and the world flipped upside down.

He shouted Nando's name as he slammed face-first into the ground, cracking a front tooth. A scream rose in his throat, cut off as the wind was knocked out of him. His head buzzed from the impact. He saw the small red light of his walkie-talkie, so faraway and useless, saw two flashlight beams converging on him as he struggled to stand up and continue running.

Gravel slid out from beneath his feet as he kicked to run. He'd lost a shoe. He held a hand to his chin, warm with blood, gathered air in his lungs to scream. He stumbled sideways, his ankle twisting on another log—or had that been the same one—and fell again. This time the log was there to catch him in the ribs, driving the air from his lungs and silencing him.

< < < < > > > >

Nando sat shivering on the cold concrete in front of the door. The isolation of knowing his dad was somewhere out in the world with the Air Force and his mom was across town working fast food made him feel tiny and alone, even with Chico at home. It was a small town. The wind blew at night. It got dark early now, and all of that led his fertile imagination to populate the dark outside not with monsters, but people he feared most: skinheads he'd seen on *Geraldo*, that crazy lady two blocks down who called him a beaner, the weird kids he saw at Chico's school who wore denim jackets with heavy metal band patches and smelled like Dad's cigarettes.

Chico had been on the radio all night, just doing radio checks. *Hey Nando. Where's Nando? Nando, come in . . .*

He'd have preferred Chico used his codename, Hawk, but at least he was playing. Walking to the school felt like it was going to be an adventure, but three blocks away he's chickened out, deciding it was too cold. There was an alleyway that ran between the houses one block over, one of his favorite places to play. He considered it spy practice, that he could watch people without being seen from the darkness. Sometimes he would sneak into backyards and slightly rearrange some of the lawn furniture, just to prove he could infiltrate an enemy base and get away unseen.

It was too cold for prolonged spying, so he decided to come home. He didn't feel like watching TV all night, but maybe they could find a movie.

The door was locked when he got there. The TV was going in the living room, he could tell by the way the colors pulsed against the curtains. He couldn't see inside. Dad always told them they had to keep the curtains drawn and the doors locked. Since Chico had been

IN THE WIND

home, Nando didn't think to grab a key on the way out. He knocked, but Chico didn't answer. None of the neighbors he knew had their lights on, and besides, going over there would make Mom look bad for leaving them alone. He'd learned that lesson the hard way once already. The phone rang inside, four times, then five.

He knocked louder, tried kicking the door a few times, but Chico never came.

Nando. I'm at the school. Come find me.

Nando beamed. Finally, Chico was on a mission. It didn't sound like him, not exactly. The voice was a little deeper and a lot rougher, but he thought maybe it was just the speaker distorting things. He was freezing and it was too dark now to go wandering. "Nah, just come home. I forgot my key"

If you don't come here . . . I can't come back. You have to come here.

"It's too cold! Come back home. Otherwise I'm gonna have to run to Steve's but we'll probably get in trouble."

I found your jacket. Come and grab it. We'll walk home together.

He'd lost it at school yesterday, concerned that he'd left Grizzly in his pocket, and he was going to take Crossbones on a mission tonight to go rescue him, but he'd decided it was too cold.

Nando, come get your jacket . . .

"Just come back home. I think Mom called and we're gonna get in trouble."

Where's home? Where is home, Nando? Tell us and we'll come find you.

Nando lowered the radio in confusion, looking off to the east, down the darkened street. It was a straight run to the school, but he was too cold now. He had to stay.

We're coming, Nando. Don't move.

There was a glint of light a few blocks away, bouncing lightly, growing closer. The static howled on his radio like a fierce wind.

OPERATION ICARUS

E.F. Schraeder

HAS ANYONE EVER told you the sky was falling? Did you believe them? This is that kind of story, I guess, but it doesn't have a moral. It's a story about a plan. My plan. The story of two weeks, a story of receiving and giving.

The two weeks started with an endurance test. Like any botmaster worth her salt, I prepared to endure a series of intense, late-night coding expeditions in anticipation of a single night of undoing as the work became the architecture of destruction. And my adventures always started and ended in the same place: at home. That may seem anticlimactic, but how many people can bring the world to its knees without leaving the house?

Encrypting was tedious business that required equal parts coffee and patience, though those two ingredients sometimes worked against each other. Like a 21st-century mystic, I detailed every line of code. I only had to wait for the final component to be delivered. Clean text had to be scrambled into cipher text, so I invented a new scrambling system for the occasion and a new key.

I needed a stronger system. Luckily, I had an impossibly rich friend who didn't ask a lot of questions. I guess he enjoyed showering his financially-challenged friend with gifts. He wouldn't have believed what I was up to, anyway.

When Henny Penny told her friends the sky was falling, who believed her?

I peeked outside. The box wasn't there yet. I stared at the crumbling asphalt on my neighbor's roof. Why weren't solar panels on every rooftop? Because the sun was free. No one wanted that. I let the screen door slam shut and went back inside. I had nothing to do but wait.

I remembered what Kennedy said about machines. About men, or was it industry? It covered all of it, maybe. Kennedy was that kind of guy, a soaring visionary of near mythic proportion. Anyway, he said, "If men have the talent to invent new machines that put men out of work, they have the talent to put those men back to work."

Of course, Kennedy was shot. *Conspiracy or lunatic?* Does it matter? Either way, he's dead. Those category distinctions were best left to others. I've always been agnostic that way.

Two years ago, my life revolved around writing policy coding language for an insurance company. It was as enthralling as you'd imagine. I invented phrasing combinations and detailed codes that enabled the denial of thousands of claims. I saved billionaires billions of dollars. *Go me!*

It was my job. I excelled, earning enough bonuses to pay off my house. Twice. For a brief, shining, glorious moment, even my student loans shrank.

The trouble was, I couldn't un-know what else was happening as a result. Those projects also cost millions of people services they needed. My perfect mathematic language, like an impossible puzzle, cracked families, couples, and individuals in half, delivered insurmountable summits and inaccessible promises. I shattered hopes in the shape of fees and disclaimers. I came to realize my job title was mistaken.

I re-named myself the Rainbow Eraser. I was the woman hovering after the storm, making sure there were no beautiful things left to break. Accomplishing this feat meant I was revered, wondrous as a shooting star. My employers led an industry crusade of sorts, and shared this genius phrasing via emails and memos with two dozen national insurers. Maybe more. I lost track.

Them: rich, richer, richest. Me: clinically depressed.

It was not the depression of television commercials where a dog whined by his leash and a sullen spouse ate dinner alone. There was no music. The nuts and bolts of depression simply croaked, tugged sinking ship feeling through the veins. My body ached with a crumbling despair. Plummeted into a deep well of isolation, I lost weight like a reality TV star. I was the biggest loser. I removed mirrors, stopped looking at myself and eventually, I stopped looking at everything.

My world shrank, and I became a long-haired, unwashed weirdo with a sixteen-inch lawn and overgrown shrubs: the epitome of what my surface shiny, self-absorbed, suburban neighbors wanted to ignore and protect their stupid children from. I was an eyesore. A spectacle. A cesspool. A nightmare. I was a lock-up-your-children-she's-out-there, sort of neighbor.

Waves of regret swallowed me from below like savage jaws clamping down on my legs. An undertow of self-hatred. I was pulled asunder. I witnessed my undoing. I obsessed over a series of ugly flashes in various moments I never managed to execute: I imagined crashing a used car off a bridge on a test drive. I imagined an "accidental" overdose on prescriptions. As if. Those were bad days. I suspected that other apocalyptic thinkers also had big ideas they later regretted a lot of the time.

Apocalypse seemed like a strange word. I imagined "a peacock lips." *What would that look like?* The probability of beak, beaks, beaking and de-beaking twisted into a confusing image rather quickly. I had other days, better days, full of plans. I waited for a computer, spent the day hovering at the door like a freak at every sound. This was the door to the future! My escape! And everyone else's. I had a duty, after all.

What would the apocalypse mean for a shut-in? Probably not much. I was already home most of the time, avoiding things. Avoiding people. I had canned food. Dried food. Plenty of beans. I didn't need much, buy much, or eat much. I already preferred isolation. I adapted to disappointment.

I didn't worry about what it would do to the world. By most calculations the world was well on the way to dead. Most countries knew this. Mine, not so much. Facts were strangely absent, like bad students, tardy, inconvenient, and unruly, so they were ignored. Panic would probably erupt. The only plausible explanation for the level of denial most people lived in was that they'd already given up. Why not watch another movie?

Just driving around like cars on a stupid coaster, going nowhere. To and from the office. Up and down the street. The wheels on the bus and all that. But I'd sort of worried that I couldn't trust my own mind. I was full of truths, yet an unreliable narrator. Like Henny Penny, my reliability depended on which version of the story you read. *Didn't it always?*

I sat in a dark room and closed my eyes. Maybe I slept. Definitely a sad hunger gnawed at me as I drifted into the mindless want of self-absorption. Anxiety grew. The thick stain of a hand pressed onto my chest. It looked like a mouth. *Whose hand was that?* Sure, I imagined and feared everything.

A fair assessment. The small eye of the computer blinked at me. I knew it did.

I sat up, looked around the dim room. True, life was a nightmare. Nothing made sense. I wanted to throw my codes like stones at the world. I unbuttoned my denim shirt and watched as a bruise erupted where the hand would've been. *Had it been real?* Sweat rose from my body like a signal. I wondered if I made a mistake, wanting innocence to visit me before unleashing a data-mining worm. I imagined that mouth hovering at my chest until it stole something from me. I never saw the face.

< < < < > > > >

When the computer arrived, the nothing box simply sat on the porch. When I saw it, I swung the door open like an eager child. With birthday-morning eagerness, I snapped it up. But it was not a box of balloons, treats. and cake. My pal Desmond sent me his discarded laptop via UPS all the way from Reno. An old laptop should not rock anyone's world.

The best explanation: unemployment. My days at home were boring and long. Besides that, I liked mail. Who didn't? Mail perked up any bland day, delivering something new. A moment of hope. An unopened box delivered a brilliant unexplored opportunity, a chance to look forward to something, even if only for a glimpse, I expected something new was about to happen. Call it a nod to my inner visionary.

The name on the address label was neatly printed in all capital letters. TAMARA BRYANT. I liked the way the letters looked when they were all capitalized. *Important*. When I was a kid, it bothered me that my initials were shorthand for a disease. I got used to it eventually. Then later, I loved it.

I AM VIRAL.

I picked up the box and scurried indoors as if I hid something significant and dangerous from my neighbors. The screen door slammed behind me from its own weight. That added a pleasing emphasis to my triumphant moment. Like music would've in a movie.

Until receiving the new old laptop, time was also lost frequently thinking. In graduate school it was called things like "unpacking" and "critical theory." That was even harder to visualize than "a peacock lips." Or maybe I was smarter then, before this.

The device arrived without fanfare. It landed here to help me record my thoughts and make a plan. I unwrapped it, carefully placing the crumpled newspaper it nested in to the side as I eased it out of the box. Unwittingly, my tongue pressed into the corner of my open mouth and my lips grew dry. Well, drier.

I felt light as Icarus. On the cusp of greatness. Or failure. *Did it matter?* I was trying. *Who could say that these days?*

Desmond's laptop was a beautiful machine. Recently, maybe a year ago, it was the pinnacle of speed, memory, excellence, and utility. It was thin, light, white, and full of promise. I didn't need the speed, but I definitely needed the power. The programming capacity. The vision of it shot through me like a lightning bolt. With white hot clarity I knew I was going to change the world. *Again.*

Planned obsolescence and boredom rendered the device useless to Desmond. I guess he couldn't load porn fast enough or whatever. Desmond the Employed replaced his electronics. Desmond the Master of His Own Destiny had no use for outmoded equipment. Desmond of the Pulled-up Bootstraps told me that many of the processing features weren't outdated, and he sent it to me graciously without cross-examination. Having more than enough, he was happy to share. My own computer was operating long past its sell-by date, and unable to compute some of the tighter codes quickly enough. Besides, I needed a second, faster machine. Sharper teeth and all that.

OPERATION ICARUS

The better to eat you with, my dear.

I had been offline so long I'd forgotten my passwords. No worries. I'd hack into my own accounts if I had to. I imagined an inbox full of invitations and awards, mostly spam. I didn't have a lot of friends. Not anymore. I jumped onto a neighbor's wi-fi network with surprising and disappointing ease. Password is not a password. Your kid's name is not a password. Idiots. Identity theft would be awesome if it weren't so easy.

I promised myself after tackling the simplicity of that first hack that if I ever wrote another internet password or built an internet network account to use sentences that people would avoid joining. My network, visible to everyone searching, would be, "How 2 kill my neighbors" or maybe "soon u2 die."

It was almost worth leaving the internet intact. *Almost.*

Working on a newer machine was ecstasy. The swift responses and easy computations felt like home. Struck by the abject intoxication, the satisfying seductive comfort of the familiar.

I began programming immediately and refused to waste time on Desmond's basic profile settings. Desmond told me he had the thing wiped, but he neglected to alter the access codes and defaults. I imagined myself flinching every morning as the computer greeted me, "Good morning Desmond." I decided to live with that. It was slightly unnerving, being called the wrong name like that. Even by a machine. But it was a manageable offense. Pixels simmered in my eyes after hours of work.

< < < < < > > > >

That night while the computer worked on autopilot, I rummaged through my old application essay to college. I had aspirations, a gift for metaphor, and a nice signature. Stupidly, I hung on to the recruitment materials. I eyed the glossy pictures of smiling students. Unlike the stack of promissory notes earned along with my education. I wondered if those photos captured real students or frauds. They looked very happy and posed. They were probably paid models. I frowned. I was too old to pursue a career in modeling. And many other things.

Hackers hacked. So I hack, hack, hacked.

Bigger fish and all that.

Two years before my cure to reimbursed claims went viral in the business of medicine, I studied propositional calculus and game theory at a small private university whose name I can no longer utter without a stinging surge of bile emanating from my stomach and burning my esophagus. None of this worked out the way I imagined. Especially the bile. I graduated with a Ph.D. from U of B.

Three weeks ago they, the University of Bile, sent me an alumni request for money. I returned the envelope with a carefully detailed resume. *No response.* Anyway, it was time to give back. I had something to give them all right. Somewhere, I envisioned my name cleanly eliminated from a database with a simple click, silent as Daedalus burying a son.

< < < < > > > >

Einstein said something like the level of thinking that created the problem has to be transcended to solve the problem. I'm paraphrasing.

Comforted by the clack, clack, clack of the keyboard, I wrote faster until the evening air through the tiny screen of the glass block window chilled me. I needed something to warm up. I saved my work and rubbed my eyes. The computer screen had a way of making me feel calm. Numb. It was like looking at a pastoral painting or a landscape of home. The glow of the screen filled the room much as a campfire would've lit a dark night. My plan was in motion, a beautiful construction of wings at my disposal. I felt ready to soar.

I found the student loan papers and I eyed my signature suspiciously. I ran my finger over the grooved pattern of the inked letters. *Yes, it was mine.* I closed my eyes and drank the Braille of unfortunate decisions. I could not calculate this level of problem. Perhaps it could not be solved. There was no calculus for failure.

In my basement, I set up an old metal trash can, filling it with paper and built a nice fire. I burned the following: drafts of application letters, admission letters, scholarship award letters, transcripts, a master's thesis. The edges of the papers tinged into a crackling golden brown before lighting into yellow flames, consuming the sheets of paper like delicate wings, sending smoking prayers up to the heavens. I did not burn the loan papers. I could've paid them off with the remaining money from bonuses, but they reminded me of my soul's debts. Soon enough, I would watch them disappear.

OPERATION ICARUS

I was hardly ever angry. Depression's sole gift, really. I was cold, numb, and shivering as I gripped the edges of my old life. As the papers burned in the small metallic cauldron, the room filled with a thick, gray smoke. It looked like smog. How appropriate to have one's past goals become ghosts, be reduced to air pollution. I felt like a witch doctor, reckoning with old demons. In a way, I was.

The basement was not a metaphor for my unconscious. No Freudian analysis, thank you. The basement had a concrete floor. Unlike my ego, it resisted burns. I knew the can held the flames securely, but why take chances? I stoked the fire with my pathetic history. As for my id, no desire fed my body. I didn't remember the last time I fucked anyone, including myself.

Depression. A bland, uninterrupted, dead landscape without music, laughter, or sex. My emotions became a burden after the depression, or right before, constructs of conscience and physicality. Software and hardware.

Levi Strauss, the French anthropologist, not to be confused with my favorite denims, sought for a structure of underlying patterns in human thought. I think the Germans made a word for that very thing. Schadenfreude. Schaden meant harm and Freude meant joy. The Germans capitalized their nouns as if they were the names of important things. I was not wrong about that. Anyway, together, schadenfreude described that sick pleasure in observing misfortune. *Go ahead, look,* it said. *We have a word for you.*

Claude Levi-Strauss was a culture maker. His was the fourth name that appeared when I googled "Levi Straus." Even spelled wrong, he appeared. That was how important he became.

I sat unacceptably long in the dark, warming myself by the low light of the smoldering past. I clicked on a small television. The television was a gift of the curb. Every week on garbage night I prowled the neighborhood after working people went to bed and gathered up bits of used lives and carried them to my home. The smaller the objects, the more I carried and the longer the walk. I probably could've bought a better one, but I liked recycling almost as much as I liked not going to the store.

The television delivered a comforting haze, another warm glowing ember in my technological firelight. I turned it on, not to watch anything but to enjoy the added blue light filtering through the room. Social unrest happened on low levels. Like a humming computer being called "asleep," as if that box of wires and circuit boards closed its unimpressed eyes. It didn't. It watched everything. I knew that much. Too many issues since the Patriot Act made sure that our little single-eyed devils told all our secrets. I stroked the clean, white edge of the flatscreen laptop, wishing I, too, could hibernate to conserve energy.

My stomach growled. A talk show host invited the daughter of a famous actor to describe her situation. The almost-famous person talked about how she puked out a $400 meal. In seconds, her suffering and her disorder became world news. Bulimia peaked, trending on search engines. She spoke candidly, sharing her pain. People loved this shit. Hers was a modern tragedy. Inherited wealth, inherited pain. Antigone had nothing on her, well, except maybe a few solid pounds. The sins of the father and all that. *Bullshit.*

Viewers wiped single tears from their weeping eyes. They praised her bravery. She announced the inevitable book release. A camera zoomed in on a woman sobbing with orgasmic release who attested into the microphone about the lives that would be saved as a result of this disclosure. I reduced the volume to an indecipherable rumble.

This was news. This was notoriety. I could sit inside my house forever. From here, with a few simple clicks, I could discover the million ways the world was undeniably ending. I could read reports and studies and confirmations of confirmations. These were no longer projections. I could take it all in, the thousands of researchers and scientists, petitions, and protests, and students, all reflecting a veritable global consensus of great minds speaking in one voice, calling out to the masses, *The sky is falling, the sky is falling!* No one seemed to care.

Sooner or later, everything reduced to Chicken Little.

I flipped open the laptop. "Hello Desmond."

I hacked into my own email, wrote to my old professors, certain they wouldn't remember me. They taught thousands of me, sent us into the world like paper swans on a river, our paper wings outstretched, ready to fail. All of us unemployed or desperate. The army swallowed some of us and our student loans, without so much as a hiccup or a belch. We disappeared. While banks were bailed out of the river, some of us died. More will die. More always die.

OPERATION ICARUS

We were the soldiers of flawed hope. We were numbers, admissions recruits, graduates. They reconfigured charts and graphs until we became their success stories. They manipulated statistics. I knew they did. They taught me how. After Icarus, I couldn't say where we'd end up, but it had to be better than here.

Schadenfreude became my favorite word. I wrapped a handmade knit blue blanket around my shoulders and repeated the word like a mantra. The smoke made me cough, so I went back upstairs. *Let it burn.*

Fire was nice, but a picture offered that sort of closure, too. I gathered together the old brochures of my past life. I clipped apart the catalogues until faces surrounded me, staring up from the floor. One snip of the scissor, and the smiles stopped making sense. Who were they grinning at? It was that easy to dismantle human understanding, simple as unplugging a cord. I decided I'd take them back to the basement to burn later. When I was done.

I typed in my directions, careful to use proper names so nothing would be lost. A Greek chorus of voices would not regret these decisions. Spellcheck overtyped my corrections. The machine did not trust my autonomy. I did not trust the machine.

I ran mental calculations and typed out universal propositions for fun. The sky was definitely falling. I was going to make it fall.

Sitting in my living room, I set up the background program parameters while a group of children played pretend baseball with a computer game next door for two hours. They played indoors. They were indoor children of an indoor generation, but my windows were open. They aggravated my sensitive hearing. They had no sporting equipment, field, bats, or gloves. They were not playing an actual game. They did not even own a ball. In the years they'd lived there beside me, I had never seen a single ball. Not one ball.

To me, this was evidence. They lacked imagination. They screamed and laughed and applauded exactly when prompted. This worried me. I imagined glossy, dim eyes hazy with a world of false home runs and stolen bases. Their soft arms waved as they clapped and cheered each other. Hitler said, "How fortunate for leaders that men do not think." That sounds true enough. Go figure.

I closed the window. Silence obtained. I realized I had not been cheered on, even in imaginary games, for years.

Icarus built the wings himself.

That was what depression looked like.

When I was young, I climbed actual trees. Unafraid, I lumbered up, pulled myself higher. I felt eager to soar above the easy, low branches. Rough bark scraped my legs and knees until thin bits of skin peeled away and revealed red bubbling dots of blood beneath the surface. I sat for hours nested in a branch planning my adult life like a squirrel for winter harvest. I had time and parents, both of which served as a pleasant reprieve. I had a safety net to ward away fearful surprises. I had neither now.

I smiled, remembering safety. I knew how fragile it was. Like a burst cloud. Now I looked forward to unraveling the net. Mine included. What'd I need it for? Where could I go from here? Down wasn't an option. Sideways maybe. More likely I'd just keep skidding.

In the dim light of the machine, I listened. The incessant, electric pulse blinked as my fingers tapped at the keyboard. There were at least a hundred thousand tasks that even the most basic computer was designed to outperform the best of human effort: equations, spelling, categorizing, organizing. At first, they entertained. Remember when we applauded the imagination sparked as coders and linguists created the first bars of computer-generated music? Computer-generated poems? How fleeting. So much work for a simple scale of notes, a stanza or two of unrhymed verse.

The monster is arisen. It's alive! No one cried. No one wept.

Within a short decade these machines became the substitute for typewriters, gaming, cameras, calculators. Then within a few more years added to the list of replacements banks, phones, and shopping. They sustained life, the purposeless boxes housed no less than human ambition and will. The impressive devices filled the homes like stars in the sky ready to blink out.

It was barely a footnote as parents and teachers handed three-year-olds a talking teddy bear who would read to little Johnny. Helping busy parents save time. No one cared when students only needed to type, not write.

Trust me, Siri never knew what you were saying. The novelty should've worn off by now. But it hasn't. The virus infected the hardware. And guess what, you're the hardware. Someone had to turn it off.

OPERATION ICARUS

I am destined to be viral. I implanted a virus in the U of B, using their system to launch a simple email story certain to have contagious impact. My uplifting tale of generosity ended with the kindest command:

Forward this to everyone you know, and give one dollar to the next person you see. Experience random kindness and freedom from greed for one second of your day. Notice that magic!

Feel good bullshit was clickbait. Within one hour it was a sensation. Crumpled dollar bills tossed around offices filled with laughing people, pedestrians smiling and shaking hands. The online videos were evidence. *Kindness works.* An end to the cruelty of greed. I predicted that such a euphoric realization would last minutes, for some.

Embedded in the goodwill message was a subterranean virus built to devour hardware. Deep code. After the message ran for a few days, I'd activate the DoSnet from a public network via a shell computer, then flood disruptive data through the system. Then I'd launch again from another system with a second password.

I dubbed the virus the "Operation Icarus." My nickname far cruder: Chicken Little. No one would find it. It would devour every megabyte of free space, dismantle every operable program on every hard drive, consume every RAM of memory, in the name of application updates. Quickly, invisibly. That hardly anyone bothered to study Greek myth was beside the point. Maybe it was the point. Icarus knew better than most of us. Even if you're going to go down in flames, it's fun to give it a shot.

My code worked like a flame, devouring and scouring the world, eliminating nonsense. I determined to shred stored data into indecipherable nonsense, erasing everything to wedge a fault line between the machine and the capacity of the human minds that are supposed to operate them. Solve this with your own ability, it said. *Think, communicate, exist. Grow. Create.*

Like a 21st Century Shiva, Operation Icarus was a destroyer. It would do more than end the claims assessment industry. It would swallow my faux pas and eliminate the errors. It would free millions of people, whose data would be erased. Finally. It was designed to launch and collapse networked systems in a matter of a few short hours. I envisioned assessors everywhere drowning in panic. Shirt sleeves rolled up. Lesser techies called. Emergencies announced. Offices closed. Buildings locked. Bank accounts drained swiftly. They toppled. *After all, I was viral.*

In short, O.I. promised an end to madness. Following chaos and despair, anyway. By the time the trash can fire went out in my basement, the trash can fire of modernity would be snuffed out as well. I toasted the laptop. "To Henny Penny!"

With my breath caught in my throat, I anticipated the world's computers screeching to a final salute. My heart raced as I imagined an end to the devices we crafted for our use. Dream of dreams, an end to the use of words like "friend" and "adult" as verbs. An end to offshore accounts, day trading, and other deceptions. No more bombshell stock announcements or victory tweets. An end to the tools of distance banking, loan tracking, and foreclosures. Would it rebuild? Though Icarus fell, Vishnu and Brahma promised to return. What did it matter? No one listened until it was too late.

I was about to witness the global removal of a seeping bandage. I cast my eyes up to watch the wings of progress darken and crisp until the body fell. I stared deep into the festering wound of life on a depleted world. I didn't know how it would rebuild itself. If it would rebuild itself. But there would be gardens. I imagined gardens, anyway. And a handful of kids, kicking a ball around empty streets.

Before the package arrived, inertia was my favorite meal. I feasted on plenty of it. But last night I typed until I fainted and dreamed of Icarus. Coding was my feast. He folded his wings into the horizon, burning with delight. The sun was close enough to taste. Sweat dripped down my face. Or maybe it was melting wax. I imagined the flavor of his success in my mouth. It was hot, heavy, filled with smoke.

I had enough for a year, maybe more already. Water, canned goods. Dried goods. When you know the sky is falling, you plan ahead. I did anyway. Did you?

I closed the laptop. "Goodbye, Desmond."

ASHES, ASHES

Jessica Leonard

THE STORM MOVED in overnight, bringing with it a record-breaking three inches of ice and five more inches of snow to top it off. The citizens of Woodshed awoke on December 24th to a world of soft grey like fallout. The old heavy trees that surrounded the tiny village were bent and broken, lacking the grace of the smaller trees planted in yards, which only caressed the ground, their young branches limber like dancers.

Electrical and telephone poles snapped and broke under the weight of all that winter. Hospitals and hotels were without power—not that Woodshed had a hospital, or a hotel for that matter. It would take a week before they'd find the frozen body of Benny Anders huddled against his hot water heater. It took only a day for the children to arrive.

Debbie looked out her front windows toward the tiny row of buildings marking the historic downtown district. There should have been pinpoints of white twinkle lights like constellations marking the store fronts. Instead, all was calm.

She was grateful for the woodburning fireplace in her living room, but envious of her neighbors who had generators. Her husband, Owen, however, reminded her that once the gasoline was depleted those lucky ones would be just as cold as they were. They could have walked to the town's only gas station, but they were under a state of emergency and only official vehicles were allowed to get gasoline because of an assumed shortage. No one was coming in or out of town.

The interior of the house was growing steadily dark. Debbie had already started rationing batteries, candles, and matches, not knowing when the power would return and having no way of contacting anyone who might. She'd turned off her cell phone last night to conserve the battery. She couldn't make a call even with it on—there was no signal.

The remaining glimmer of day cast mile-long shadows across the yards of her neighbors. It crept through the windows and masked her Christmas decorations in obscurity. The distended shadow of a crucified savior stretched from the wooden cross on the living room wall and bled down onto the bare wood floors.

"At least I don't have to look at the Clarks's tacky inflatable Rudolph," she muttered.

Beyond the forest that lined the opposite side of the street, the sun continued to sink, getting lost in the space between thick woods and horizon. The last shimmers glinted off the ice, reflecting and moving as a stubborn wind still insisted on trying to make the burdened branches sway. Light, then shadow, then a brighter flash played across Debbie's vision, and for a second the trees seemed to move forward. She closed her eyes tight and tried to stop the trick of the changing light.

When she opened her eyes again, the sun had all but disappeared, taking its secrets with it. Only reality was left, and the truth of what made the trees appear to move stopped Debbie's breath. Her forehead broke with the kind of sweat that normally accompanied stomach cramps.

"Owen." She called her husband's name as she stepped out onto the porch. The rubber grip of her tennis shoes tried to make purchase on the ice, but she skidded a few inches before coming to a stop just in front of the railing.

"What are you doing out here?" Owen asked, carefully following her out. "You're letting the cold in."

ASHES, ASHES

Debbie reached back toward the sound of his voice, pawing at the air until her trembling hand found his large confident one and squeezed it tight. Her eyes never left the woods.

Owen followed his wife's gaze out across the field into the deepening night. His face was blank. His eyes widened for an instant, and then squinted out into the dark.

"What is it?" he muttered. He could now pick out small bodies moving through the grass in the direction of the house.

At that moment, he heard another voice and looked to his right. His neighbor, April Joseph, plodded down the steps of her home. Her hands were pressed against her chest as she shuffled into the snow and ice toward the woods.

There seemed to be dozens of them, although their numbers were impossible to guess in the failing light, their individual forms blending and turning into a large bobbing mass. It wasn't until they reached the street and began gathering in the yard that Debbie was able to pick out individual children.

They weren't dressed for the cold. Their clothes were dirty and torn, none of them had coats. Their faces were smudged with mud and brown bits of decayed leaves stuck at odd angles from their hair. They were all young girls. Debbie guessed their ages to be anywhere from six to nine years old.

"What are they?" April asked, her voice ringing out in the ice. She'd stopped halfway between their houses as if her resolve to reach her friends had suddenly been squashed by the sight of the children.

"They're just kids," Debbie replied.

The girls stopped at the edge of Debbie's porch, their dirty faces looking up at the couple standing there. Fear clutched Debbie's chest, but she pushed it away. Sucking breath deep into her lungs, she edged off the porch and down the graying wooden steps. The moon was full and bright, giving the world a pale glow. Owen remained on the porch.

"Hello," Debbie said.

They studied Debbie and she in turn looked them over, unsure of what action to take. One of the girls shuffled forward through the snow. Her pale blonde hair glowed like it was made of the moonlight and not just reflecting it. Her used-to-be-white dress was torn and stained dark brown at the bottom.

"I need help," she said.

The words tugged at Debbie's heart, stirring compassion for the daughters she never had. She wanted to go to the child, hold her, promise her that everything would be fine, that her salvation was at hand. But something held her back.

"What is your name, honey?" she asked.

"Lily."

"Like a flower. That's lovely. My name's Debbie." She smiled at the girl. "And who are your friends?"

"They're lost," Lily replied.

"Can't they talk?" Debbie's brow furrowed.

Lily just giggled and looked back at the other girls. Her eyes were dark.

Debbie looked at Owen for support. He was still on the porch. His face crinkled up so that he appeared to be crying. Debbie turned to the girls in time to see one of the youngest dart toward the porch.

"Evie, don't!" Lily yelled.

"I'm not afraid," the girl shouted back over her shoulder. In a second, she was up the front steps and next to Owen. Her eyes were wide, and even in the dark Debbie could see her small form tremble in the below-freezing night air. The girl reached up and touched Owen's hand, her fingers sliding down to meet his. Without a word, she backed away from him and went back to the group of girls and dissolved among them.

"Where did they come from?" April asked.

Owen was silent. With the night enveloping him, Debbie couldn't see his face anymore, but she understood he was afraid. They'd been married for fifteen years. If there was one thing she knew, it was Owen.

She turned her attention over to April. "Just came out of the woods. We've got to get them some place or they'll freeze."

"What about town hall? It's got a generator hooked up. It's the only place big enough."

"I don't have a key."

"Just knock on Dean's door, not like he isn't gonna be home. Take the girls up that a-way. I'll stir the neighbors, call a meeting." April was already heading to the next house down, her resolve returning now that she had a plan of action.

"Where do you live?" Debbie asked, looking at Lily.

"Somewhere else," she replied.

"How did you get here?"

"The man brought us here. He brought all the girls here, and I found them. They were his girls. Now they're mine." Lily stepped forward, separating herself from the pack.

"You can't help them." Debbie spun sharp at the sound of Owen's voice. She waited for him to say something else, to explain himself, but he only stood firm in place on the porch.

"I'm taking them to the hall. Get your coat and meet us," Debbie said. Looking back at the children, she tried to smile. "We're going to go up the street a bit. Can you walk a little farther?"

None of them moved. Every face watched Lily. She bobbed her head and stepped next to Debbie. Lily laced her small fingers together with Debbie's and smiled up at her.

A small noise rose from Owen, something like a yelp. "Get back, devils. Leave my family in peace," he cried. His breath came in quick heaving pants, leaving condensation puffs hanging in the thin, frozen air.

"They're just girls," Debbie said, with a confidence she did not feel. Owen preached about the devil on Sunday mornings, but that devil was a vague idea: a drinking problem, an infidelity. These were flesh and blood children standing in the snow.

"Devils come to us in all forms," Owen said. "Satan himself masquerades as an angel of light, or are we just forgetting second Corinthians?"

"Don't quote scripture to me, Reverend," Debbie warned. "I know the Good Book well enough to know God'll judge us for turning away children."

"Judge?" Owen repeated. His eyes shifted from the girls to his feet. He shrank back further onto the porch as Debbie led her small army down the street toward the cluster of old two-story brick buildings that was downtown. The moon lit up the snow lit up the trees lit up the ice until the whole world seemed like maybe it *was* the moon. The stillness made Debbie's bones ache. All calm. All bright.

It only took one minute to bring Dean to his front door, but the cold had already seeped through Debbie's clothes and was stinging her skin. She had no idea how the girls were managing in their thin rags.

"What's going on here?" he asked.

"Not sure I know. These girls just up and showed up on the lawn. They came out of the woods, Dean."

He squinted. "How many are there?"

"I don't know, has to be at least twenty. Listen, we have to get into the hall, get the generator going, decide what to do about them."

Dean nodded and backed into the house, leaving Debbie and the girls adrift in a snow-filled world. A moment later, he jangled a set of keys in front of her nose. He had a hat on. Still dangling the keys in front of him like a lantern, Dean trudged out into the cold, led them a block further to the town hall, and let them all inside.

"It'll take a second to get that generator going, but it's hooked up to the main box, so the heat'll kick in quick enough. Only trouble is the gas. I have enough for the night, but I don't know about much more."

"At least it's something."

Debbie stood in the dark of the hall, unable to make out anyone around her. She was dizzy as pitch black consumed her. Her body swayed in an ocean of nothing.

Then from the nothing, there was the sound of a motor.

The overhead fluorescents flickered once, twice, stayed steady, made the room hum with the sound of modern technology.

Owen was standing directly in front of Debbie, and the unexpected sight of him startled a yip out of her. His hand shot out and latched onto Debbie's arm. The intensity of his eyes matched the hum of the Fluorescents, the Heater, and the Holy Generator.

"They're unnatural, Debbie," he hissed. "All together in one room. It looks like so many gathered up like this."

"It's only maybe a little more than a classroom full." She thought on that for a moment and then added, "Do you think maybe they're from a field trip that got lost?"

He didn't answer.

Ten more citizens wandered in, looking tentatively at the girls who were huddled together at one end of the meeting hall. April smiled at Debbie, clearly proud she'd rustled up such a good crowd in the middle of the night in the aftermath of an ice storm. She also had an armload of quilts that she began passing out to the children.

ASHES, ASHES

Debbie turned to one of the girls. "Is this your class? Did you get separated from your teacher?"

The girl did not answer. Her gaze remained steady on the floor.

Dean made his way to the front of the room and smiled humbly out at the weary crowd. "Looks like we have a bit of a situation," he started, chuckling at his own understatement. "As you can see, some unexpected tourists have arrived, and I wouldn't be doing my mayoral duty if I didn't make them comfortable as I could. I don't rightly know what we should do about alerting anyone tonight. Debbie, do we have any ideas on where they came from?"

"No, but we have to figure someone's out there looking for them."

Dean nodded, "I guess they can stay here, unless anyone else knows something better. Brother Owen? Did you have any thoughts?"

Owen strode up beside Dean, his eyes dodging the girls as best they could. "We can't keep them."

A rabble ran through the group. Debbie eyed her husband in disbelief. The stress of the situation had driven him mad. She shook off her disgust and walked up next to him, placed a hand on one broad shoulder, and smiled out like the good preacher's wife on a Sunday morning.

"I think what Owen means," she began, "is that the girls will need to be tended to, they're so young after all. Maybe we should divide them up, each of us take some of them home for the night. Who knows, by morning we might have cell service at the very least."

"Yeah, that might be okay," Dean said. "We'll need them going home with couples, in at least groups of three or more. Just so everything seems up and up."

"Forever the politician," April said.

"Well, I don't really want to see the town getting sued or something. I have no idea what the protocol for something like this is." Dean was flustered. Debbie guessed he wasn't too comfortable having young girls in his home unsupervised.

"If we take them into our homes, we will be liable for what happens," Owen said.

"I'd say it's a better alternative than being liable for what happens to them in this weather if we don't take them in," said April.

"It's Christmas, Brother Owen. Are we going to deny these girls a room at the inn?"

"It's not right. I'm telling you, telling all of you, I know it's not right."

"How?" asked Dean. "What makes you so certain?"

Owen opened his mouth, but only sputtered the beginning of three different sentences. Bright red crept up his cheeks. "You're supposed to trust in me," he finished.

Debbie surveyed the group. Most of them had their heads down as if in prayer. Lily's eyes were on Debbie. The girl seemed so small in this room, smaller than she had in the void left by the ice storm. Wind rushed by the hall door, took hold of a frail limb and snapped it off. Debbie watched the ice-covered branch glide by the window in silence. There was no traction in this new world.

"Okay, who do we have that can take some girls in?"

"You can't be serious." Owen looked at his wife, outraged. She ignored him.

April raised her hand, not heeding Dean's instruction that it should be couples. Besides, what he really meant was that he didn't think single men should take four girls into their houses during a blackout. Janet and David Clark raised their hands as well; they had a generator and didn't mind having five or six girls, so long as they were fine camping out in the living room. Four other families volunteered and soon the girls were divided into small groups among their impromptu foster parents.

Debbie corralled Lily, Evie, and one other girl, whom Lily introduced as Laura, around her.

"No," Owen shouted. "This is an abomination. These girls are going to be the end of this town."

"Stop it." Debbie didn't raise her voice, only her eyes. "These girls have done nothing but exist in this world. You'll stop now." She could tell he wanted to argue more but didn't know what else to say. She watched the struggle in his eyes give way to the muted panic of a hopeless loss.

The town dispersed with their new daughters, each trudging back up Main Street toward home. Dean stayed behind to shut down the generator. Owen walked ahead of them at a brisk pace.

On the way out of town, the girls came to life. Instead of the forlorn silence they had arrived with, they were now dancing up the street, holding hands and singing Christmas carols to each other. Lily laughed and became a figure skater, sliding her feet across the slick road, twirling without any of the awkward balance of youth. The gusts threatened the trees and shook down icicles, which shattered as ice met sturdier ice.

Debbie ushered the three new girls into the chilled house—the fire had died out while they were gone, and Debbie gave a quick thanks that the place hadn't burned down instead. She lit a candle next to the door and handed a flashlight to Lily.

"Shine this on the fireplace while I get it started," she directed.

After a few minutes, the logs took flame and brought the room into a new light. Debbie looked down the hall, noticed the bedroom door closed, and presumed Owen was pouting in there.

"He doesn't like that we're here," Lily said, bringing Debbie out of her thoughts.

"He's just tired."

"No."

"I have a couple of air mattresses in the hall closet. It'll just take a minute to get a bed ready."

"Everything will be okay," Lily called after her.

Before long Debbie had the two camp mattresses inflated side by side, a king-sized sheet spread over them. She handed a stack of quilts to Laura and watched as she carefully tucked Evie in, tickling her sides playfully as she went.

"I'm going to get some sleep. Holler if you need anything."

"Please wait," Lily said. "Could you maybe sleep with us tonight?"

Debbie hesitated, her eyes on the closed bedroom door.

"Please," Evie echoed. "I'm scared." Her big doe eyes reflected the firelight.

"I guess so, but it's going to be tight with all of us," Debbie relented. She took off her shoes and slid in next to Lily. Lily smiled at her. She closed her eyes and let exhaustion take her away from the day.

"Everything will be okay." Lily's voice followed her.

< < < < > > > >

Something was pecking at the window and the noise brought Debbie from the mattress to her feet. She was sweating. The house was too warm. The fireplace roared, flames lapping out at the shining hardwood floors, threatening the fake pine garland stretched across the mantle. Confused and drowsy she shuffled to the window. The bedroom door was open. Tiny fingers tapped against the outside of the glass. There were no bodies, no faces, not even arms visible in the shrouding dark. Only tiny hands with tapping fingers drumming nonsense rhythms on the glass.

The mattress was empty. Evie and Laura danced in a playful circle around the Christmas tree. Their bare feet thudded on the wood floors adding to the volley of rhythms closing in on Debbie.

As they danced, they began to sing, "Ring a-round the rosie . . . "

The hands on the window left no smudges.

"Pocket full of posies . . ."

In the kitchen, Debbie could now see faces in the windows. The chubby too-pale faces of the girls looked in at her and smiled.

"Ashes, ashes . . . "

Lily was standing in the center of the living room watching her friends play.

"We all fall DOWN!" The two girls plopped onto the floor with the last word, erupting into squeals of laughter.

"That song is about the plague, you know?" Lily said, not looking at Debbie.

"Everyone knows that."

"People never know as much as they think."

"Shouldn't it be Christmas carols?'

"Joy to the world," Lily whispered.

"Where did you come from?" Debbie asked. She kneeled beside Lily.

"The woods."

The tapping on the glass was getting louder.

Voices rang out and echoed off the ice. "Come out! Come out and play with us!"

"Lily, how did you all end up in the woods?"

"No one will hurt you. But you should stay inside." Lily watched her friends climb off the floor and go to the coffee table. Laura and Evie started leafing through the large decorative family Bible displayed in the center.

ASHES, ASHES

"The family tree is in the front," Laura told Evie, showing her the names of generations past.

Evie looked over the illegible cursive names. "No more children?"

"I can't," Debbie began.

Lily stopped her. "Your unborn daughters are lucky."

"Why are you here?"

"He took me into the woods," Lily said. "He held me down and shoved his prick inside me and when I cried, he moaned and when I screamed, he bashed my skull with a rock." Lily paused. Debbie wiped tears from her eyes, trying to clear her vision. Lily's image kept blurring, flickering in and out of perception. "That's when I found the others."

The tapping was now banging so loud that the windows rattled in their frames. Debbie heard footsteps on the porch. She saw the doorknob twist. The terror in her chest escaped in a faint wail and she closed her eyes.

"Come outside and play!" The children's voices were inside the house now. Tears streamed down Debbie's cheeks. She didn't want to look. She didn't want to look.

She opened her eyes.

The shy quiet girls from earlier in the evening were now crawling over each other to get through the front door. Their filthy limbs tangled as they smashed into the house. Debbie watched a small forearm crack and bulge—bone splintering through flesh. The mass of children screamed out as one. More snapping. A sound like slick rubber on rubber. Taffy stretching to its limits before consuming itself. The skin crushed and fused.

"Come in, come in!" Evie squealed in delight, urging her friends inside.

"He's in the bedroom," Laura laughed.

The girls had become a mass of garbled bodies and appendages. Their little mouths snapped at the air. The tongues could no longer articulate. A harsh gargled moan rang out from what was left of their throats. The skin was wet with blood and sweat. It smelled yellow. Knees, elbows, and jagged bone propelled it forward and the scraping squeak of it made hot bile rise up Debbie's throat. She retched and sobbed, fear making her feeble.

Lily held Debbie's face in her hands and forced eye contact. "Everything will be okay."

"Why are you doing this to us?" Debbie whispered.

"Haven't you always known?"

"What are you?"

"Just ashes. Nothing but ashes now. But once we were girls. Until Owen collected us." Lily's voice was calm.

Debbie forced herself to look at the creature sliding down the hallway toward the bedroom. The creature that was once children who were once alive. Debbie began to pray.

"Don't worry," Lily said, "God is already here."

The creature had reached the bedroom and Debbie could hear Owen now—his screams and pleading. Soft wet noises and frantic animalistic scratches. Owen's cries became muffled as the waterlogged splatters heightened.

"We are God, Debbie. Look upon us and weep."

THE PROTOPTERYGOTE TAPES

Joshua Chaplinsky

[TAPE #1]

THE JUMPER EDGED towards the rim of the crater, nylon suit rippling in the crosswind. He stared down five hundred yards to where shadow met sun. The former joined the latter in a neat seam across the middle—a slash through a nought.

Movement behind him sent gravel skittering down the limestone. He bent at the knee to center his gravity, looked towards the cause of the disturbance. A hand entered the frame, giving a thumbs up.

The jumper scowled, then turned back to the expanse before him. He let out a controlled breath. Then he left his hesitation standing at the lip of the crater.

The cameraman followed. He'd gone with a wide shot to minimize the need for tracking. Before long the jumper was halfway to the bottom of the crater.

At that exact moment—unbeknownst to either of them and unseeable by the human eye—the objects appeared, like needles poking through the fabric of space. They converged on the jumper in unison.

JOSHUA CHAPLINSKY

At regular speed they looked like mere streaks of light, but when played in slow motion the footage revealed further details—translucent cylinders, approximately six to eight inches in length, with paper thin membranes on either side, rippling like an eel's fin. Years after they uploaded the video to the nascent web, intrepid AV geeks had color corrected, rendered, sharpened and zoomed, giving birth to the definitive version we know today. It was a video taken by Cammie's father, the first of many, and one she'd watched hundreds of times since his disappearance.

He had christened the objects *Protopterygotes*, but in colloquial terms they became known as "flying air fish" or "rods." He took dozens of videos, but due to the limitations of dial-up only the best made his Angelfire page. Cammie pressed pause on video 001 - 031995. The receding jumper was a pinprick on the verge of winking out of existence. Tiny trails of blurred light surrounded him. He had been none the wiser when he landed at the bottom of the crater, exhilarated and unharmed.

Cammie's eyes drifted to the shelf where she kept her father's original tapes, spines labelled 1 through 27. The plastic case for tape #27 was conspicuously empty. She scrolled down the webpage to the final Real Player link, for video 027 - 060998. June 9th, 1998 was the last time she'd seen her father. The upload date on the video was August 21st, 1999.

[TAPE #27]

All the girls Alex knew had daddy issues. Whether it manifested as a lack of trust or an overeagerness to please, it only meant one thing—trouble. B-I-T-C-H. Trouble.

Maybe that wasn't fair. She'd never understood the big deal about fathers. She felt pretty ambivalent about her own. He was a nice enough guy, but he had his life and she had hers. Maybe ambivalence was *her* daddy issue.

Or maybe her current course load was too steeped in Jungian rhetoric. All she knew was her best friend Cammie hadn't been the same since Joe Sanchez disappeared and left a father-sized hole in her life. We're talking into thin air, John Krakauer style. No warning, no note, no nothing. One day Joe was living the life of a happily married family man, and the next he was gone.

THE PROTOPTERYGOTE TAPES

There were rumors, of course. Whispers that the happy marriage hadn't been so happy. But most people dismissed this as idle gossip. After all, he'd taken his video camera with him. Most likely Joe had fallen victim to an extracurricular mishap while running around the forest chasing fairies, or whatever it was he did with his free time. But Cammie refused to accept that explanation. Since Tape #8, Joe had never gone on an excursion without her.

Alex looked down at her Motorola Bravo Plus. Cammie had paged her 9-1-1, so she skipped her three o'clock psychology class and drove straight there. She arrived as Cammie's mother was leaving for work in her not-so-freshly pressed nurses uniform.

"Good afternoon, Mrs. Sanchez." Cammie's mother hadn't changed her last name. "How's our girl today?"

"Don't ask me," Mrs. Sanchez said as she passed. "I'm only her mother."

Alex smiled a straight line. Cammie had frozen her poor mother out after Joe's disappearance. Classic daddy's girl behavior.

She went inside and found Cammie sequestered in her room, obsessively monitoring Joe's old web page. Cammie had a passion for the latest in consumer computing, like her father before her. Compared to Cammie's souped-up desktop PC, Alex's pager resembled a carrier pigeon with a broken leg. Alex flopped onto the bed beside Cammie's desk.

"What's up?"

The tattoo on Cammie's forearm twitched imperceptibly as she clicked the mouse. A yellow hand with four fingers gripping a winged green cylinder. The words below it read, "In Rod We Trust." Raised pink threads of flesh surrounded the image.

A Real Player window popped open and Cammie hit play. The video consisted of a static black frame accompanied by the thrum of insects. It lasted all of fifteen seconds.

"That's it?" Alex tried to read the lines on Cammie's furrowed brow. "I don't get it."

Cammie pointed at the video's timestamp.

"Someone uploaded it this morning."

Alex couldn't help looking over at the bookcase and the line of DV tapes that took up the shelves.

"I know what you're thinking," Cammie said without taking her eyes off the computer. "I still haven't figured out his password."

Alex turned red.

"What do you think it means?"

"I'm not sure." Cammie pursed her lips, made a show of mulling it over, but Alex knew she'd already made up her mind. "I think it's a message from my father."

FIELD JOURNAL: TAPE #8

Last night the woods were clear and quiet. Minimal fauna activity. On the hike in I saw a black squirrel missing a tail. The thermometer read 62 degrees.

We set up the camera in a small clearing not far from the tent, one Dad said had yielded good results in the past. He calls it his "go to" spot. It's where he goes whenever he has doubts about his research and needs to reassure himself. Ideal for my first excursion.

Unfortunately it yielded nothing. Dad had trouble hiding his disappointment, but I was content to roast marshmallows and tell scary stories. In that respect I consider the outing a complete success. Dad spun a yarn about three crones who shared one eye and one tooth between them. They'd been alive since the dawn of time and could read the future via a giant loom. If you managed to brave their lair without becoming food they would answer your questions three. I told Dad that if they could read the future, they'd be one step ahead of any adventurer and never go hungry.

For my turn I cribbed from a chain letter that had been going around school. The one about the little girl who could predict people's deaths. She was too young to speak, but when she stood by your bedside it meant your time had come. The townsfolk became so afraid that they sewed up her eyes and mouth and left her in a cave to die. But that didn't stop the girl. She continued to appear at people's bedsides until the entire town was dead. If you didn't send a copy of the letter to ten different people, the girl would appear to you in the middle of the night with a giant needle and sew your eyes and mouth shut. I didn't tell Dad I'd had to sleep with the lights on for a week after I'd heard the story.

THE PROTOPTERYGOTE TAPES

[TAPE #28]

Another video appeared on Joe's Angelfire three days after the first. It was labelled 028 - 082399. Cammie paged Alex 9-1-1, but Alex forced herself to sit through her History of Psych class before heading over.

Once Alex arrived, Cammie turned down the lights and cranked up the volume. They huddled next to each other in front of the seventeen-inch CRT monitor. Alex felt Cammie's scars brush against her arm.

In this video, a canopy of trees accompanied the darkness. The camera drifted left to right, like a lilting ship. Alex didn't want to acknowledge what kind of ship. She pushed the word *ghost* out of her mind.

There was something else, something she couldn't put her finger on. She noticed Cammie watching her instead of the screen, waiting for her to get it. Cammie turned up the volume as far as it would go and there it was, just beyond the drone of insects.

Breathing.

Ragged, possibly human.

Alex smoothed down the hair on her arm, the skin underneath dotted like braille. She didn't know what to say. She wanted to be supportive without enabling her friend's burgeoning conspiracy theories.

"Someone definitely . . . filmed this," It was the best Alex could come up with.

"Someone," Cammie said. "But not just anyone."

FIELD JOURNAL: TAPE #11

I've captured my first, bona fide image of a protopterygote! One of the best he's ever seen, Dad said. And it wasn't even at his "go to" place. It was at a spot of my own choosing. The specimen's larger, more tapered than previous ones, and has a small loop at its tail. I've named him Terry. Terry the protopterygote! Dad says first thing tomorrow he's going up on the Angelfire.

Rod hunting with Dad has been a lot more fun than I expected. I only agreed to help him so Mom could have some space and study for her nursing exam, but now I look forward to it. Me and Dad get to hang out and go on cool adventures, and the next day there's a surprise waiting in the form of new footage! It's not always great (like the time a couple drunk guys mooned the camera for twenty minutes straight), but once in a while we score a new clip for the website. At this point I'm genuinely curious—what are these creatures, and where do they come from?

[TAPE #29]

The third video appeared a week after the second. It was labelled 029-083099. It had been filmed at dusk, making the landscape easier to read. The camera looked out onto a small clearing lined by a ring of sturdy pines. Cammie recognized it immediately.

"Don't you see?" she said.

Alex squinted.

"No."

"This is Dad's go-to spot. He wants me to meet him there."

"What?" Alex turned to her friend. "How can you tell?"

Cammie grinned and pointed to the timestamp like Alex had missed the most obvious thing in the world.

"This date is a week from today."

FIELD JOURNAL: TAPE #14

Dad seemed preoccupied last night. I thought maybe he'd had another fight with Mom, but I kept catching him talking to himself, like when he's trying to figure out a riddle or solve a complex problem. I knew from experience not to interrupt. As soon as he resolved the issue he'd come back to the land of the living.

Which is exactly what happened. We were sitting around the fire when suddenly his eyes came into focus. He smiled like he hadn't seen me all day.

"You sort things out?" I asked him.

His smile got wider as he explained. The common theory on rods was they were one of the world's first flying organisms, an ancient, long thought extinct insect that managed to survive millions of years by appearing virtually invisible. Others believed they were of extraterrestrial origin, alien life forms or tiny UFOs.

Dad had a different idea. Rods weren't terrestrial, but they weren't extraterrestrial, either. They were extradimensional. His reasoning had something to do with string theory and the multiverse, which I didn't quite grasp, but basically he believed these organisms existed across dimensions, maybe even served to bind them together. Every so often we'd get lucky and catch a glimpse of one in action.

Unfortunately last night wasn't one of those nights.

[CAMPING]

Alex didn't question her friend's motivation. She just nodded in agreement when Cammie told her they absolutely had to go. She'd never been camping before. It was something Cammie and her father had shared, something Alex had always been jealous of. She told herself she'd deal with Cammie's eventual disappointment when the mystery uploader pulled a no-show. For now, she couldn't stop thinking about the two of them alone in a tent.

Distracted by anxious thought, Alex didn't notice the patch of loose rock. She pitched forward, coming down hard on her hands and knees. A high-pitched gasp escaped her mouth as she clutched her right hand to her chest. Cammie dropped into a crouch beside her.

"Shit. You're bleeding."

Alex scrunched up her face.

"Is it bad?"

Cammie whipped off her pack and produced a first aid kit. She tore open an alcohol swab and wiped away the blood on Alex's hand. Alex winced at the sight of the inch-long gash across her palm.

"It isn't bad, but it's in a bad spot. It could probably use a couple stitches." Cammie took a needle and thread out of the first aid kit.

"What? No!" Alex pulled her hand away.

"Relax. My mother's a nurse, remember? I've seen it done a thousand times. Why do you think we always had those pig's feet in the fridge?"

Alex's head went light at the thought of detached pink trotters sitting on a shelf next to the OJ, but it wasn't enough to gloss over what Cammie had said before that.

"*Seen* it done?"

Cammie fixed her friend with a look, then hiked up the leg of her jogging pants. A number of faded pink lines hid amongst the calf stubble. A series of faint dots flanked the lines. You could almost picture the threads criss-crossing between them.

"I've had to stitch myself up a couple times, too."

Alex looked from her friend's leg to her face. Cammie held her gaze for a brief moment, before self-consciousness reared its head and she launched back into surgical mode.

"If you don't let me stitch this, it's gonna get infected. And I'm not turning around now, you understand?"

Alex nodded.

"Look the other way, it'll only take a second."

Alex complied. It didn't hurt as much as she expected. She'd practically forgotten about the injury as Cammie led her through the woods by the uninjured hand, regaling her with tales of camping with Daddy. Alex hadn't seen Cammie that excited in a long time. It wasn't until they had set up camp and were sitting around the fire that the mood turned somber and Alex began to worry once again.

"So . . ." she said. "When do you think he'll show?"

He. Not *dad*. That word was too concrete, too real.

"I don't know." Cammie jabbed a stick into the fire, watched the embers float upward.

"Maybe it's like one of those Santa Claus situations. He won't show up until after we fall asleep."

Cammie responded with a wan smile. Light and shadow danced across her face.

"Maybe."

The hum of insects filled the silence that followed. A familiar silence, one that signified a subject unbroached, even by best friends. But eventually the silence grew too loud.

"You don't know any reason why he would have left your mother, do you?"

Cammie looked up, as if Alex had stuck her with a knife, a frightening resolve behind her eyes.

"Maybe my mother," she said. "But never me."

Alex drifted on the cusp of wakefulness and sleep, the details of a pleasant dream floating just out of reach. She knew it had been a good one because she felt a familiar warmth between her legs that radiated outward through her body. Eyelids heavy with sleep fluttered open, which is when she noticed the shadow looming over her.

THE PROTOPTERYGOTE TAPES

She stiffened. The shadow had pulled away the sleeping bag and positioned itself between her legs. It leaned in close, and despite the almost total darkness Alex recognized the shape of its face, remembered where she was, who she was with.

The swelling in her chest exceeded the feeling between her legs.

Cammie sat back and lifted her hand. It glistened in an unknown light. A gossamer strand hung between her fingers and Alex's body. Cammie gave a wry smile. She leaned forward again. Alex closed her eyes and pushed against Cammie's hand. Cammie pulled away. A low groan formed in the back of Alex's throat.

"Please . . . "

She opened her eyes and followed the thread back up to Cammie's hand, where it looped through the eye of a slender steel cylinder.

A needle.

Alex's muscles contracted and her entire body went cold. Cammie smiled as she leaned in for another stitch.

Alex jerked awake and threw off her sleeping bag. She grabbed the flashlight next to her as she shoved her hand down her pants. She clicked on the light. Her hand came back wet with blood.

"Fuck."

She turned to ask Cammie if she'd had the foresight to bring tampons, but Cammie wasn't there. Alex unzipped the tent and stuck her head outside.

"Cammie?"

The only answer was the hum of the insects. It reminded Alex of Tape #28. She listened for ragged breathing beneath the woodland noise. She jumped when she heard it. It was her own.

She tip-toed towards the camera. They had set it up five yards out, facing away from the tent so the spotlight wouldn't keep them awake. Standing by the beam comforted her—light offered protection.

She scanned the edge of the beam's reach. Seeing nothing, she grabbed the handle and panned the spotlight across the camp. Grass rustled in the illumination as disturbed animals fled, but no Cammie.

Not wanting to be alone in the dark, Alex didn't bother repositioning the camera. She left it pointed at the opening of the tent, almost 180 degrees from where it had started. She hurried across the frame as she returned to the tent.

She sat up the rest of the night to keep watch, rationing her blinks. Chunks of time started to disappear. One moment she was staring at her friend's empty sleeping bag, the next she awoke to find Cammie inside of it. She shook her head to make sure she wasn't dreaming then shook her friend. Cammie bolted upright, alertness at one thousand percent.

"Daddy?"

Alex's heart broke a little inside her.

"No," she said, voice small. "It's just me."

Cammie hid under her sleeping bag and gave a Charlie Brown groan.

"Then why the hell did you wake me?" She sounded far away, voice muffled by down-filled flannel.

"I . . ." Alex trailed off. Maybe she'd dreamt the whole thing. She thought back to the dream she'd had and felt even worse. "Do you have any tampons?"

"In my backpack," Cammie said from under the blanket.

Alex rummaged around in her friend's bag until she found them.

"You sleep alright last night?"

"Like a log."

"I woke up in the middle of the night and didn't see you. Thought you might've stepped out."

Cammie pulled the sleeping bag away from her face and gave Alex a quizzical look.

"I didn't even get up to pee. Speaking of which."

Cammie pulled on her boots and exited the tent. Alex watched through the nylon as Cammie's shadow straightened up and stretched in the morning sun, then stopped, arms forming a giant V above her.

"Hey, Al? Did you move the camera?"

[THE CAMPING FOOTAGE]

Alex paced the room as Cammie connected the camera to the television.

"Will you cut that out? You're making me more nervous than I already am."

THE PROTOPTERYGOTE TAPES

Alex plopped down on the edge of the bed and gripped the duvet. Cammie reappeared from behind the television.

"Ready?"

She picked up the camera and pressed play. A familiar expanse appeared on screen. After some minor jostling the frame assumed the position it would maintain for the next few hours.

Cammie hit fast forward and the sun set in record time. A couple sped-up hours later, Alex stepped into the frame. Cammie took her finger off the button.

"The elusive Alex in her *un*-natural habitat."

"Funny."

But neither girl laughed.

They watched as Alex stepped behind the camera. Then, after an uneventful scan of the treeline, the frame came to rest on the tent. Alex huffed audibly offscreen before speed-walking back to safety. She gave one last look at her surroundings before disappearing inside. All became still. A flash of white filled the frame, accompanied by heavy digital artifacting, and then the screen went black.

Alex started to cry.

"You okay?" The television backlit a concerned Cammie.

Alex folded her arms across her stomach.

"I don't feel so good all of a sudden."

"Could be motion sickness. DV does that sometimes."

Alex shook her head.

"I feel like I've just seen something horrible and can't remember what it was."

Cammie studied her friend's face. Alex wasn't one to get emotional. She rewound the tape to right before it whited out and started moving forward, frame by frame.

Tent.

Tent.

Tent.

White.

And in that white, Cammie, arms outstretched, feet hovering an inch off the ground. Her hair stood out from her head as if charged with electricity. A dozen rods circled her body, forming a sphere of light around her. Some of them entered her flesh, could be seen coming out the other side. One pierced each hand. Another stabbed her chest.

They stared at the image for a small eternity. Then the video moved ahead one more frame and it vanished. When they closed their eyes they could both still see it.

FIELD NOTES: THE CAMPING TRIP

In an instant it all came back to me—communing with the Seamstress, her outline painted in protopterygote streaks. Threads of light piercing my flesh, stitching me into time itself.

I sensed another presence as well—my father. Why had he led me there? I could tell he did not want this but was powerless to protect me.

A sudden burst of emotion diffused in the air, drawing the attention of the Seamstress. An anesthetic that numbed the pain I felt and relaxed my limbs. I found strength and pulled against the threads that bound me. The fabric of infinity began to tear. Then a shockwave of psychic energy, a feeling of great anguish slammed against me, and I woke up in the tent next to Alex. In that moment of fading sleep, I knew my father had sacrificed himself for me. Then the feeling passed, an image burned into a single frame of video the only proof of what happened.

Maybe someday I'll tell Alex what took place in that split second of time, but for now I don't think she can handle it. I can barely handle it myself. In the wake of viewing the video we crumpled into each other's arms and cried. Then we climbed into bed, curled up next to each other, and slept.

[THE AFTERMATH]

Alex woke early the next morning. The feeling in her stomach had not subsided. Light haunted her periphery. When she looked at Cammie, her uneasiness intensified. Psych 101 terms like *engulfment* and *abandonment* dominated the rational part of her mind as she tried to explain her irrational fears.

She slipped out of bed, slipped out of the room, and after taking one last look at her friend, slipped out of her life completely. She would come to understand it wasn't a decision she made in that moment, but one she'd made many times over the course of their relationship. Years later she'd go as far as telling herself the decision had been made *for* her.

Cammie's mom stood in front of the bathroom mirror, getting ready for work. She raised an eyebrow at Alex's departure but said nothing. Alex drove home on autopilot. Floated through her classes in a daze. Every time she blinked she saw Cammie suspended in light. She could handle the cutting, Cammie's obsession with her father, but this . . .

That night Cammie paged her 9-1-1. Alex didn't respond. She didn't respond the next day either, or the day after that. She thought about getting rid of her beeper. Nobody used them anymore. A week later Cammie continued to page her, so Alex took out the battery. A month later she saw an item on the news about the local girl who had mysteriously disappeared, like her father before her.

Alex spent the next six months in a guilt-ridden fugue.

Then, one day, a sliver of clarity, the potential for closure. An unexpected package arrived in the mail. It didn't have a return address, but the postmark indicated it came from somewhere in Mexico.

The envelope contained a piece of paper torn out of a spiral notebook and a mini DV tape labelled "Tape Zero." She only knew of one place she'd be able to play it.

Cammie's mom didn't say a word when she opened the door. She just led Alex to Cammie's room. It looked the same as the day Alex had left, DV camera still plugged into the back of the TV. It made Alex wonder about the tape in her hand. How had it been made? She pressed eject, half expecting to find the tape from the camping trip, but the camera was empty. She inserted Tape Zero and closed the cassette holder. Before she pressed play, she reread the note.

FIELD NOTES: TAPE ZERO

It was with a heavy heart that the Seamstress took up her needle to darn the fabric torn by man. I know this now. My father knew it as well. His memory is here with me, and though it was not his intention that I join him in his fate, it soothes me to finally know the truth. His attempts at contact were not an invitation, but a warning, that I might be discouraged from following in his path. Sadly, they achieved the opposite.

If only you'd been there to convince me to stay.

Light and heat pierce my flesh as I am woven into the veil that separates this world from ours. She is the Mother of Needles, the Cutter of Threads, and she uses our being to repair the damage done. That is our punishment.

Please do not try to find me. You will find only pain.

—Cammie

[TAPE ZERO]

The camera panned to reveal the yawning expanse of the crater. Wind beat against the microphone, dominating the soundtrack. Five hundred yards below, darkness engulfed visibility.

The camera pushed forward, as if trying to get a closer look, and then it was hurtling downward at a frightening speed. Alex's breath caught in her throat as she watched.

The black of the crater rushed towards the camera, widening to engulf the whole of the frame. Soon the screen went completely dark. Alex thought maybe the video had ended. She looked and the timer had in fact stopped counting.

But then the texture of the darkness changed. It became sharper, grittier. It appeared as if time had slowed, the camera and the darkness no longer rushing to meet one another, observing each other instead.

A spec of light illuminated the frame. It streaked past the lens, a glowing tail in its wake. Another appeared, then another. The frame whited out completely. A flash, like the darkness had ended and the camera had pushed through into the light. Everything turned blue, like the sky—although that couldn't be right—like the camera traveled up instead of down, rocketing through the atmosphere, through its various layers, beyond where weather existed, beyond where satellites flew, all the way into the vastness of space, except it couldn't be space, because there were no stars. A limitless nothing, a complete absence of light.

Unless the video had ended and Alex hadn't realized. She paused and unpaused the camera numerous times, to no avail. She checked the cables. She thought about pulling the plug on the TV, but instead settled in and continued to stare at the blank screen to make sure she didn't miss anything. She stayed that way until Cammie's mother asked her to leave.

THE PROTOPTERYGOTE TAPES

[SURVEILLANCE VIDEO: 071405]

In 2005, surveillance cameras at a Chinese pharmaceutical company produced the clearest images of a protopterygote to date. Scientists set up nets to ensnare the creatures, and the cameras documented their capture. Upon inspection the next morning, the nets contained only insects.

A few years later, a group of intrepid television personalities armed with the latest high-speed cameras trekked into the forest under cover of night. Their footage corroborated the Chinese evidence—the blurry, elongated images of rods captured by traditional video cameras were an effect due to the slow frame rate. High speed cameras revealed the creatures to be nothing more than common moths.

The footage aired as part of a cryptozoological television show on a previously respectable cable science channel. Though true believers persisted, what miniscule mystery the subject contained for the larger public vanished. By that point, Joe Sanchez's website existed only as a nostalgic archive of the internet past, although all his original videos have been made available on Youtube.

Alex never uploaded the footage of Tape Zero.

LIFE BEGINS AT INJECTION

Hailey Piper

"AND THIS WILL make me straight?" Camille asked, eyes fixed on the syringe.

Across the white examining room, Dr. Scott drove the needle into a brown glass vial. Amber fluid filled the syringe. "As an arrow, potentially," he said. "Barbaric conversion therapy is a thing of the past. We're all free citizens of the state and deserve to be treated as such."

"We want to get right with the state, don't we?" Dad asked. He stood sentinel against the wall in his tan business suit, face etched with worry lines as if Camille might change her mind and charge from the room. A rack of brochures stuck out beside him, where a familiar blue paper read: *Don't fret what you are—volunteer at your local research facility and together, we'll fix you. Normal family, normal life, normal happiness.*

The examining table's paper crinkled beneath Camille. She wasn't going anywhere. "Am I the first?"

"We've successfully treated several young men of deviant same-sex inclinations." Dr. Scott drew the needle free, its tip dripping yellow tears. "Side effects were mild stomach irritation and faint headaches. You'll be our first young woman, but there's no reason to believe you're any different."

Camille glanced longingly at her purse, which sat across the room. She would've felt better if she could make her one pointless phone call. "How does it work?"

"Think of it like an electrician for your brain," Dr. Scott said, nearing the examining table. "A little rewiring from deviant to normal, and you'll have bagged the quarterback by your school's Spring Fling."

Camille pictured girls her age hunting across Miller High's football field, sweeping up their high school crushes into giant cloth bags, the mouths cinched with electrical wire. She stuck out her arm. The imagery didn't please her, but then neither did the thought of statesmen hauling her off while her belly filled with confused butterflies over Leesi Thompson.

Camille never made A's in math class, but this equation seemed simple. Bagging football boys, she'd survive. Gazing at girls, she wouldn't.

Dr. Scott flicked the needle, and another yellow teardrop fell. "Gene therapy means we'll soon be fixing the better nature of babies in the womb, born normal. We get closer each day."

"See?" Dad piped up. "Even babies struggle. Doesn't matter how it works, only that it works."

"Yes, Daddy," Camille said, eyes downcast. "Sorry for asking."

While she wasn't looking, the needle pierced her skin.

Dad stopped at the front desk to finish paperwork. Camille left him for the outdoors. March's chill offered no sympathy for her aching arm, and she plucked out her phone to find some warmth.

"Mom's office," she said, and the phone dialed. When the receptionist answered, Camille added, "Monica Kates."

A long pause stood outside the doctor's office, breathing cold air down her back before the receptionist returned.

"I'm sorry, it appears she no longer works here."

Camille already knew that. The long pause had been her hollow space to pretend otherwise. She hung up.

<<<< >>>>

Two weeks later, she tore across her moonlit back yard in pajamas, a bulging, blood-drenched pillowcase swinging from her fists.

Beyond the yard, dark pine trees climbed a slope overlooking I-316, its lanes streaking with headlights and roaring engines. Camille's problem would end there.

An hour after she first fell asleep, she'd felt dampness between her thighs. No preemptive cramps or spotting this past week; her period brought sudden onslaught. After tampon, pad, change of underwear, and an ibuprofen, she hoped to sleep until morning.

Instead, she'd awoken past midnight to something larger and bloodier sharing her bed.

She stopped running just past the trees. Headlights swept the hillside at regular intervals, their visual rhythm beating in time with her heart. Trembling hands pried open the pillowcase. She hoped that it bulged because it had somehow become filled with socks, or the dream of a bagged football boy, and that she'd imagined the thing in her bed. Maybe she'd swept like a phantom through the night for nothing.

No—her nose wrinkled at the dead raccoon's hairy stink.

She didn't know where he might have come from or why he was dead, but he couldn't stay. She tilted the pillowcase toward I-316, and her problem disappeared down the lee side of the hill.

Back home, she scrubbed amber-colored streaks from her bedroom window sill—raccoon residue?—and swapped the bloodstained sheets for new ones. If Dad noticed anything amiss before she did the laundry, he'd assume "lady troubles." Nothing worse.

She found him asleep in his office, one hand cozied against a beer bottle, the other wedged between the black covers of his and Mom's wedding album. They'd had the traditional big wedding, the kind that rocked the world. Across dozens of photographs, he smirked while she beamed, her skin an almost sickly pale compared to his, and yet she'd seemed much more beautiful than Camille would ever be.

Leesi Thompson's mother must've thought the same. Why else had their two mothers risked being stolen away forever? Now they were gone. The statesmen had brought that fate to both houses one night nearly a year ago.

Camille supposed every life torn away by the statesmen left behind ragged ends of spouses and children. The dead rode a palanquin carried by the living, and their ghosts weighed heavy. She couldn't wake Dad over new dead things when his wife and marriage were already crushing him. A little perseverance on her part, and they might have a shot at being a family again. She closed his office door and hoped they both had pleasant dreams.

And that nothing like tonight would happen again.

< < **< <** **> >** > >

She tried to push the dead raccoon out of her mind at school the next day, but every time one of Miller High's assigned statesmen stormed past a classroom door in his thick, clacking boots, she couldn't help but think of deviancy. Maybe the treatment had cured her straight— normal—but would the state tolerate bedroom roadkill? Not unless everyone kept some.

Two statesmen slowed behind her locker while she swapped her history textbook for chemistry. Their presence jammed icicles through her veins. Everything would be fine if she could only behave exactly right at every possible moment. A shock collar would've been handy. Offer those to students, and she would be first to bare her neck.

She watched the statesmen pass down the lockers, yellow metal jutting toothlike from the walls, and at the end of the row stared Leesi Thompson. Where a swarm of friends once buzzed around her, now she stood as alone as Camille. Both girls had shed social standing after their mothers' arrests.

They looked over each other, Camille's eyes full of questions: What did my mother see in yours? How could she be worth throwing your family away?

Leesi probably wondered the same.

The bell buzzed, and Camille hurried to chemistry. A statesman faced her from down the hall, gaze hidden by his helmet's black shield. His blue uniform looked disheveled. Today must have been another student's birthday. Eighteen years old, time to sign an agreement toward normal marriage, normal happiness, or else.

Yet absent mothers proved the agreement was no guarantee.

"I bet they dissect your freak brains," Leesi said, sweeping past Camille, into the classroom.

Camille almost said she was sorry for standing in the way but bit her lip.

"There's no fixing people like you, but if we sift out what's wrong from the muck, next comes antibodies, cure, vaccine." Leesi rapt her fist against her chemistry textbook in time with the last three words. "Dead deviants make a normal future." That she was talking about her own mother, too, didn't seem to bother her.

The rhythm of statesmen's boots pounded through Camille's bones, and she scurried to her seat. That same percussion had thrummed down her driveway when they dragged Mom to their white van, the men wearing blue uniforms and black boots, Mom wearing cotton pajamas as white as her eyes that night. They hadn't let her get dressed.

Camille envisioned hers and Leesi's mothers being taken to some remote facility. There, knowledge scraped from a thousand deviant brains might swirl in a syringe filled with yellow fluid. Their mothers' brains, too, might float in jars. Deviation worth studying.

Camille glanced at her arm, still bruised where Dr. Scott had plunged a needle through her skin. If the treatment didn't work and the statesmen hauled her off, maybe they'd scrape her brain cells into the next test tube.

Antibodies, cure, vaccine. A long pause for each phone call to Mom's office that never amounted to a cheerful *How's it going, sweetie?* anymore, and never would again.

No, Mom's fate wasn't Camille's anymore. The thought of kissing a boy's face only slightly turned her stomach, but it didn't entirely repulse her. Boys might even dance with her at Spring Fling in a few weeks. She couldn't imagine getting butterflies for Leesi anymore, at least.

Maybe the treatment was working.

Three nights after the racoon, Camille plucked a dead squirrel from her bed. The same panic sent her flying through yard and woods to the hill overlooking I-316. Four nights later, another squirrel, and then a cat that she hoped was feral; he didn't wear a collar. A slender hole had been dug into each animal's head. That first racoon might have had the same.

Someone would eventually find their carcasses beside the interstate, but that wasn't her problem. She needed them gone. Each time she cleaned her sheets, she wondered if she owed the animals apologies. They weren't coming to her bed to die; something inside her had changed, gone hunting at night, and found prey. Was it her fault that she couldn't remember? Questions clawed at her dreams.

Daylight brought no relief. Instead, knives twisted in her gut. She'd heard of other girls having cramps between periods, but this intensity was new to her.

So were the headaches. Some mornings, something punched behind her eyes, as if her injection's metaphorical electrician had wired up her spine and rooted around deep in her brain, plucking out what it wanted and leaving nightmares in exchange. Mom's face swirled in dreams, auburn hair swaying past her pale shoulders. The way she'd looked before the statesmen stormed the house.

The dreams might have been premonitions—like mother, like daughter, the deviant apple didn't fall far from the deviant tree.

Only Mom never had an electrician in her skull.

In the morning, Camille tried Mom's office again, and the long pause settled its arms across her shoulders, an eager grin plastered over its face. Happy to indulge in her misery, but it wouldn't speak to her.

Neither would Mom, of course. "I'm sorry, miss," the receptionist said. "Is there someone else I can connect you to?"

Camille hung up. Someday, the office would block her number, but for now she could keep pretending that the long pause would bring a different outcome.

< < < < > > > >

"It's not like I regret the treatment, it's just—" Camille chewed her lip. "Side effects."

Dr. Scott didn't look her in the eyes, instead fixated on a clipboard as if its papers were his patient, fretting about normalcy only a scant couple of months before her eighteenth birthday. "Side effects," he repeated.

Camille clutched her still-cramping abdomen. "You said only boys were treated before, but I'm the first girl, and since my last period—"

"Probably growing pains," Dr. Scott cut her off. "No need for details; any trouble would show in monthly blood tests. What about your same-sex inclinations?"

Camille shook her head. Had her mother ever been asked that question?

"And toward boys?" Dr. Scott asked.

Camille shrugged, head still swimming with nighttime yard runs. Growing pains? At seventeen, she should have finished any significant puberty-driven changes.

No, Dr. Scott wanted her to get with the program, be normal, and sweep any contradicting trouble under the rug. She could rationalize away nightmares, cramps, and even that constant intrusive sensation in her head. She couldn't explain the dead animals.

And she didn't want to. Maybe most straight people woke up to bloody wildlife in their beds now and then, or felt intrusions pawing inside their brains. She hadn't noticed that in Dad, Leesi, or the other normal folk in her life, distracted by her—what had Dr. Scott called them?—same-sex inclinations.

"Sorry, you're right, Dr. Scott," she said. "I guess it's nothing."

He walked her out from his office, chatting amicably about how she would be crushing on some boy any day now, when the pale walls and hard floor echoed with hollering. At the hall's end, a statesman clad in blue dragged a teenage boy by the arm and neck, while a second shoved him along from behind.

Camille recoiled, but Dr. Scott placed a firm hand on her shoulder. "Not everyone's trying as hard as you," he said, and gave a squeeze.

The boy flashed pleading eyes toward Dr. Scott, but he and the first statesman passed the corner. He would never be seen again except by a vial to be filled by amber fluid. The second statesman thrust one arm in a shove and then turned down the hall to Camille and Dr. Scott. Eyes hidden behind his face shield, Camille understood he was staring at her. Every statesmen had to see deviancy in the youth, potential to lose control and become wild creatures that craved raw flesh. He held the line between normal happiness and unknowable chaos.

Camille waited until both statesmen went unseen for two minutes before she sped through the parking lot and into her dad's car. No white van idled elsewhere on the asphalt. The statesmen were already gone. She would have called Mom's office again if she could get a moment alone.

But Dad was here. "Good?" he asked, checking his mirrors.

LIFE BEGINS AT INJECTION

Camille nodded, her head tied by marionette strings of expectation.

He drove them out of the lot before adding, "Spring Fling's soon. Got a date?"

She had disclaimers she wanted to say, about how even a thorough rewiring would take time to find acceptance in her soul, but in his silence, Dad went on speaking: *Don't break my heart, I'm begging you.*

Camille didn't look at him when she said, "Sorry, zoned out a sec. Yeah, a boy on the football team, like we both wanted." She kept her eyes fixed out her window, but his smile spread like too-hot sunshine across the back of her neck.

"I'm happy for you, really," he said, chuckling. "And don't think of it as commitment. It's one night out. Not like you're getting married, or that you're pregnant."

He wouldn't mind that though, would he? Pregnancy meant the treatment had worked in his eyes, as if that had saved Mom from being dragged out of their lives. Camille knew from watching old TV shows that men used to threaten all manner of death and dismemberment against boys who so much as glanced at their daughters. Nowadays, any lecherous goon was preferable to seeing Camille become an echo of a mother long gone.

"No, nothing inside me," she whispered.

She found one more squirrel in her bed the night before the dance. Exhausted after so many sprints to I-316, she dumped it out the window of Dad's office. He likely wouldn't notice.

< < < < > > > >

Spring Fling filled Miller High's gymnasium with white and canary yellow streamers and matching plastic flowers. Boys stood two feet apart in their ill-fitting suits, only touching when they punched each other's arms. Girls gave careful compliments toward clothes, hair, and jewelry, never faces or figures.

Camille swept through the gymnasium doorway in a flowing teal gown, slender purse over one arm, date's hand on the other. He wore a baby blue suit and a dazzling smirk.

If only she could remember his name.

Leesi stood at the punch table, no date in sight. She stared until Camille turned to the dance floor. She could hate all she pleased, but she couldn't know the price of standing here. Neither girl would ever get closure with her mother. If Mom had known she could have kept her family and her life by stomaching a few dead animals in her bed at night, would she have stayed?

Or would Camille's treatment have been impossible without her mother's arrest? Brain scraps in vials, amber serum in veins. Camille might not have agreed to the treatment trial if not for Dad's anxiety.

She scanned the dance floor, where the girls might have once caught her eye. Tonight, she saw only dresses, Miller High's gymnasium haunted by decorative ghosts. She was normal now, a creature of—what had Dr. Scott said?—her better nature. These were absences she would have to get used to.

Her date's arms encircled her. They wiggled and loped to silly pop music for what felt like hours, action akin to dancing. When a slower song nudged him to hold her close, she didn't fight. His arms and chest were safe, hardy furniture she could lean against. That had to be normal affection, right? It only seemed natural when he pressed a gentle hand under her chin and tilted her face upward. Toward his face, his approaching lips.

But she didn't kiss him.

A wet lump wriggled up the back of her throat. She gagged, terrified she would vomit all over him right in the middle of Spring Fling. She would've turned away, but he held her chin.

A tube of narrow, clammy flesh rolled over her tongue and past her teeth, where it brushed the boy's lips. His tongue slipped into her mouth and caressed the tube. She spotted it briefly at the edge of sight as he let her go, a chalk-white thread that prodded at his face and then swept back into her mouth.

It had to be a tapeworm. She'd heard they could come up the esophagus at night, hadn't she?

Her date didn't comment. When he drew his lips back, his smile turned awkward. He hadn't seen the white flesh.

Camille covered her mouth. "Excuse me, sorry." She darted out the back of the gymnasium, through the girls' locker room, and into its adjoining restroom. Her swinging purse reminded her of a carrion-filled pillowcase.

The wet lump wriggled up again, desperate this time. Camille's stomach lurched. She'd never heard of parasites this strong. She ducked into the first stall, pressed palms to either wall, and doubled over.

A bundle of fleshy ropes spilled past her lips toward the toilet bowl and dangled there. She grasped one slick white strand, but tugging it felt like pulling her own tongue.

These things were no parasite's entrails, but parts of her.

They slid back inside her mouth, some down her throat, others up into her skull, systemic as her blood vessels. Dr. Scott's metaphorical electrician—that had to be her trouble. The treatment had changed her. Now fleshy muscle stretched from her body and hunted animals' brains at night. They had prodded at her date's head same as any squirrel's, eager to break inside.

But they didn't look like her. Their flesh came in various pale shades, sharing her mother's sickly tone. Camille hadn't seen skin like that since Mom disappeared.

The pieces crashed together, unstoppable dominos: Statesmen. Capture. Dissect brains. And then what, antibodies, cure, vaccine? Experimental treatment. Injection.

She leaned deeper over the toilet bowl. "Mom?" she whispered. She fished her phone out of her purse. "Mom's office." The long pause packed itself into the stall with her, now waiting on a nighttime answering service somewhere in the Midwest that had too many clients and too few ears.

The restroom door creaked open, and high heels clicked the tile floor. "Camille?" Leesi called. "Where'd you go?"

Camille hung up, stuffed her phone into her purse, and then coughed globby amber droplets across the toilet seat. "Not now."

Acrylic nails tapped the stall door as two legs' shadows filled the gap underneath. "It has to be now, before I change my mind," Leesi said.

A tremor stirred through Camille's body. Could she be sure these worming arms belonged to her mother? Many things were pale. Maybe most straight people coughed up tangles of white flesh.

"Do tentacles come out your mouth?" Camille asked.

The tapping stopped. "Tentacles?" Leesi asked.

"Do they kill animals while you sleep, and dig inside your skull, and wear skin like your dead m—" A cramp tore through Camille's middle, forcing her to double over and cry out. Mom would never hurt her like this. Tentacles meant her serum's electrician had confused what aspects made a person normal. She should've changed from gay to straight, but the electrician had turned some other, forbidden dial from human to other.

The stall door squeaked; Camille had forgotten to lock it. She leaned against the wall, weary and aching. Leesi had to see the toilet's amber stains, realize something was wrong, and show mercy for once.

"I came to apologize," she said.

Camille wasn't hearing this. Especially not now, after a year of glares and taunting. "Apologize?" she coughed.

"I'm sorry about your mom," Leesi went on. "It wasn't your fault what happened to mine. You're not like them, same as I'm not like them. I saw you with your date, and you looked—you were normal. Everything we dream of. You'll have that big wedding someday, and normal happiness, and you'll never have to worry about the statesmen. I should've been better to you."

Camille's guts rumbled. Why couldn't this have come some other night?

High heels clicked, but not to leave. A hand grasped Camille's shoulder and spun her around to face Leesi, another decorative ghost in a violet dress. Any thoughts to fill out that dress with a girl seemed intrusive, Camille's brain gone haywire. Maybe her desperate electrician was looking to unplug the tentacles cord and had to try everything before it could get the settings right.

Or maybe Mom really was alive inside and watching the echo of the woman she'd loved. Leesi's mother might be alive too, bits of brain now floating in a jar somewhere, waiting to be injected and revived in some girl's blood, stomach, and skull. She might have been injected into someone already.

"The hell happened to you?" Leesi asked, eyes trailing the stained gown.

Camille forced a smirk. "Being normal happened."

Leesi peered closer, and her eyes widened to binoculars. "Are you pregnant?" A delighted scream lit the back of her throat and transformed into a warm word: "Congratulations!"

"Not pregnant," Camille tried to answer, but Mom's slimy arms tossed at the back of her throat. Leesi knew nothing of screaming inside.

LIFE BEGINS AT INJECTION

She kept spilling compliments, but Camille couldn't hear the rest. Her head filled with cold flesh, Mom's muscly arms tearing through the back of her skull. The electrician must have unplugged her eyes, as darkness stole her vision. She couldn't see Mom's milky tendrils, but she felt them reach around from behind her and speed toward the stall doorway.

Leesi must have started screaming in earnest—her mouth felt open and unresisting. Teeth, palette, throat, skull, brain, *there*. Whatever Mom had sought out in wildlife, she found it inside Leesi, too.

When their work was done, the arms slipped back to Camille's head, and they did not return empty-handed, grasping pieces wet and warm. Her hearing snapped back as Leesi hit the bathroom tiles.

Camille's heel slid in an unseen puddle, and soft floor lumps threatened to trip her. Leesi was dead, same as any squirrel. Camille would never be normal. The statesmen would come for her.

Fleshy ropes trailed from the back of her head like thick, muscly hair and unspooled down her shoulders, arms, and spine. Their firm squeeze was the closest she'd felt to a hug in months. Tears didn't clear her eyes, but it wasn't like she tried to open them. Maybe she didn't need to see anymore, and that was why Mom had taken her sight.

Mom's wet arms patted at cool walls to guide Camille back through the locker room to the gymnasium doorway. The slow song was gone, replaced by some decades-old tune that demanded its dancers clap their hands to its beat. Camille wouldn't lift her arms, but Mom reached out to join Spring Fling.

"Mom," Camille whispered beneath the thunderous clapping. "Don't hurt them."

No promises. Much as she felt the tentacles' every twitch, she didn't seem to command them. Whatever procedure had scraped away Mom's cells to develop the serum had also scraped out her love. Pain filled her, and she would push it into everyone she touched. She grasped the gymnasium doorway and dragged Camille inside.

Without seeing the other students of Miller High, only listening, they seemed huddled closer together than she had ever known. They smelled closer, too, music encircling them in a thick cloud of teenage excitement. For a moment, they seemed empowered to dance to their own tune. None of their fear was their fault any more than Camille's love was hers.

She scarcely felt love now. Like daughter, like mother.

"Camille, where've you been?" a boy asked. "You okay? What's that stuff in your hair?"

That was her date, right? Camille couldn't be sure. She hadn't really learned his voice any better than his name. She supposed she owed him an apology for both.

One wet arm thrust from the back of her head. She couldn't see her date, but she felt his skin, skull, brain. Poor boy; sweet little ghost.

The rest went quickly. Arms shot in every direction and found another skull, and another, and hundreds more. The fleshy ropes seemed to lengthen, fatten, and multiply the more ghosts they made. Camille's couldn't count them, her eyes still blinded, but she felt muscly flesh tug the gymnasium's doors shut.

There was no way out.

The clapping broke into screams. Camille pressed her hands over her ears to muffle them, and the music's bass quaked down her bones, overtaking the world. The song went on for two more minutes. By the time it ended, so had the screams.

At least the deaths were quick. In and out and done.

Camille lowered her hands, and another quiet slow song seeped across the gymnasium. Several of Mom's countless arms had grown elephantine, their muscles so thick they had no trouble coiling around Camille and lifting her off the ground. The floor beneath her feet was a subtle sensation anyway; her nerves stretched in every direction. She seemed one with the gymnasium's walls, ceiling, and bodies, football and non-football boys bagged alongside the girls. Mom was doing something to them that Camille didn't understand and didn't want to. Firm, muscly arms drew her to their center, where she curled up as if Mom's flesh was a soft nest. Without seeing the dead, Camille could almost believe this was okay.

Not normal, though. The only way she and her mother would be normal now was to change normalcy's criteria. If they killed the statesmen who would soon come for them, the doctors, the military to follow, and then everyone and everything until they were the only two living creatures in the world, then they could be relatively normal.

They had to start somewhere.

Camille reached into her purse and felt for her cellphone. No need to call Mom's office anymore. If Camille could see, she might have deleted the number, but instead she told her phone who else to call and then waited to hear him pick up.

"Come get me," she said. "I'm in the gym." She hung up without explanation and let her phone slide to the floor, where it hit something soft. She imagined the long pause lay dead among the bodies. No more waiting for an answer that wouldn't come.

Mom was here.

Twenty minutes passed before she heard dress shoes clack the vinyl floor in Miller High's hallway. Dad was still dressed for work. Mom uncoiled from the doors so that he could yank them open. Once he staggered into the gymnasium, the doors slammed shut behind him.

Camille guessed at what he saw—a heap of corpses cocooned in flesh beneath her at the dance floor's center, encircled by fallen streamers. A web of thick white limbs stretched in all directions, his daughter cradled at the center.

She turned toward the sound of his footsteps. "I'm sorry, but I couldn't tell you or you wouldn't come," she said. "Please don't be upset. This is a good thing. Look—I found Mom. You were right about the treatment. We're together, like you wanted, like we both wanted. Mom wanted it, too, and now we all get what we want. What are you saying, Dad? Your noises don't make sense."

A wet surge twitched through her scalp and across the gargantuan flesh web. Every inch of her mother went taut. One long arm of flesh twined around Camille's father and pulled him close. He was hurting, but so was Camille. Same as when Mom died, now again that she was resurrected. That was how families survived, by sharing the pain.

"See, Dad? It's going to be okay." Camille forced herself to smile, and she hoped that when Dad noticed, he would smile back. And maybe Mom, too, in her own way. "We can be a family again."

12 Modern Ruins

MODERN RUINS

Rebecca Jones-Howe

BEHIND THE VALENTINE'S DAY card display stands a wall that separates Target from the abandoned interior of Sahali Summit Mall. Brad removes a row of cards and presses his hand to the display fixture, imagining the decaying mall concourse on the other side. He used to throw pennies in the fountain when he was a kid, used to wish that he'd be a better hockey player so his dad would stop harassing him to make goals like Gretzky.

Mall management had the fountain filled in the early aughts. That was the beginning of the end, when franchise stores started to vacate and the remaining local tenants saw a growing decrease in foot traffic.

Brad recollects when he got his job at the already-struggling Sport Chek. Dawn worked at the neighbouring store called Summit Music. A strip of magenta neon lined the store's perimeter, burnt out in places. Most of the CD stands were dented and rickety and replaced with wire discount bins. Brad bought a copy of Franz Ferdinand's *You Could Have It So Much Better* back in 2005 just so he could talk to her.

"Well, do ya? Do ya, do ya want to?" Dawn asked, singing the tune of the album's single. Brad started spending his breaks on the bench outside of the mall's side entrance, hoping that Dawn would come out to smoke her honey-flavoured clove cigarettes.

Now, he picks out a card with a red heart over a pink polka-dot background.

IT'S VALENTINE'S DAY AND YOU TOUCH MY HEART

Something about the word *touch* sets him off. Not just physically, like he hasn't been touched in months, but deep down, like a fist pulling his throat into his body. A pressure that roots itself within. He digs into the slot for the card's matching envelope, hasty to leave because he still hasn't picked up the groceries yet.

He passes the display of Valentine's Day chocolates on the way out. They sit in a heart-shaped box, an impulse, a temptation, but Brad knows that his wife's favourite chocolates are at the Rocky Mountain Chocolate Factory.

He decides to make one last stop before heading home.

< < < < > > > >

He tucks the gifts beneath the seat of his truck and carries the groceries into the house. Dawn gathers the dinner plates and piles them into the kitchen sink. The baby cries in the high chair. The toddler cries in her booster seat. There's still a plate of Hamburger Helper beside his eldest child, Ethan, only it's not actually Hamburger Helper but a homemade version that Dawn makes because it's healthier.

Dawn scrapes half of the cold pasta and ground beef mixture into a Tupperware container for Brad's lunch tomorrow.

"How was work?" she asks.

Brad shrugs, has nothing to say about the bland monotony of the mail sorting plant.

Dawn sighs, tending to the baby instead of nagging him for coming home later than he promised. Brad eats his dinner out of the pot, appreciating Dawn's efforts while still missing the overly salty taste of the real Hamburger Helper that his dad always made after his parents divorced.

After eating, Brad scoops the toddler, Casey, out of her booster seat, and takes her upstairs to brush her teeth. He tries to wedge the brush past her screaming mouth, hoping to scrub away all the grime. Then it's to bed with a story and a lullaby, followed by a long session of coaxing to get her to sleep with the lights off. Then he returns to the table to help Ethan with his spelling homework.

SCREAM

QUIT

DEFENCE

Brad drills until his son's frustration starts to show, brows furrowed, fists clenched tight. Ethan's too old for stories or lullabies, so when he puts his son to bed, Brad has nothing to offer but a calming pat on the shoulder.

"If you fail the test, it's going to be okay. There will always be another."

"Okay, Dad."

Brad shuts Ethan's bedroom door, realizing that he probably said the wrong thing.

< < < < > > >>

Brad takes off his hard hat in the locker room. He shrugs out of his orange vest and digs his phone out of his locker to find the new picture of the grocery list that Dawn has sent. The list is always written on a chalkboard that hangs in their kitchen.

Most of his exchanges with Dawn consist of photos of the same chalkboard, her cursive handwriting telling him all the things he must collect in order to sustain their family for another week. It's what their marriage has become.

After work, Brad goes to Safeway.

Safeway isn't the family's usual grocery store, but it's the only other remaining anchor at the Sahali Summit Mall. He finds himself parking in front of it only to glance over at the old scar of the cursive neon sign that once hung in front of the mall's main entrance.

Brad swallows. The pressure returns in his throat. A tightness. An unsteadiness. It feels like an infestation, like it's something his body needs to fight.

Fresh snow falls over the empty mall parking lot. It starts to stick to the windshield and Brad gets out of the truck and hurries toward the grocery store. Safeway still has a florist counter, and Brad peers through the aged display case at a vase of roses, ultimately resorting to buy six for Dawn.

Just a token. A little perk. An apology for not being able to be a better man.

He packs the flowers in with the groceries and heads out. The snow's heavier now, its thick pack dampening his footsteps across the parking lot.

That feeling in his throat returns. It pulls at him, forces him to turn back.

The mall entrance waits, shadowed and still. His footsteps trudge toward the doors. They're boarded from the inside with plywood but that hasn't stopped vandals from smashing the glass. Shattered pieces slip under his feet. Brad puts the groceries down. He tests one of the doors. The metal handle wobbles. Broken pieces of tempered glass rattle as he shakes the door. Still locked. Still secure. He moves to the next door and the next, thinking of Ethan's spelling test.

SCREAM

QUIT

DEFENCE

He kicks the plywood that covers the last door on the right. The panel budges just a little. He kicks harder and knocks the wood loose.

Then he hears it.

White noise. Water rustling.

Kneeling down, Brad stares into the black vestibule. He sees himself in the glass of the interior doors, his face blue and warped. The pressure builds in his chest, coaxing him toward the darkness inside. He considers climbing through the small opening, but then thinks of how much it would mean to Dawn if he could make it home in time to have one dinner with his family.

Brad stands and hurries back to the truck. Upon putting the groceries inside, however, he realizes that the roses are missing. He traces his footsteps back to the mall entrance, but the sound of the fountain has ceased. The red flowers sit before the quiet mall entrance, trampled in the snow.

Dawn sends him a message, just a new item for the grocery list.

I need an onion for the soup. Is it too late?

It isn't, not really. He could go back to Safeway and give her what she wants, which is to make a healthy homemade version of Campbell's Chunky Vegetable and Beef.

He doesn't go back.

< < < < > > > >

Dawn's sobbing when Brad gets home. The kids sit in the living room. A movie plays on the television but none of the kids pay attention. They all look up when Brad places the groceries on the counter, and he hurries up the stairs and finds his wife laying on the bathroom floor, tearing at her hair.

She's past the point of consoling.

Brad goes back to the living room. "What happened to Mom?"

Ethan shrugs. "She burnt Casey's grilled cheese, I think."

"Oh," Brad says. He squeezes his hand over Ethan's shoulder and preheats the oven for a frozen pizza. Then he goes back upstairs and pulls his wife into his arms. He doesn't have the heart to tell her that he didn't get the onion.

He runs the water and pours the honey-scented bath salts in.

< < < < > > > >

At night he can't sleep. He digs through the photo albums on the bookshelf.

Brad finds a picture he took inside the mall with his old digital camera. The shot captured his father in mid-conversation with Dawn, standing near the planters placed where the mall fountain used to be. He remembers taking it the day he introduced his father to Dawn. It had already been several months into their relationship, but Brad wanted to keep the meeting casual, just lunch from the fish and chips stand.

Brad squints at the background, at the shuttered stores, their entrances either gated-off or boarded over completely.

FOR LEASE

"Make sure you treat her nice," his dad said after the meeting. "I didn't do the same for your mom, you know?"

He suffered from a heart attack two months after the photo was taken.

Brad got his dad's urn from Debbie's Fine Jewelry and Keepsakes, which was one of the last tenants inside the mall before it closed permanently.

He bought Dawn's engagement ring on the same day.

< < < < > > > >

On Friday night, Brad takes Ethan to his junior hockey game.

Ethan plays defence and spends most of his time defending himself instead of his side of the rink. It was like this when Brad played hockey too, only his dad always screamed from the stands, expecting more, expecting better.

Brad stares at his phone the entire game, only raising his head when the parents around him break into fits and cheers. Brad stands to watch his son get slammed into the sideboard.

The other parents gasp and clutch their hands over their mouths. Brad's heart pounds. He forces himself to breathe but that tight feeling is back again, strangling him. His breaths sound like they're underwater. Ethan takes a moment before getting up but his skate slips beneath him and he plummets to the ice a second time. The referee offers a hand. Ethan takes it. He adjusts his helmet and skates again, pretending like it didn't hurt.

Maybe today will be the day that Ethan will beg not to do another year of hockey.

Brad secretly hopes this but will never say it.

It was Dawn who wanted to put Ethan in hockey. She wanted to put Casey into dance. Brad can't exactly blame her. The moment she found out she was pregnant with Ethan, she threw her cigarettes away, replacing her only vice with the pressure to cook healthy foods and enroll all the children in extracurricular activities.

A modern life. A happier one.

Brad wishes he could spend money on a therapist instead. It'd be a better gift than chocolates and a card with a shitty sentiment.

He spends the rest of the game watching urban explorers walk through abandoned malls on YouTube.

"Urbex", the videos are called.

Ethan's team loses the game by four goals.

< < < <   > > > >

Brad tries to make the loss easier, allowing Ethan to pick out whatever flavour of ice cream he wants from the Safeway freezer. They walk out with mint chocolate chip and Brad nods at the dead mall entrance.

"Your mom and I met in there," he says.

Ethan doesn't say anything. The mall's been closed for most of his life. The boarded doors must look like some kind of relic. *Old school*, which is what the kids in the urbex videos say.

"Dad, what are you doing?"

"Come on," Brad says, walking toward the entrance. "See, there's a hole in the door? We could go inside if you want."

"We can't go in there, Dad."

"Sure we can. The hole's big enough."

Brad kneels down to look through the broken panel, surprised to find that all the interior doors of the vestibule have been opened. He pokes his head inside. The echo of the fountain sounds again. Whispers.

"Do you hear that?" Brad asks.

"Hear what?" Ethan asks.

"You can crawl in and unlock the door," Brad says.

Ethan shakes his head.

Brad stands, puts his hand on his son's shoulder and coaxes him toward the opening. "Don't you want to see all the things you missed?"

Ethan's face crumples, looks just like it did when he lost the hockey game. Still, Ethan does what is asked of him. He crouches down and peers inside.

"It smells so bad, Dad."

"Just unlock the door."

A white vehicle pulls up in front of the mall. The security guard leans out and shines a flashlight. Brad yanks his son's jacket and Ethan falls out of the opening and onto the pavement, his gasped sob cutting into the night.

Brad squints against the light's glare. He raises his hand.

DEFENCE

The guard lets them off with a warning and they both heave sighs of relief inside the comfort of the truck. Brad turns the key in the ignition. The engine's rumble fills his gut with dread.

"Don't tell your mom, okay? It was stupid. I know that. I just wanted you to see."

<&< < < > > >

Dawn rolls over at night, awakened by the glow of Brad's phone.

"Can you turn that off, babe?"

He pulls his headphones out and apologizes.

He continues watching in the dark of the living room. It's a video of Rolling Acres Mall in Akron, Ohio, the most famous of all the abandoned malls. The camera pans across an empty store wall desecrated with a series of graffiti.

MODERN RUINS

YOU CAN'T HIDE
I WILL FIND YOU
I WILL HURT YOU
I WILL KILL YOU

Former mall patrons post comments below the video. They share memories. They mourn.

Brad goes to the truck and he digs out the Valentine's Day gifts he bought for Dawn. He fidgets with a pen for an hour, clicking it again and again, listening to the echo in his own house, and he wonders what the pen would sound like in the vast empty space of the mall.

His mall.

Ballpoint to card, he writes what feels like a last testament.

< < < < > > > >

Ethan told me what you did last night. What is wrong with you?

Brad's only got five minutes left on his lunch break. Today's leftovers are tacos. Dawn made the seasoning herself, but a part of him still misses the over-salted Old El Paso that his dad used to swear by.

If Brad leaves the message unanswered, Dawn will replace the conversation with another picture of the chalkboard on the fridge. This isn't the right thing to do in a happy marriage. This isn't obeying his father's last demand of him.

Make sure you treat her nice.

Brad dims the screen of his phone before heading back to the warehouse floor.

I WILL FIND YOU

When the five minutes are up, he puts his hard hat back on and returns to his forklift. For the rest of his shift, he moves packages full of Amazon orders. Valentine's Day gifts, he imagines, set to arrive within two days of purchase.

< < < < > > > >

Dawn reads the Valentine's Day card, her expression fading his message. Brad smiles, his lips feeling plastic and mannequin-like. He opens his arms for a hug but her touch feels like nothing.

She opens the heart-shaped box from the Rocky Mountain Chocolate Factory and eats a praline. Ethan asks for one. Then Casey asks, and the box Brad spent forty dollars on melts in the greedy grasps of the children.

He wishes he'd gone back for the roses.

< < < < > > >

Rolling Acres is to become an Amazon Fulfilment Centre, so says the article on Brad's phone.

Something about the word *fulfilment* sets him off. Not just physically, like he hasn't felt useful in months, but in the tightest part of his throat. It feels like the hand of his father reaching from death to choke him.

SCREAM

I WILL HURT YOU

Dawn sends him a new picture of the chalkboard.

Brad glances up from the phone and stares at the mall entrance.

Sahali Summit Mall

His mall.

There are pictures of him inside of this mall but there is no history online, just a couple photos of the old sign.

He hasn't shared his memories with anyone. He hasn't mourned the loss.

Brad thinks about what would happen if he didn't buy any groceries. Just went home. Just found his wife crying. Just lay down on the floor beside her, the cold ceramic tile against his cheek.

The illuminated screen of his phone blacks out. Red shines down over his thumbs. He looks up again, where the neon's glowing. He hasn't seen that glow in years, the red of it warming, pulling him out of the truck, luring him across the parking lot, welcoming him home.

< < < < > > > >

He kicks at the plywood but it's been reinforced.

Hugging the shadows, he rounds the graffiti-tagged side of the building to the back employee entrance. The old bench remains, its seat covered over with snow and flimsy cardboard. The stench of piss radiates around the doorway. Plywood covers all the doors on the outside, but he tests one of the handles and finds the lower pin lock broken on the leftmost door.

Brad wrestles it until the loose lower hinge breaks. The metal wobbles on the frame and he ducks down and squeezes his way through. He goes in feet first, wedging the door open as he goes. Broken glass slices at his wrist.

"Shit." He stumbles as he stands, clutching over the torn flesh.

Blood drips down his fingers but the cut doesn't look that deep.

MODERN RUINS

The warmth is welcome, like a hand touching him, pulling him along like Dawn's lips in the darkness of her old dorm room.

The stench of mold pricks his nasal passage. It stings in his eye sockets and makes him squint in the dark. The mall's silence floods his ears. Blinking, adjusting, he pulls out his phone and turns on the flashlight. The white beam hits the tiled walls.

Cream and salmon and teal.

The mall was never renovated. It's a relic, a piece of the past. *Old school.*

Moonlight bleeds through the skylight over the mall's main concourse. The barricaded Safeway sits to the right. He turns to the left, where the flicking neon light casts shadows along the span of the corridor. The shadows move like people fluttering past, making Brad blink again, rapidly, like a seizure of time.

The light illuminates, directing him over the steps littered with shattered glass from all the broken shop fronts. The first place he enters is Summit Music. Only one line of neon radiates with magenta. It reflects off the broken pieces of glass at the shop entrance, little stars sprinkled over the moldy floor.

He traces his fingers over the old display cases, now void of the CD's he used to buy just to see Dawn, to talk to her. He'd never been all that great at talking to women. He once thought he was good at pretending, but even she caught on to that.

"You don't actually like Arcade Fire, do you?" she once asked. *"You don't seem like the type."*

Brad doesn't remember the last time he spoke to her. Really spoke to her.

A few posters still remain pasted to the walls above the checkout desk. He doesn't recognize any of the artists, just pop star remnants of the years that cast the mall into obscurity.

He walks over patches of black mold and fallen ceiling tiles. The material disintegrates beneath his feet, sticking to the soles of his New Balance sneakers. He passes the dollar store, the Sport Chek. He stumbles against the plastic spiral wishing well. Mall management had it put in shortly after the fountain was removed. It was a replacement home for everyone's hopes and dreams, loose coins looping around the yellow whirlpool of momentum, unable to prevent themselves from slipping into the black hole of a dying cause.

Packed snow from the roof slips through the broken panes of skylight glass. The flakes land over the tiles where the mall's fountain once stood. A vandalized exit sign sits on the floor now. The metal cables splay out like dead limbs. Brad kicks at the metal box. The sign appears to flicker, but he shines the flashlight over the letters and everything goes dull.

Brad's footsteps sound like gravel over the debris. The tightness in his lungs only worsens. The stagnant water and mold clings to the inside of his throat. Infests it. He shouldn't be here and yet he is, face to face with the cinder block wall that severs the Target from the dying remains of the mall. Reaching out, he touches the spot where he picked the Valentine's Day card a week before.

REMEMBER THE MALL? REMEMBER HOW WE FELT AT THE MALL? I STILL THINK OF YOU THE WAY YOU TOUCHED MY HEART AT THE MALL.

He wrote that.

In his delusion, he'd written that.

In this delusion, Brad draws a breath and chokes on the mold. Spores fill his throat like a fist clutching, tightening, a vice grip. He coughs. Sputters. He wipes his nose and the blood drips from the wound on his wrist. Neon red streaks the cuff of his jacket, drips down the sleeve. His phone slips out of his grasp and clatters across the floor, the screen landing face down.

He blinks hard, adjusts to the dark. He turns back toward the concourse, toward the fountain.

The working fountain.

Water shoots from the spout at the top level and spills down the sides. The ripples glow with movement, with promise, with life. Brad approaches, his wet shoes slipping over the glass. He takes a knee, taking a moment before getting up, but his foot slips beneath him and he falls to the floor a second time.

Spouts of water reach out like tendril fingers.

Brad crawls toward the fountain's edge, reaching into his pocket for a coin.

THE NEW CHILDREN OF THE FLOWER FOLKS
Muhammed Awal Ahmed

A **BAD PRIEST** hurries through the dark, carrying something molded with clay in his hands; a bowl filled with seed. In the distance away, you can see torches burning, glowing like hot coals. You can hear shouts and howls, and distant calls for more men. These are angry men with axes and cudgels headed for the door of the Priest's school, and the skull of the Priest's head. I know you have no idea what is happening, but no one ever knows what the end of the world is like. So put the babies to sleep, and relax the arc of your back.

He slips into his school like a thief, this Priest, and down into the dark of a classroom where he finds them crowded around each other; the Fulani's Children, their eyes dark pooled and homesick. Nothing about the way they look at him and each other says they are all about to die. The sun is still buried deep, just starting to peek a little out of the horizon. The Priest wipes off his sweats; the thin streaks of tears that just keep coming.

He drops the bowl he has been holding all night, down on the cracked floor of the class. He looks around the room one more time, and they nod back at him. He reaches into the bowl and brings out a handful of flat black seeds; seeds you cannot trust to sprout in a thousand years, but the Priest drops three seeds each in outstretched palms. The girls swallow the seeds down their throats, look around at each other's idle faces, and wait and wait to bloom beautifully in the Sun.

< < < < > > > >

Onu Enebenele II was a green-bearded bastard with more silver earrings than all his wives. He was more interested in collecting things than ruling us; that sturdy foot of an elf hanging from his royal regalia; the long-boned blue tails of mermaids, crushed as an aphrodisiac spiced into dishes for his harem. The man had a quiet belief inside himself; that Aljannah, Paradise was somewhere breathing and blooming on this earth, waiting for those who could find it.

Regardless, he had thirteen thousand soldiers in his army. Cockless men, and even women armed with ropes, spears, and long swords. Those fools marched with him in the wettest of days: in the dry crack of harmattan. They trooped through marshlands, greened evil forests, sandy planes and steeped dunes, following quirky compasses directing their journey to Paradise. They never fought any people as they went, never took anything from farming hamlets and fishing villages, except maybe only the things they found to be queer.

We hear how his army would ride down on gangs of Djinns basking in the sun, far in their preternatural world of the desert. They could only have done that for those skin of theirs, blue as the big bowl of the sky, awful smelling, and powerful talismans. The dead poor Djinn's eyes his men gouged out and kept for themselves, as protection against the desert's Evil Eye, against its hotly breathed curses of bad luck on their days.

I saw an eye once, hanging down a thread like a trader's purse, strapped around the waist of one of those cockless men. They always seemed to stare back at you, no matter where you were in one of those crowds that gathered to welcome Enebenele II back from his explorations. The eye swung like a pendulum, covered thinly in a white sheen of fear, and deep with something tempestuous aching within, blackening the inside with rage. It didn't look like the peaceful oceanic blue eyes of the home Djinns a hunter finds sometimes, lying among the wide soft bedded vegetation you encounter as you make your way through giant trees and soft shrubs of the forest beyond the River Olamaboro. I can at least tell you that.

They say the Onu and his men made it so far into the desert that they came upon a whole city buried under a sandstorm. They say the storm whirled furiously, shrieking and wailing, a thousand disfigured faces appearing and disappearing in the whirling sand. All night his men swung blindly, stabbing and slashing helplessly in the dark, through the thick gust of wind and sand as they made their way deeper into the city.

They say in the morning all that remained of the faces in the sandstorm were men, women and children with skin pale and fickle from age, eyes poisoned with Djinn rage. It seeped out of their body slowly, that terrible shadow of fear that constantly jolted through their transmogrified bodies held captive in the howling sandstorm of Djinns. It trickled out of them in their last breaths and returned to the desert. They say everything returns to the desert. They say some of the faces were so disfigured from old and new gashes of sword wounds that you could only recognize them as humans from their eyes, still widely open; black eyes, green eyes, and hazel blue eyes of normal folks.

They say as the men marched out of their slaughter, the city was littered with eyeless corpses rotting in the sun. Ugly business. This was the day he stood in the light of the sun scorching his men and swore to them he'd never retreat, or stop the exploration penetrating deeper into the desert, searching for the elusive heart of Aljannah.

All he found was one flowered city.

< < < < > > > >

Far away in the desert, wildflowers broke through the minaret of a Mosque, the only thing the Onu could see on his way into the city; petals of deep hues of blue and indigo reflecting brightly in the blazing sun. On arrival, the rest of the city walls and the Mosque turned out to be barely standing. And in the city were alien structures rising from the ground, standing high, half-fallen on each other like mermaids kissing above water. All reddened with time and dust, their bodies bursting with deep crevices that had flowers creeping through them.

There were vines everywhere and strange unnamed flowers filled empty fountains; green growing moss spread all over the buildings, waves of heat rising off of them so that the whole place looked like one green shimmering dream of the beautiful paradise of Aljannah.

There was no one in sight. They say they found ponds filled to the brim with dahlias and daffodils, but no water for the men or the animals they rode on. They say this city was only an eerie silence condensed with the sweet smell of roses. So the Fool thought it was Paradise he'd found. The Onu and his men cut through stems and roots with their swords and daggers, broke down walls and doors with hammers and boots, as they made their way into the biggest structures in any civilization they'd ever seen or destroyed until they came across what looked like a fortress.

It was where all the folks gathered; standing, falling, folks running as they turned into the flowered structures whose soft leaves the Onu fondled in amazement. As the men looked up, they found grey stone-carved statues of Djinns and elves staring down at them solemnly.

On the right wall of the fortress was a wide mirror with a silver frame. Whether the folks of flowers were running away from the Mirror or towards it, Enebenele II couldn't tell. He could tell it wasn't Aljannah he had found but maybe some things to build one with. He ordered his men to take down the shiny Mirror from the wall and wrap it up in fine silk, that it may not be scratched on the way back.

They say the Onu lost half of all he stole on his way back to Anpka; his men wandering into strange portals to strange lands; finding themselves caught in ancient mirage spells. So they marched backward, back to where the day started. Again and again.

In the cold nights—their camps of tens of thousands of tents and praying mats spread all over the cool sand of the desert, the sky clear and plenty with stars, like a rash—things they couldn't see fought them, disemboweled them, stole from them and their loots. I hear there are bands of Walis everywhere in the desert. Those half Djinn half men roaming the desert floor forever in caravans; of lost merchants, and undead camels, and frayed silks, and threadbare cottons and rotten baskets of dry and decayed fruits.

The Onu lost all his best scouts into the desert night. Scouts whose bodies they never found. And some days when nothing happened, the desert calm and airless like it was holding its breath, his men would hunt tiny Effrits in the sand like they were crickets, and they were back home. Inside gourds and kettles, they went; the angry squealing Effrits; tricksters of the Djinn kind that gather together and appear far away in the scorching sun like a pond of water, or an oasis filled with a party of queer folks.

It was what drove some mad with thirst, I hear. Not the actual thirst but the promise of water in hot scorching land, the rush for it, losing sandals and whips and ropes, only to find nothing but more arid land stretching farther before them.

At the end of all this, the desert was strewn with corpses rotting in the sun, whips and odd pairs of sandals, treasures with extinct qualities; broken bottles of rare cures for rare diseases poured and sizzled in the desert sand. And among these was the Mirror, in its fine silk cover, half-buried in the sand, reflecting the blazing sunlight from afar. Lost forever.

< < < < > > > >

No one thought they would find their way back from Aljannah, but they did. It was all everyone could talk about in those early days of their return; the dust-covered men, the dangling eyes like a trader's purse, the worn foot of camels, the golds, the tough skin of desert Djinns spread across camel humps.

And in the middle of the procession was Wutsia, the Onu's camel, heavy-laden with the loot of loots; jars of myrrh, pepper and queer desert spices, fresh plump dates and grapes, and the gangly Flower Folks with their flat black seeds exploding from their bodies time after time, fascinating us and drawing deep gasps out of us. We'd watch as the palace servants scampered after the seeds, delicately picking them from the floor, prying them out of our clenched fists, from inside folds of our celebratory garments, drawn out of our beautifully styled sword sheathes, and put away in the newly baked bowls.

Folks of Gardenias, Folks of wild Roses and Dahlias, and the tender upspring of their seed were dug into the ground of the royal garden. I wasn't there but I heard the soil of the garden came forth with delicate sprouts that bloomed in the first hour of planting, or the first hour of sunlight, unfurling bright petals in the sun. I hear old Wutsia, probably tired from being laden with too many boxes of cardamoms, maggots stuffed with gold, and parts of creatures heavier than they looked, slumped down on his side, as long stems of the growing flowers crept over his body.

They say he slept for so long you couldn't see the brown of his hide under those strange flowers.

Enebenele II, never one to pass up an excuse for a good feast, ordered his guards to slaughter the beast of burden and prepare a banquet. I hear Wutsia's eyes opened, white with fear, wild with irrepressible rage as he climbed out of the flowers. The royal guards were thrown into panic. He ran, his face and hump covered in strings of fledgling and faint flowers. He charged through the set banquet tables running headlong into the Olamaboro River and was never seen again.

I think it wasn't long after that that little babies who couldn't walk started disappearing from their homes. Children we found far in the outskirts of the city, by the root of lone flowers, cherry-picking and chewing away at buds of Gardenia, or furled petals of roses growing out from the exploded seeds.

In those dark nights after, bush babies you never see in the deepest parts of the forests sat fat on their hind legs, distant in the dark of the Royal Garden. And if you were curious enough to come close, to sneak past the royal guards and scale the palace fence, you could see their fat panda-like figures; their furs glowing, you could hear them plucking and chewing away at delicate stems of roses, marigolds and dahlias. And not so soon after that, they became what stole our babies and plagued our farms like goats.

It wasn't long after the last day of celebrating his arrival ended before a terrible nostalgia gripped the Onu. It crippled his right foot, seized his tongue. He was suddenly filled with an overwhelming feeling of disgust, dissatisfaction, and disdain at everything, and everyone. He woke up after the nights of missing children and wild bush babies in his garden, and decreed that growing and tending to of the Flower folks was henceforth illegal. The thriving flowers were to be cut down; vine by vine; root by root.

Strange gangly flowers were trampled together under muddy guard boots in that gloomy soil you see today. It didn't stop anything, definitely not the Djinns possessing children and blackening their tongues with flower juice. It wasn't long before

THE NEW CHILDREN OF THE FLOWER FOLKS

visible traces of bush babies—those bright colorful furs that shimmer in the dark, and their long and sharp canines—appeared next to cocoa fruits and beans in the Ankpa market.

Now every time we ask for a new doctor to treat typhoid that comes from shitting in the Olamaboro River, we ask for an exorcist, too.

< < < < > > > >

Let me tell you about our First Exorcist. A Fulani man, tall, stooped in the shoulders and gaunt looking. They say he came with a stomach ache and died from one; the lining of his stomach, his lungs and throat bruised with acid refluxes as he trekked and trekked down from beyond the Northern desert, from where he was summoned. They say, as he made his way into our city mad with hunger, he came upon a small boy drinking a bowl of pap. He snatched the bowl from him, and drank all its content. The bruised insides of his body could take in pap; he never ate or drank anything but pap, ever again.

In the days after his arrival, he was already staring lasciviously and licking his lips at our women bathing in the Olamaboro River. We built a small house for him at the outskirt of the city. The Exorcist settled in the small rooms of it, where childless women came to him to be given a baby to hold and to love. The Exorcist gave lots of women lots of babies to hold and to love.

Abominations, I'll say. Soulless babies, I'll say. Babies that grew light with holes in their spirit. Holes that were easily filled by one of those Djinns invisible to us, roaming around, sniffing for the last of the Flower Folk's Body, fighting to still bloom under a guard's boot.

Those babies grew into what you see today; young girls and queer boys who open their mouth too wide when they laugh, those who shout too loud in the markets, stare too long when you look at them or tear at their hair at the slightest provocation. Small girls, whose insides swirl with madness, a tempest of euphoric emotions, and the boys touched with the left hand of femininity.

Those children who are easily stunned by how fast they're growing, how subtle and sudden they find hidden under their tongue; new languages, arithmetic disorders, endless and useless poems and stories by dead poets and great storytellers rotting in forgotten graves.

Today, you can always pass by one on your way to the farm or the market, and they wouldn't greet you. Rather, they'd have their ear by a flower, listening to the music of bees buzzing inside, as they smile sweetly in self-indulgence. I can tell you one thing, even before The Mad Priest showed up on our doorstep, we were always shaken by how stubborn and aloof they are; how easily these girls could fling an undesired hand off of their bodies

I hear when the daughters of the Fulani's Children started menstruating, they did on the same days. So there were days they would disappear from our gaze, and we would find them beyond the Olamaboro River, in that land of ghosts and frightening noises. They'd be gathered around in a circle, together with their queer boys, like they were all still little children. We'd watched them from trees, as they sulked and argued among themselves; one furiously scribbling down Akpoto poems with a forefinger dipped in the muddy ground, only for another to wipe it off with a palm, and then replace it with the lost ways of writing messages invented by dead Igala scribes in hidden crypts.

Unaware of our presence, they'd stand around the circle, on the tips of their toes, bending in perfect port de bra, like their bodies were not filled with bones. We'd hear them reel off songs our grand and great mothers had forgotten on their death beds, and move to strange dance steps to strange songs only pausing to howl obscenities.

We'd watch for as long as our stomachs could hold away our disgust, and hunger, then out of the bush we'd spring, all arms wrapped around mad bodies. It wasn't easy, I can tell you that, but someone had to do it. The Exorcist would be in the house we built for him, sipping from his bowl of pap and relishing memories of naked women.

He'd startle as we drag one child or two we caught in our strong arms, into the room. We'd look on as he chastises the room, or everyone standing around, or the Djinn inside a child; the way his chin rose as he spoke into the air, you couldn't really tell who he was talking to.

Sometimes we'd be fortunate enough to hear a Djinn speak out of a mouth. Have you ever heard one? That deep humming sound that scratches at the back of a throat before coming out like the voice of a really old man, or a newborn baby?

THE NEW CHILDREN OF THE FLOWER FOLKS

It could say it had never done a wrong thing in all its life cycles. Or that it flew so long, for seventy days and seventy nights, across oceans and oases to find a rare flower that only grows here in the lost garden of Aljannah. Or that he lives here with us, inside a bat in a dark cave or above us, folded in the air of our city and it dissolved into holes in the soul of a body it was supposed to fly through.

It never mattered what the Djinn said, anyway, or what we said when we dragged one of them into the house we built for the Fulani man, he'd still pull out his whip. The child would cry; the Djinn grind their teeth together. He would slowly bring out crude instruments used in the cruel methods of Northern Exorcism from his only bag; a large cask of zam zam water, bronze cuffs of different sizes, a double-edged dagger, several bolts and links, and lay them on a black sheet of cloth in front of us and the Djinn-filled child, as we watched in a mixture of horror and excitement.

You could never predict what he would do. He would pour so much zam zam water into a poor girl's ear until she began to hear our voices like drowning sounds. He'd slowly squat down to the writhing body, wipe off the hair matted across an anguished face, calmly ask the Djinn to leave, and say nothing else.

But later in the day, a mother would dance and sing and scream when we brought a Fulani Child home, back from beyond the Olamaboro, her whole body shivering like it is dissolving into molecules. You have to understand that we just wanted to help, someone had to. We didn't take any pleasure in the songs of praise for the brave men who dared to cross beyond sanity, beyond the dark cold waters of the Olamaboro just to bring children back to their grateful mothers.

(When the Djinn leaves, it is usually in the form of a dry air through the mouth, and weak threats and promises of return, for revenge against us, the Exorcist, and the city that trod boots down on the most precious of flowers.)

In Enebenele II's absence, we'd heap the last remaining loots of myrrh and cardamom and well-oiled praise on the Exorcist, his lips pursed thin, his face placid, never betraying a smile or a smirk. More women would come dancing into the house we built for the Fulani, singing in the dull light of the full moon, singing for a child to love and to hold. More Djinns would not see where they were going and get trapped in these children with punctured holes in their souls.

MUHAMMED AWAL AHMED

It was a confusing period for us, but things moved, good things happened. We became a city of a million folks; our raffia roofs replaced with zinc from the South. Enebenele II, our Great Fool laid sick with despair and depression, for years. A new servant one day found the last of his wealth under the great frame of his sickbed; a silver-gray lamp covered in soot and webs. He rubbed the sides of it, cleaning the dust, and rubbed out a massive army of tiny angry Effrits, trapped for years inside the small hard space of silver.

They surged through the room like ants, past the fear-frozen servant, climbing the bed and spreading quickly all over Enebenele's body, every inch of his skin covered with them, like a rash, or a smudge of stars. He died that afternoon, his soul shared among the tiny mouths of Effrits. But I hear the quest for Aljannah lived a little longer, only coming to a sudden and inevitable end when that guard removed his boot from the ground, after so long, too long, the body of the last Flower Folk, dead and withered, blown away in the wind.

One day we gathered around, watched and marveled at the Fulani Children, playing games they invented at an instance; complicated games with complicated steps that made them laugh and point fingers at one another, as they stood over the dry and whittled body of the Fulani man.

The Second Exorcist came through a portal that opened in the market one day and stayed breathing out dust and sand from the desert. We tried to cover it with a veil but the wind blew it away. So we paid it no attention after a while. A little after our Onu's death, a man dressed in an old and tattered scout uniform stepped out of the portal, in pomp and pageantry, loud talking drums and musical horns, a caravan of riches and naked women with smooth olive skins. We liked this one immediately. He renovated our Palace and painted it blue. He had the Onu's maids and servants working again. He had flutists blowing royal tunes in the palace courtyard every morning.

This one was a big man who liked fine-fine things, shine-shine things. He only drank from silver cups. I never looked inside his mouth, but I hear he had more gold nuggets in his mouth than teeth. Every Friday, he gave sadaqah to us, fed our children alele and oje uchu. He exorcised Djinns in mass; waved his hand as we held up a Fulani Child to him, and that was it, gone, cured, healed. A miracle.

THE NEW CHILDREN OF THE FLOWER FOLKS

He let the children stay in his Palace even when their parents were still alive, and too grateful to object. The rest of the time, we left him to his business of entertaining wealthy men who trouped down to him from the East.

Wallahi, we find out about things too late in this city. We lynched him, pulled out gold nuggets from his mouth and into ours, and burned down the midnight blue Palace when we found out he wasn't exorcising Djinns from our children, but casting silence spells on the Djinns in them.

While he kept our children in his Palace, he taunted and tortured the Djinns inside them with hot zam zam water and whips, as he inquired from them, details about the fate of the rich men; about God's Unknown Cosmic answers. He'd cast a Djinn out of a body, and up into the sky above, up among the stars, where he'd listen through their ears, eavesdropping on God's plans for the rich men from the East.

When they returned into the body, by the Second Exorcist's command, half the body would have burns from the scorching flames of God's vigilant Comet.

(One of the clients he promised would become rich again before he died, was carried heavily indebted on his deathbed, into the city; it was already over for him before we found out what he was doing to our children.)

< < < < > > > >

This Exorcist is so young, he doesn't look like an Exorcist at all, or a Priest. He has blue burning eyes, and pale skin we hear is very sensitive to sunlight. We will soon nickname him the Oyinbo. He's never seen during the day. Services are held close to sundown. He'll stand tall and lean on the pulpit of the Palace we have converted into a church, wiping his face intermittently with a handkerchief, smiling and peering at our faces with those deep blue eyes.

Our bad luck with flowers and flowery words and quick exorcisms makes him hard to listen to. We regard him in the market with distrust and disregard. Maybe because of his smile, his overly kind smile that nudges you towards him when you're on your way to do something better with your time. Or it's how he treats the Fulani's Children roaming around aimlessly, still mad; too close. Too conspiringly close, I'll say. Like he's not here to save us, or them, but to save *them* from us.

An Exorcist should be gaunt looking. An Exorcist should sniff the air and wrinkle his nose in disgust at a body farting and shitting itself during an exorcism. But this Exorcist is nothing like that. As a man in the wrong profession often does, we see him playing with the Fulani's Children.

Playing o, neither smacking his lips at them, nor locking them somewhere in a cage to purge out the Cosmic Force of God's unanswered questions. We even watch him create a game for them; hide and find the Djinn!

He has built a little school out of the ruins of the house we built for the Fulani. There, we see him teach them how to read and write, again, like that wasn't what brought us into this mess. We have schools for our boys, and girls who don't laugh too loud. You have to understand; you can't be too careful. Also, I don't like the Fulani's Children. There is this thin air of authority around their small eyes. You ask them a question and they study your face like you are mates.

These days, we can't watch over them like we used to, the Priest's blue eyes can spot you from far away as you hold onto the fat branch of a tree and peer down his school. But we hear things. We hear when the times comes for their madness, and their eyes turn dark with Djinn panic, this madman gathers the rest around, gives the crazed one a piece of chalk, and watch them teach the rest and him the new languages that emerged at the break of dawn.

He calls our children his little sisters and brothers, this man. He even bathes the little ones himself, plaits their lice-infested hair with the dexterity of a loving sister, like they don't have us for that, if they weren't so mad; their mothers and sisters and aunts. I hear since he came, the children no longer become possessed by any random Djinn. Each child has a Djinn their age assigned to their body, each class with a wise and ancient Djinn assigned to their collective spirit. A most queer thing.

(I think this man has hopes, hopes borne only by a fool; that soon, one day, the children and the Djinns will learn to live in each other's bodies without one trying to dominate the other. A Wali. An Abomination.)

He invites us to the remains of the burnt down palace, climbs down from the charred steps, preaching. What a dramatic man. He wipes his face, looks around at us, opens his mouth slowly like we are retards and he says, with a finger pointed to the sky, "The Djinns are also God's 'loving' creations, and much like mankind, there are good and bad Djinns."

Can you even begin to imagine? A man of God!

He says there have been Djinns in Anpka before the days of the 'Collector' King and there'll continue to be. He lowers his head, smiles and says stupid things about a certain Neferetti; her wit, her mind, like we don't hear stories about The Nymph, so he says these things like you would about a lover no one wants for you, but you do; with affection and understanding. Neferetti who does not know it is wrong to take children from their mother's womb and replace it with air woven into fibroids because she wants to 'play' with it. Neferetti who panics and flies away when she realizes, in each life cycle, that she can't give a baby back to its mother.

(We gasp and cover our mouths in horror; wide-eyed and disturbed that he'd gather us here and mention such unholy names on such a holy altar, while still claiming to be of the Lord.)

It is Sunday, again. This time he calls on us and our baggage of humanity, to give him another piece of our land, to shelter the Djinns inside.

Wallahi, we find out about things too late in this city. There are rumors Djinns have a strange bond to flowers, and since that day we saw those mad Fulani's Children trooping after each other, never heeding our calls and our jibes, their eyes dark and onlooking. These children filed themselves into the grounds where the royal garden used to be. Now dark and damp, and with their fingers they dug up wet and loamy soil as they tried to bury themselves. To grow.

That day our eyes opened to our problem. Now, he asks for this, to our face.

This man is a problem, we know that now. For the first time in years, I've been going to city hall meetings, youth and peerage group meeting, because this is a serious issue. It's a fight for our survival, against madness. Elder meetings are being held every night, under kerosene lanterns and small fires lit in the dark, all coming to the same conclusion: Burn the Priest and his children before giving an inch of the city to Djinns and their flower lovers.

MUHAMMED AWAL AHMED

At every meeting, we are thrown into the chaos of complete confederacy of words and woes and awes. We curse our fate. All night inside our houses, we curse the dead; Enebenele II, his army of women and eunuchs. We gather and exchange stories about the years before The Exploration of the Desert, when we were just a little unknown city, and not Aljannah; about the first flower that ever sprouted out of the Ankpa soil, blue and poisoned with beauty; about Wutsia; about that Exorcist who brought madness to our mothers' wombs. Now we even bless the name of that Exorcist who only locked them in cages.

I just heard the priest took a digger and a shovel, and broke into the Royal crypt. It is where pots filled with bodies of the Flower Folks are kept.

(By noon, news of the crypt-robbing Priest has spread through city districts like wildfire. It has plunged itself into cries that vibrate in throats like a stuck bone of fish. Everyone is angry now.)

< < < < > > > >

The angry people reach the door of the school, and hack on it with their axes and their cudgels. They howl and hoot. They burn things and dance around the fire, machetes glinting. The sun watches, creeping out from beneath the clouds, early and red. The girls fall to the ground like falling forest trees, their bodies collapsing one after the other around the Priest, as he weeps and weeps into himself, for himself.

He wonders if he has done a wonderfully wrong thing. But the rising sunlight is already filtering into the class. Light falls on his pale skin, ringing a violet undertone. The girls lie dead; dead eyes looking up at the direction of the sun, dead eyes blinking softly, dead eyes turning wet with a crimson red.

More of the sun's rays slant into the room like a sharp razor, go in open eyes. Roses squeeze out, unfurl and bloom wet out of pupils. Long stems grow out of dead fingers. Their skin turn green, green roots rush down their follicles like tiny tender arms of vines. It slithers around the floor, spreads through the foundation, crack through the walls of small classes.

The priest looks away from the rising sun hot on his skin, as giant thorns of giant roses cut through him, pinning him to a wall. The sun is fully out before the angry people realize too late, that it is

THE NEW CHILDREN OF THE FLOWER FOLKS

happening again, not in a story or a land long lost in Aljannah, but here, inside them, flowers unfurling out of open mouths, eyes, armpits, other holes in their body. They drop their axes and their cudgels and they try to run, again.

THE NEW CHILDREN OF THE FLOWER FOLKS

FIRST, A BLINDING LIGHT

Betty Rocksteady

THE HEADACHE IS brief but leaves you dazed.
Floaters dance across your vision, disappear.

You breathe in, step onto the path. Uneven gravel crunches beneath your feet. The trail winds a slow wave up and down hills, bracketed by overgrown weeds and rotten leaves that pulp beneath tangled trees.

This road leads home, or if you turn around, it leads everywhere else. You could walk it with your eyes closed, and you have on occasion, blurry-eyed after some endless party, bushes shifting in the wind, guided by instinct around curves that may as well be the curves of your own hand. It's wide enough for two people to walk comfortably, but you've rarely ever passed anyone on your solitary trips home.

You've never seen whoever maintains the path, but every spring the trees and bushes are mown back to allow your passage through. When the long days of summer stretch on, the trees claw across the stones, reaching for you, tearing your clothes and grabbing fistfuls of hair. They begin to withdraw in autumn, when the foliage falls to reveal skeletal branches and whatever lay twisted within their grasp.

FIRST, A BLINDING LIGHT

You breathe out and a red-violet leaf twists on the breeze, a shocking flash of color against the greying sky. A tremor vibrates through your tailbone, creeps up your spine.

The bushes nearest you rustle. Between their shaggy leaves, movement. You peer into the configuration of rotten berries and broken branches and it moves again, the shining flank of something much too large to be contained here, something that growls and the muscles in its neck twitch and you glimpse sharp sharp teeth and you barely catch yourself from falling and that's when you see her, coming up the path behind you, her pale face, a smear of dark hair and the sunken green glow of her eyes.

The girl approaches and you didn't see anything in the bushes and you force a smile and you use the halfway smile you use when passing a stranger. She doesn't smile back. Not quite. She looks familiar, her movements strangely liquid as she closes the distance between you.

"Hello," she says, and then she speaks your name.

Her eyes flash from green to yellow, something alive in the irises.

"Do I know you from somewhere?" Your mouth doesn't open all the way. Your voice is not your own.

"Yes, you do." She nods ahead. "We're going the same way. Would you like to walk together?"

You don't say yes.

You fall in line with her, the rhythm of her feet. She tilts her chin up as she walks, as though she is watching the sky. You still feel the presence of her eyes on you, the way they saw past your skin, past muscle and sinew and blood and meat and all the way down to the cold hardness of bone. Something boils in your gut, expands, contracts, you can't take your eyes off her, the way her skin is shadowed grey by her dark hair, that tangled cloud that moves to reveal only a sliver of cheekbone or the pale cracked edge of a smile.

Her features are single puzzle pieces that you can't coalesce into a whole. You can't place her, you've never known her and it makes you uneasy to hear your name on her lips. She did say your name, didn't she? She keeps her head tilted to a sky where no sun shines. You follow her gaze and you don't see anything, nothing at all, and gravel fills your throat and when you swallow it your insides cramp.

BETTY ROCKSTEADY

You wish you were home, your chair, your books, your bed. It hurts to be here. It hurts. It hurts.

You're almost home. Echoes of your own footprints scuff across the path, each step one you've taken hundreds of times, thousands of times before. You feel your feet press away from the ground and a nameless fear wakes. "I'm sorry," you hear yourself saying, "but I can't place where I know you from . . . "

As if in reply, her mottled hand brushes through the pine needles of an encroaching tree. Does something else move in its branches? A cloud blots out the dim light of the sun and in the flutter of her fingertips you find a memory.

Her name hangs on your lips but your throat is too full to speak. Your neighbor, or maybe she lived down the street. Dark hair, pale skin, those glowing eyes. Rainboots splashing water, caterpillars accidentally squashed before transformation, a purple sunset, a smile at recess, and then nothing. She was gone.

They plastered dozens of posters of her face downtown, on every pole, in every window of every corner store. They used her school picture and photocopied it over and over, so many times that eventually her darkened eyes looked scribbled in charcoal and her face distorted into a horrific caricature of the girl you knew. Your parents ushered you from the room for weeks when the news came on but that didn't stop the fear from boring into you, a new fear that was too big to be contained within your body, so it leaked out and moved through every shadow in your bedroom at night. You had nightmares for years. How could you forget?

You speak her name but don't hear your voice. Everything trembles a little looser. You want to touch her, you want to turn her face toward you, you want to look in her eyes, but you are afraid to know and already you are certain.

She was dead. You always believed she was dead.

Your feet keep moving, keep crunching gravel, crushing errant leaves. The trees stretch taller here, reaching overhead, bony fingers that touch a sky where no birds fly, where nothing moves at all.

The girl is smiling. Even if you can't see her mouth, you can feel how sharp her teeth are. You want to ask a question but your tongue is thick and slow and something deep in your throat is pulsing and ahead there a turn in the road, a fork in the path, a different way home.

FIRST, A BLINDING LIGHT

You think this is the perfect time to step away. The rightward fork leads back to the street, a safe street, just a few blocks from home, a street with houses and fences instead of bare trees and dark eyes.

You could walk away from whatever is happening here.

You owe her nothing. There's no need to say goodbye. You turn, you take a step, and your feet seem *fuzzy* but finally you make them move, and then her cold, small hand brushes your arm and it feels like all your muscles are stretching out at once when she whispers, "It's not safe, stay with me," and that's when you see them.

Sharp angry bushes surround the exit of the trail and within those brambles you catch a flash of teeth. A hot huff of breath releases the stench of rotting meat. Huge eyes blink yellow, they stare through you, and a forked tongue hisses through the air and though foliage shrouds its face you can tell what it is but you won't say it out loud.

"Don't go that way," you hear, and it's unclear if she said it, or if it's your own voice in your head.

You listen.

You've made your last choice.

"Shouldn't we . . . get help?" The words tumble from your mouth, splash like raindrops on the stones, and you realize you don't have your phone. Or your wallet. Or your clothes. You don't have anything at all. You are just a body, but even that feels so far away now. You are just a soul, a flash of light, a thrumming vibration of energy following a woman up a path you have walked a thousand times before and really, truly, you are almost home.

You keep walking.

The sun peeks from behind the clouds and the hazy light bleeds to a warmer hue. Something cracks open at the crown of your head, spreads with a pleasant tingle down your neck, through your shoulders. It curls down your biceps, past your elbows, into your wrists, your fingers, and something seems to leave you. You realize the girl is speaking. Something about how you never kept in touch.

A shudder moves through your shoulders and creeps down your spine and you wonder if you're really still walking, and though the crunch crunch crunch of your feet is reassuring, it is not enough.

The girl is smiling. You want to ask what happened to her. You should ask her where she's been, and you try, the words are halfway tumbled out of your mouth when you remember and your voice shrinks.

Sometime last year maybe, maybe longer ago, wrapped in sweaty sheets, unable to sleep, sunken shadows under your eyes reflected in your phone, you saw her familiar face in your suggested friends list. That same golden glint in her eye, that tangled mess of hair. You clicked on her profile, amazed she had survived, amazed to see her grown up even if you couldn't quite make out what she looked like from her photos. You intended to friend her, to catch up, but instead you scrolled through cryptic updates and then, finally, the videos.

You followed the bread trail to her YouTube profile and under the covers, your headphones projected her voice directly into your ears and you don't remember anything she said but you remember how you felt. You remember the damp tangle of hair stuck to the drool on her chin when she spoke of us.

We took her and we helped her and then her skin started to melt like the sky is melting now.

Every word you don't remember was the truth.

The trees droop like candles, the path turns slow and orange and liquid and the girl turns and her smile is a slash across her face that tumbles into the dirt and her teeth shatter and break. Her skin writhes with translucent worms and then they too disappear, leaving only her eyes that hang in the sky, distorted, scratched out, burnt in charcoal.

Then there is nothing.

You've always been walking this trail.

Alone.

You want to run. There is nothing here to run from but still something inside you insists and then there is a tugging on your spine, a *yank* that makes you feel sick and this time when you wrench your chin to the sky there is no sky, there is something massive and shining and you see yourself mirrored, at a distance, bathed in ultraviolet light.

You can see that you're at the beginning of the path.

You think maybe it is time to let go.

You think maybe you don't need to hold on.

Let these new thoughts come.

FIRST, A BLINDING LIGHT

You've been holding so tight. The vibration rumbles through you and your body feels too heavy and you want to let go. You should let go. The light is so soft and it is pulling but it is gentle and insistent and the vibration intensifies and you are thrumming with light and you forget what you were trying to hold on to.

You don't have to be afraid.

You are not afraid.

You open your eyes and see nothing.

The vibration settles in your forehead. You relax. You notice how it slows, how it ebbs and flows, how it seems to breathe and you relax and it thrums but it doesn't hurt and you relax and it peels open and now you can see.

Your mouth opens. The light fills you, this holy song.

Loosen your grip. Let the tingle spread again, from your forehead through your throat, down your spine, through your hips, your thighs, your knees, shake your toes free, one by one. Let yourself rise.

Your body peels back, ripples of flesh swallowed by the earth.

You are almost home.

IT TAKES SLOW SIPS

Michael Wehunt

SEVENTY MINUTES TO drive eleven miles, and the daylight was souring over the trees behind the apartments. He had left in the dark and only just made it home before the dark. For a moment he sat in his car and watched a white dog being walked in the park across the street, its fur almost shining. People were wearing coats now, but it was only September. It had gotten cold two weeks before his favorite season, the one with her name.

He had been standing all day. His feet ached through the foyer and up the stairs to 312. A long envelope the color of butter lay on the carpet, wedged a few inches under his door. COLIN was written in black marker ink that had seeped out in tendrils before it dried, causing the letters to blur. The reddish words PINE ARCH RESEARCH had been stamped within a beveled rectangle in one corner. Neither name had an address, as though it had been hand delivered. He picked the envelope up and something shifted from one end of the package to the other with a hoarse whisper.

The light inside the apartment was like stagnant water through the blinds. His laptop and phone waited on the kitchen island, and a dryness spread through his mouth. He hadn't seen her face since before the sun rose. He couldn't get used to missing her, but leaving these devices behind was the only way he could keep a job. The job was the only thing stopping him from moving back to her early. Before autumn.

He said her name twice as though greeting the phone and computer. Autumn, her hair a yellow darkened to brown like a turning leaf, waves crashing against her neck. Colin liked to picture her in the tiny pottery studio she had set up in the house she rented, streaks of gray drying on her arms, dabs of gray in the hair she kept having to tuck behind her ears. Barely five feet of her on a stool, spinning clay through her delicate small hands. When she paused and looked up into the distance, through her walls, what hung there in her thoughts?

While his soup heated in the microwave, he tore a side off the envelope to postpone the comfort of looking at her. Two halves of a CD slid out onto the counter, each a wedge of iridescent mirror. He turned them over and saw WA Y written on one half in perhaps the same black marker from the envelope, TCH OU on the other. The disc had been snapped neatly into its two useless pieces.

He couldn't make sense of the letters. He opened the microwave to end the piercing tone that wasn't loud but always dug into his head. When he pushed the CD halves together, WA Y TCH OU stretched in a line that was almost perfectly straight above the center hole. Careful lettering. WAY. TOUCH? It clicked and he saw WATCH YOU. The disc had been broken on purpose. Otherwise the Y and the OU would have been written below the rest.

Colin wondered what the point of the package was. He'd never heard of Pine Arch Research, and the person he had hired online wouldn't have traveled up here to deliver a package in person. But even as the thought rose, it fell away. Autumn was all that mattered.

He checked his phone and saw an email notification on his screen from mid-morning. He tapped to open her full message and smiled into the phone light washing up onto his face. *A man was following me last night. Outside my window and scratching at the door. You promised in court. Leave me alone!* He turned on a lamp and the kitchen light and sat down to eat the soup.

He typed out with his thumbs: *Are you okay?? You should maybe call the police. I told you I have this job in Durham until*

October. Why would you think that was me? It was just one bad mistake. I thought I'd left something at your house but wanted to know if you were up before I knocked, remember? Please be safe. I care about you.

The soup was too hot, it couldn't cover the taste in his throat of days without sleep. He closed his eyes tight and felt the burning under the lids. He listened to the warm song of his blood pushing through him, cresting in his ears. Sometimes when his eyes were pressed shut this hard, the sound of his blood was almost the sound of mountains shifting far away.

He counted the number of times he had typed *you*, each one an intimate touch. He deleted *I care about you*. The words ached as they disappeared, but he had to build to it. He needed her to realize some things on her own. He sent the text and closed his eyes again.

What was she doing in this moment, as the sun bled away? He pictured her out for a walk, in a light jacket because it was a little warmer down in Atlanta, he almost felt the vibration of his message against her thigh. She stopped and a man with a dog curved around her, the dog's tongue hanging out of its mouth like one of the cozy socks she'd had in her dresser drawer. She slipped her phone out of her pocket and read his words. What did her face look like? Did it light up? Did lines crease her forehead? He would need to know before he was near her again.

He checked his social media accounts, but they'd been dormant for three months. It was as though Colin had died and no one had noticed yet. These profiles only existed now as doors for Autumn to open, to walk back through into his life.

She had changed her Facebook, Instagram, and Twitter passwords weeks ago, but he didn't think she had figured out he had them because he could still get into her email. He had been careful ever since he found the list in her desk the only night he ever spent with her. He handled this last password like a delicate glass structure that could collapse in his lungs at any moment. Even his breathing changed when he was in her account.

There was nothing today that caught in his throat or twisted cords in his gut. No cute messages from Brandon, and she had lost interest in Cory in July. She was working on herself, just like he was.

He logged out and opened his own email. There were message

replies from the forum where his friends lived. They thought his strategy was solid. They reminded him that "celibate" didn't need to apply to him anymore, so why should "involuntary"? There was a time when you took what you deserved.

He saw a money transfer request from username paroo0600606, the words *went out with some females, went home alone*, and a video clip of Autumn, sleeping, filmed through a gap between her curtains. It was ten minutes long, and at the end the scene changed to three seconds of the window of a different house, a dark figure stretching up the wall, before cutting off. He watched the clip again even though it was grainy and the angle didn't show much, then sent the second half of the payment and asked if he was available to follow Autumn the day after tomorrow. He needed more. He needed it to elevate. He needed her to need him when he returned.

He felt he could sleep now, but he sifted through her social media photos. There were only two new ones, and no men in them. One had the caption, *Still scared of the dating scene but #selflove is my hashtag*. He tapped the heart on a select few images. She had blocked Colin everywhere not long after their one date, the day after she caught him fastening his pants at her window. He hadn't been careful enough. But he could still see her because the profile swooning over her pictures was a woman he had made up. An older woman who sold pottery online just like Autumn did. This woman was safe, she had watched from a casual distance at first and only last weekend started messaging her, praising her work and promising to order some pieces.

It takes slow sips to not waste a good thing, he thought his father had told him that once. But he was still there when the night was gone, looking at her face. He memorized it all over again, and the first pink light pushed at the blinds.

< < < < > > > >

Colin came home and the sun was still hanging above the trees, clawing at the sky as it fell. Its blood caught in the low clouds. He was tired again, his senses were dulled by patience. For the first time since moving here and leaving his access to Autumn at home every day, his work performance was suffering. The manager asked if there was something wrong after he got another order wrong, and Colin had looked into the perfect sunlight through the café windows and come close to saying the restraining order was choking him at this distance. He shouldn't have moved this far away from her, two hundred miles was playing it too safe.

There was another envelope outside the door of 312, the same weight sliding across as he picked it up, but he placed it on the counter as soon as he walked into the apartment. He had missed her so much today. It was difficult to remember the way she smelled. He went straight for the phone and the home screen was empty, just the washed-out background image of Autumn asleep on that April night. Her windowpanes had been poorly cleaned. He was still bothered by the streaks getting in the way of a good view of her. But it was still her face.

The stamped PINE ARCH RESEARCH was smeared this time on the yellow envelope. His name seemed to have been written with less care, with fewer tendrils of ink soaking into the paper fibers because the marker had slashed the letters instead of dragging them. The CD inside was whole, it slid out onto his palm with a corrupted image of his face staring up at him on one side and the words WATCH YOU on the other in a nearly perfect line.

He thought of the "par" initials in the username he had paid to follow her. Maybe they stood for Pine Arch Research. Maybe this was more footage of her. His laptop was just old enough to have a disc drive, and it dragged the CD in with a sound like wasps caught in a jar. A video player appeared and he filled the screen with it.

It wasn't her face. It was his face. It was the dark of 312 and he was in bed, a camera was hovering over him. He lay in half-shadow and seconds sifted into minutes in the bottom right corner of the screen. There was no sound, he could almost hear the blankness in the speakers where the ambient noise should have been, or the breathing of the person with the camera.

After eight minutes he began to smile in the video. It was slow, only the corners of his mouth creeping up into a curve, as though he had been dreaming her face. Eleven minutes and his eyes opened on the screen. He couldn't tell if they saw anything.

Colin watched his body shudder, gentle like an old memory coming back. The camera stayed hanging over him, the person holding it must have been near his feet. Thirteen minutes and a dark smudge leaked out of his smile, into the darkness of the bedroom. It spread like a stain. It stretched up toward the camera and swallowed the lens in its mouth.

And he stepped away from the laptop, because something dark seemed to peel away from its screen into the kitchen. Like wet smoke, like a flaw in a photograph of this moment. But he hadn't turned any lights on yet. He wasn't sure. Something landed on the back of his neck, it pushed into his hair at the nape, but it was gone before he swiped his hand across the skin. His eyes crawled around the room, up into the corners and across the walls, along the carpeted floor. He flipped on the kitchen light and brushed his fingers behind his head again.

He looked back at the laptop screen. He was still sleeping there, the smile gone from the corners of his mouth, and there was something dead about his face until static filled the video like a swarm of digital moths and the clip cut off.

A group of moths was called an eclipse. He thought about this as he switched on a lamp and sat on the sofa in its pool of light. The video and the thing that seemed to lift out of it. The feel of a heavy moth on his neck. The walls were still empty. He wondered what would happen if he replayed the clip.

He opened his phone and was about to go online to see what Autumn had been doing today. Only she could calm him. But there was a sudden feeling at the back of his neck, as though the flesh was lifting away from the bone, and something pushed through the fold of skin. A pinch and a numbness that ebbed through him.

Colin thought he jumped up from the sofa. He thought he screamed. But he was still seated, and he reached back and touched his neck. His fingertips came away stippled with a greasy black dust, a bead of blood clinging to his thumb. It was becoming hard to concentrate. A tired cloud seemed to spend minutes drifting over him.

He fought it because he needed to see her face. He typed her name into Facebook, but she didn't come up. He switched to a different fake account to be sure. The same thing happened on Twitter and Instagram. Had she locked down her privacy, was she taking a social break? He went to her online pottery store, her Etsy shop, but the URLs wouldn't load. Other profiles appeared normally, people he had known before he met her. Other websites were functioning. She was even gone from LinkedIn. He noticed he was shaking. The back of his neck throbbed like the beginning of an itch.

Autumn's email account was still there, and his throat unlocked. He was able to swallow. But the inbox stopped two nights ago, with an unread message that hadn't been there when he checked yesterday. He hadn't deleted any of her emails. He was always careful now. The subject line read WA H TCH IM, and he tapped on it. The message was from pinedemon@z.z. Nothing in the body of the email, only blank space his finger had to drag up the screen to reach the bottom. Everything in her trash and spam folders was at least two days old.

He felt an awful drop in his stomach. He switched to his own email account. The message from paroo0600606 was still in the inbox, but the tiny video player was no longer embedded inside it. He should have downloaded the clip when he had the chance, grainy as it had been. He hadn't seen her face since before the sun rose, and now it was dark again.

But he didn't need to go online. He had his phone, the hundreds of images downloaded from her profiles over these last silent weeks. He opened the photo app, but it was a clean white sheet he swiped at in a panic, until he started seeing worthless pictures from before her. Above them, each of her photos was an empty square, the brightness shining up at him, too much light and too new, like spring or summer.

He stood and stared somewhere near the microwave for a long time. The cloud of fatigue settled into his pores. His phone fell asleep and he woke it up. The background image was still there, but it was different now. With the screen held close, Colin saw that it had been altered somehow. Her window was dirtier and he couldn't see her face at all, it could have been anyone.

He looked up Pine Arch Research on Google and could only find a video of an indistinct figure outside a house at night, reaching a long impossible arm or movie prop toward a window. It was the house he had glimpsed at the end of the clip of Autumn sleeping, from the man he had paid to follow her. A different woman was pursued through trees, a different man tried to find her. He didn't know what this could mean. It was from years ago. It felt like someone else's story. He watched the video until he was sure Autumn's face wasn't going to be in it.

The one thing he couldn't do was call her. She had changed her number and he had no way to get it without her guessing he knew her email password. But he caved and it rang twice before a humming static filled the line. He redialed and the crackling started as soon he pressed the call button. Where was she right now? Was she in trouble? He wanted to feel her heart slamming under his fingers. He wanted to calm her heart. He would have to quit his job and go back home early.

The night stretched ahead of him without her face, like a sickness. His eyes burned. His eyes ached. He tried to eat a can of soup and fell asleep on the sofa while waiting for it to cool.

< < < < > > > >

The café windows poured light at him for hours. At lunchtime he felt something grip the back of his neck again, just under the collar. It pierced the skin. He reached his hand into his shirt, pulled it out to find a trace of black dust caught in his palm, a rill of blood in the seam between two fingers. The manager came in to help with the rush and said Colin didn't look well. The café filled with chatter like a swarm of voices. An eclipse of one great voice murmuring.

In the restroom Colin looked in the mirror. He avoided his face when he could, it reminded him that Autumn had only taken him home the night they met because she'd had too much to drink. He had kept buying her drinks, the kind of door that opened maybe once in a life. He was used to the sunken flesh under his eyes, bruises from looking at her face instead of sleeping each night. It was difficult to remember waking up next to her that one morning, the way the light had come in between the curtains to swirl in the shadows like cream. Her smell mixed with his, and the quiet beatitude of the world.

He turned away from the mirror and something was clinging to his back, in the corner of his eye. It shifted, it crawled to the other side of him. It was gone as he twisted in a circle and scraped at his back. There was a hint of darkness under his fingernails.

After the second mistake, the manager sent him home. The drive was fast before rush hour. There was no envelope at the door of 312. He called her and there was only the void of distorted rings at the other end of the line. Her face was still gone from the internet. There was such a profound tiredness, soaked in his muscles and his bones. The course of his blood had slowed in his head when he squeezed his eyes closed. He couldn't hear mountains out on the horizon.

He moved toward the laptop but then moved away from it.

The pinch came under the collar of his shirt again, the flesh pulling out and punctured by a tube or a blunt needle. He felt small hands moving across his shoulders. He tore his shirt off and the shirt beneath it. But there was nothing in the bathroom mirror. He tightened the blinds and sat down. The phone lay empty of everything beside him on the sofa.

< < < < > > >

Colin opened his eyes in the bedroom. He didn't remember coming in here, getting under the covers. A face was looking through the window at him, two eyes in the space between two blind slats. For a moment he thought it was Autumn. He let the moment stretch into a floating island of moments. He didn't remind himself he lived on the third floor.

But the eyes seemed too much like her eyes in certain pictures, when she was trying to look serious. He couldn't take it. He slipped out of the bed because he was too weak to stand. He had to crawl to the window and pull himself up with his hands on the sill. The eyes were gone. When he spread two slats apart, there was only the ghost of his own eyes in the glass. He thought he could see a trail of dark grime smeared along the wall and around the corner of the building.

The door of the apartment creaked open. It clicked shut. He waited in the quiet, watching his eyes watch him in the windowpane, until something climbed up onto his back. He felt the pinch again, the dig in his neck. He cried out in a high voice that was only breath and scrabbled a hand behind him. For a second he had it. It writhed out of his fingers and he felt the small weight of it sliding down toward his waist. Colin said her name, he put all of himself into it as he managed to get to his feet.

The laptop was still open on the kitchen counter. He woke it up but the video player was gone. The CD wouldn't eject and there were beads of black paste around the mouth of the drive. He rubbed a finger down the screen and drew a line in the dark film coating it.

He opened a browser and searched for her, as though telling

himself there was something wrong with his phone and not the reality of her. He would see her face in a few seconds. But she was nowhere. He logged in as the woman potter and checked the Instagram messages, and only what he had written was there. Her replies were empty spaces beside empty circles. Search engines were no use, all he found were endless tributes to the season and empty, ugly Autumns with the same last name.

For a minute that felt like the last five months without her, Colin couldn't find his phone. He was weeping now. He remembered sitting on the sofa, and there it was, slipped down between two cushions. Her name was gone from his contact list now, her texts had faded from the messaging app. He struggled to remember her number, he could almost feel it leaking from his heart. It rang six times before silence picked up, the distant sound of wind like a place outside of existence. He made a gap in the blinds and saw the trees in the park shivering. A man was crossing the street toward them with the sleek white dog.

He felt a breath across his ear. He felt the nape of his neck bunch up. The tube slid into his skin. A wire of pain straightened down his back, numbness pulsing out in strands. He tried to go still as a warbling voice said his name in almost a whisper. What would it do if he let it, he wondered, he would find out if he didn't move.

It took a slow sip of him. His bones were like syrup, like the black paste beneath his fingernails, and he was folding down onto the floor. The voice spoke to him in crackles and gasps. He thought he heard it say Autumn was safe now, without him. She could sleep well again. He thought he heard her name over and over again, an eclipse of names. Soon it was only wet noise instead of the perfect sound he had held onto for so long.

< < < < > > > >

There was something he had not seen. He had forgotten what it was, that it was a beautiful face, that it had turned itself away from him. He had forgotten the face was hers. He had forgotten what name he had called when he needed a reason to go on. There was only a remote impression of her still in his blood when he closed his eyes against the slanting blare of sunlight through the café windows. Leaves skirled past outside in a breeze, in the overture of fall.

Each day it took more of him, it drank the fact and the idea of her from him. It let him watch the white dog on the leash in the park when he got home from work. It let him sleep through the night. But it took the color from even these things.

Colin carried two plates over to the small table closest to the door. He set them down and one of the women raised her face with a faraway smile. She didn't quite look at him, her eyes seemed to graze the line of his shoulders as though trying to crawl over onto his back to look there. Her hair fell in waves some would have called dirty blond but he called the color of the leaves starting to cover the world. And for an instant—but the instant was gone. He asked if they needed anything else. She shook her head and turned to the taller woman across from her. Their voices built their own secret murmur.

Back at the café bar he glanced into the antique mirror as he took a clean mug from the shelf. He saw a face rise up behind his shoulder. It was his face but smaller, small enough to belong to something that could cling to his back. There was something dead about its eyes. Its mouth opened, and a black growth pushed out over the tongue. He watched his face lower itself behind his head. He felt the pinch, and the tube going in.

THE ARBORGLYPH

Sofia Ajram

TEARING DOWN THE road in Peter's '98 Buick LeSabre, that jasper green bitch with the wide girth. We loved to go shooting through those streets of rural Aurora, along that wild stretch of road that tilted and turned like a carnival ride.

Since high school we'd done this, another Peter and Sebastian classic born of boredom, him and I in our everlasting stupidity, me riding shotgun and Peter at the wheel with his idiot grin, beers galore and taking that road like a rocket to the moon. Up and down and up again, the end being the steepest curve. The thrill of looking—not over the crest, the hill a platform to the stars, but at him—in his eyes a wild, endless summer; the sharp line of his jaw twisted into a mischievous grin; my mouth a wide line of disbelief each time our asses lifted from the seats.

With enough speed, we could really catch some air and shoot off the top, like we were trying to outrun the wind, right off the edge of the damn universe. That last time I felt like I was soaring off into the stars. There, him and I, mid-twenties with years of practice, Peter pushing the Buick a hundred kilometres an hour, and dark outside, that *thick* kind of darkness, just the light of that big blue marble and one dim headlight—the other one Peter said he'd get fixed—and us screaming at the top of our lungs down that last hill like bats out of hell. And wouldn't you know it, that one time, the impossible: dead of night, some couple in a hatchback; high beams on, blinding like sun after a night of hitting the bottle—came flying out of nowhere.

Wheels crashed down. Slamming on the breaks, but no good—immediate suspension collapse—and Peter lost control, hands flying over the wheel, veering off-road toward that towering sycamore, the stench of burning rubber, and bracing for impact, too late to really see anything until explosive pain and complete darkness.

< < < < > > > >

Irene said I struck my head on the dash and died of blunt force trauma. Peter, smooth as an oiled tit, suffered no more than a few scratches and a fractured rib.

That was the first time I met Irene. Peter brought me to her. I was dead for four days, cruising in a womb-like warmth among the stars before the world rocked back in around me.

I awoke with them standing over me: Peter, face caged; Irene, a shape of a shape of a face in a strange hue assembling before my eyes. And me, her canvas: intubated, sallow skin drained of blood, with a headache like the toll of a church bell inside my skull. I've heard being born is always painful.

My thoughts felt muddy for a long time. Peter took care of me. We were roommates after all, best friends since childhood, cut from the same cloth. Peter, whose flash of youth changed my life. Peter, whose velvety aura I drank like rich coffee. Peter, who tasted of everything I wanted.

Peter, who I was in love with.

How he knew someone like Irene who worked at the crossroads of neuroscience and metaphysics was beyond me, but that was Peter, always with an ace up his sleeve, a bastard with a knack for making friends with the most unlikely people.

Days resumed the mundane. I went back to the humdrum life of a handyman. Everything was exactly as it had been, minus the totalled Buick, so life downgraded to the glamour of three hours in transit to and from work. Things were fine for a week: bland normalcy of the daily grind. Lazarus, back from the dead just to work hand and knee grouting some rich suit's bathroom tile.

THE ARBORGLYPH

After a day on my knees, I shuffled outside for some air, and leaned back under the porch light, sweat stinging my eyes. I could have used a beer, but I was too lazy to pilfer from my patron's garage. I thought about Peter, about how he would sometimes join me, pretend to be part of the work crew, and would sit and DJ the dials on some old portable radio for us to have music to work to, spend all day like that in silent company, *for fun*, and how we used to follow that up with the delicious tradition of shotgunning a joint.

Sagging back against the rusted frame of the garage I searched the darkening sky for stars. It was still summer and at times the constellations would fulgurate before the sun kissed the horizon. Pools of sweat around the grooves of my miserable body had drawn mosquitoes and I swatted away their irritating drone from around my ears. A prick on my arm, and I found a rogue bastard bloating itself on my bloodstream, and slapped my gloved hand onto it, expecting a bloodied prize. No evidence of such, but already, I sensed a mounting itch there, writhing up my arm. Too acute to have been a mosquito bite. Probably some stupid oversight, exposure to tiling cement and all that. Cement burn always carried an insidious onset. I pulled off my gloves and, wouldn't you know it, right at the site of irritation: a dozen iridescent, ulcerated lesions, initially painless but throbbing, increasingly tender. The more I looked at it, the stranger it became. I tore inside to the kitchen sink to flush it under cool water and,

God help me,

my fingers glistening under the cascade of water began dancing of their own accord. Silly Punch-and-Judy puppet show, twitching about like a nightmarish shadow play. And me, "Oh!" in playful amusement, staring, entranced at this *thing*,

my hand.

Those pustules changing, no longer supposed contact dermatitis but popping open like extracted cysts borne into eyes,

dozens of eyes, eyes of all sizes, wriggling and darting on my hands and fingers, the wiggle of their irises slippery against my skin and my face settling into a mask of horrified incomprehension.

I, ever good at compartmentalizing, shoved the glove back on hand. I didn't know what was happening—perhaps I'd left my mind on the other side of life's tracks—but I didn't want to deal with this here. Not now. Out for the bus, boss on my tail and me waving him *goodbye! goodnight!* over my shoulder. Stomach in knots as I felt the wiggle of fingers beneath the glove, my own funhouse Deadite hand, gelatinous tissue of soft eyes pressing against the fabric as I sat on the bus on the way home and willed myself not to look.

I didn't know what to say to Peter when I got home so I didn't say anything. Found him dragging the trash out back into the dumpster. Then, trotting up the stairs beside me into the four-story, some derelict tenement over by Happy Valley and we passed an old Greek woman slapping dirt off a colourful rug in the hall.

"How's it hanging, Baba Yaga?" Peter grinned. Another one of his friends. Island of Misfit Toys, the lot of them, but who could not fall in love with that easy, affable smile?

As I moved to pass her she grasped my metastasizing arm with a viselike grip. Then, inspecting me—one eye a mossy green and the other a milky tiger's eye— she said, her breath a fragrant ochre: "You come to me when you are ready."

All of which is to say, I didn't know what that meant but there was something conveyed in her gaze, and she released my hand with a flourish and turned back in and closed the door.

"What was that?" said Peter.

I stood for a silent moment, then shrugged. "That why you call her Baba Yaga?"

In the apartment, I ripped off my coat and stalked to the bathroom. Peter jumped ahead of me, hands splayed like placating a feral stray.

"You alright?"

And I was trying to keep my cool. "Yep," I said. "Real cool, cool as a cucumber," but in my voice the low vibrato of panic. He was blocking my way to the bathroom and I stared at him through heavy lids.

"Emily's having a party tonight," said Peter.

"Great. Have fun." I was trying to move past him, but ever since this car accident he wouldn't leave me alone. His presence hovered over me inside the bathroom as I ripped open cupboards looking for anything to help. Treatment, a cure—

—for *what*? Had I even seen it right or was I just tired after a long day's work?

THE ARBORGLYPH

No.

Something was definitely there, stirring beneath the sheath of my glove. I shut my eyes, swaying on my feet.

"Want to come with me?" Peter asked. "It'll be good to get out of the house. For something normal."

"I work every day, Peter . . . " Ripping drawers open then, finding providence in the last: a tube of antibiotic ointment, squeezed out around the middle and crusty at the cap. "I haul ass out of bed an hour and a half earlier each day to catch a bus because we don't have a car anymore."

You totalled it. Thanks for bringing me back from the pearly gates to all this, you selfish prick, I thought to say, but didn't.

I turned to him but I didn't want to take my hand out of the glove. I hadn't braced myself to see what it looked like now, with its necrotizing deluge of eyes, and I didn't want Peter to see my little circus act. *Come one, come all, get a hand job from the freak show!* No, so I dropped a few aspirin into my gloved hand and leaned under the sink for water and gulped them down.

"That shit's not good for you," he said.

I braced myself against the sink, eyes closed as the overhead lights flashed behind my eyelids with a crash of pain.

"You eat ramen noodles every night," I replied.

He ignored that. "Anyway, *fun* normal is what I meant. There's a lake; they're planning a bonfire. It's Friday night and you have the whole weekend off."

I could feel something writhing against my glove and up my sleeve.

"Give me an hour to wash up."

I slammed the door in his face.

Turned the shower on to drown out the noise. Sure, that place was a shithole but we got it for the seemingly endless hot-water tank. There was something healing about a hot shower, like a home-cooked meal or a good fuck.

I ripped my work gloves off and twisted my arm to see, like a magic trick—ta-da! And the eyes, all open, Medusa stare, the sensation of their shifting pupils constricting in the sudden light creeping across the skin of my hand, and I thrust my arm into the scalding shower like a five-year-old sitting over a plate of brussels sprouts. All the eyes—blinking like tiny pustules—stopped at my wrist and instead, up my forearm, what looked like honeycomb lenses, like some grotesque wasp hive. I joined the appendage in the shower and washed off, bandaged it up, and pulled the gloves back on like useless condoms.

I lay down for a rest and passed out. Came to with Peter hovering over me, shaking my shoulders, and a car horn sounding outside.

"Let's go," he said. My mouth was dry and my head felt groggy. Peter looked down at my hands, the stupid work gloves. "You okay?"

I grunted.

"Do you want me to get Irene?"

And that got me out of bed like a shot. No, I did not want Irene. I did not need her further fucking the order of my biology. I went through puberty once and in no scope whatsoever had something like this ever fucking happened.

I pulled a shirt on, one with long sleeves, and looked outside. It was dark out past the dirty windows.

"Let's do this," I muttered.

< < < < > > >

We headed for Emily's. No Buick. Stupid me, kept forgetting. We shared a ride with some other people I didn't know.

I leaned my head against the window as they passed a joint around and my breath fogged the glass. Peter shifted around me—I could smell his skin; that warm soapy scent of laundry—to reach past and draw a little smiley face in the steam. I liked how he looked. The thickness of his brow. His sparkling eyes and soft, curly hair. He had the longest dark eyelashes I'd ever seen. He smiled so disarmingly that I intuitively grinned back. Those moments with him were treasures. I thought about how I must have looked, though, my repulsive hand and disheveled appearance, and I turned away to face the window. Looking like an ugly frog prince, my grappling desperation finally bleeding through my attempt at stoicism. I ran my gloved hand through my hair, pulling away a clump of it, and felt myself unmoor.

"You cool?" Peter said as we stepped out of the car. I dropped my fist into darkness, the mess of hair floating gently to the dirt, and nodded. *Sure, arctic.*

Let's get this over with and oh, the minute I was in there I wanted

THE ARBORGLYPH

to leave. Everyone there was so young—were these kids even legal?—
and they'd built a bonfire out by the lake, just like Peter said, trying
to live like teens in San Diego. But this was Lake Simcoe, we were in
butt-fuck nowhere Ontario; crisp summer air, croak of toads, and
there was trash all over the shore already. I sat down for a beer.
Relax, I told myself. *Take it easy.*

I made small talk with a girl at the bonfire. Young, with dangling
earrings shaped like iridescent apple slices. She wasn't from here,
name melodic in my mouth, but already forgotten, arms crossed and
huddled before the heat of the flames.

I gave it a few hours, then stalked off to find Peter to leave when
he raced past me trailing a beautiful girl by the hand: the elusive
Emily.

"Sebastian!" he shouted. I looked up and over to the shore where
Peter was comically tearing off his trousers, face broken out into a
blissful smile. "We're going skinny dipping!"

You are twenty-eight years old, I wanted to say, but that felt
wrong. There was no expiration date on an endless summer youth.
Not the kind Peter had.

"Wanna come with?" he said with a lilt. I shook my head.

I had always been that way. A stubborn bore; no good at parties,
never really fully understanding what Peter ever saw in me, let alone
for this long. Absolute wallflower, a shut-in, and so I kept to myself.
I watched, waiting for my turn, a lull in conversation where I could
interject, but I never did. I only let Peter pull me in, Peter make
space for me, Peter coax me into sharing a story. Like there he was,
back on the shore, skin gleaming wet, body like a Greek sculpture,
with my cell phone in his palm and backing toward the water. I stood
slowly, towering over him, hoodie pulled up and my face
downturned in a scowl.

"The way I see it, you got two options," he said. I knew where
this was going. "Either you come willingly, or I might just
accidentally slip and drop this old phone of yours into the water."

My face flared red. I did not want to be a killjoy.

"Peter," I said. His face lit up like a supernova.

"Sebastian," he said. Slow, delicious. My name in his mouth
made me want to melt. "Live a little?"

And my shoulders dropped. I caved, because with Peter I always did. The man had a fierce stranglehold on my heart. We all have our love language and that was mine. He tossed my phone back near the flames, sinking in the sand there, damp with spilled beer, and I pulled my shoes off, my pants, hoodie, briefs, and hesitated, watching the glow of the bonfire illuminate the gloves and what was masked underneath, lost somehow to the biology of something else.

I made my way to the water and he stood up in the shallow, buck-ass naked, hair glowing in the light of the moon and his mouth turned up in a wry grin. His glance lingered on me and he jutted his chin at my gloves. "Aren't we a little overdressed?"

I gave a weak smile—I didn't want to take them off—and thundered into the water past him and sank myself under.

It was black and cold, pinprick needles against my skin. The sound of the party drowned out of my ears and I soaked into the pleasant reverberation of the waves around me. I kicked up for air and Peter was there, rubbing water from his eyes, easy smile gracing his features. He moved close, dipped down beneath the water to his nose and pushed my hair out of my face. I looked at him and felt myself stir under the waves. Watching him, I was hot as a restless animal. Peter, larger than life, the mischievous and competitive troublemaker, the boy who always led me to adventure.

We had kissed, once, that night at camp years ago. He slid his hand into my sleeping bag and explored there, culminating in my first ejaculation. He had kissed me so softly on the lips, it might have been a dream, then rolled over, too afraid to speak, and fell asleep. And I, not built to perceive these things, let it slide as a moment of pubescent lust, but I had ached for him ever since. We kissed once more, at a party years later, on a dare. Peter had a bit of the devil in him. He'd go for anything that moved, anything interesting. I melted into that kiss and had sustained myself on the fantasy of another for years, but there was nothing of interest in me, no; just a shell of a man, some haunted ventriloquist dummy stumbling its way through life.

Peter got real close, close enough to whisper in my ear, and I felt something brush against my skin and a razor-sharp pain against my ankle, and pulled away. There was a feeling like snagged-tight barbed wire snaking up my leg. Peter looked confused.

"I think something bit me," I said, and palpated my shin under the water. There was a lump there. Someone—Emily—had already pulled Peter away. My face blanched as the growth moved up my leg. I waded through freezing water and then through the crowd and started putting my clothes on, sopping wet.

Peter was yelling my name, but I waved him off over my shoulder.

I raced out into the street in search of our car before the memory seeped in and I remembered it was totalled. I took a deep breath and called a lift. The night air was ice cold against my lungs but the feeling was good; I needed that numbing blaze of pain to pull me out of going crazy and gnawing off my own foot like a fox caught in a hunter's trap. I grazed my face where Peter had touched me and felt myself getting hard against my jeans. *Christ.*

Back at the apartment, I tore into the bathroom, finally alone, and ripped my wet clothes off. I pulled down my pants. There was a mass of scaly pustules up my leg, and thin membranes between the toes of my foot, the skin there rippling a sick translucence. The flesh all up my legs purple and red and the top epidermal layer peeling like a nasty sunburn. I twisted back in horror and crashed against the stall, fumbling for the shower knob.

I turned it on and dropped to my knees, tearing down a smorgasbord of cosmetics across the shower floor. I shoved them all aside. The water shot out, scalding heat and I let it burn my skin. I curled fetal by the drain. There was a lingering pain in my lap, the hot ache of desire, and I jerked off tight against my body. I came, and collapsed back against the wall of the shower, steam curling around me, hands a sticky mess. I lowered the back of my head against the wall and shut my eyes.

I don't know how long I sat there. I was in the dark and shrivelled like a prune when I heard a gentle knock on the door, and Peter softly calling my name.

"Can I come in?"

He let himself in and I didn't bother to hide this time. I saw the silhouette of him, backlit from the hall.

"Sebastian?"

The shower door distorted his figure as he squatted down. He looked at me through the glass. I felt disgusting. A caged animal; freak-sized sea monkey. *Just add water!*

"You okay, man?" Peter said.

I sat in the shower and he pulled open the door and shut the water off. Looked to see a creeping texture on the backs of my legs. He stared down in awe and got me a towel.

"I'll get Irene."

"I don't want to see Irene." I wanted a fucking doctor—a priest.

He brought me to bed and I grabbed his shirt collar. I was drained and scared and his after-image shivered and warped before me.

"I don't want to see her."

I went out like a light, facedown in a pillow.

< < < > > >

I came to, feeling the ripple of something against the back of my neck. I snapped up, disgruntled, my sight filmy with rheum, and clapped my hand there where I felt, oh shit—

eyes wide now, that rich foreboding,

something *alive* absorbing into my skin. It was screeching, struggling, tiny feet sinking into my backbone like mud. Irene was standing over me, Peter too, and suddenly I was up and yelling, twisting, feeling blindly with my hand at the soft fibers of it curling in and under my skin. Oh, no way—a deep revulsion when already my physiology was changing in spots along my back and down my arm, and I was screaming, "What did you do!"

Irene glared at me, grim-faced. "We needed to see how far along it was," she said, like I was in on this insane experiment, and I whipped around and gripped both her arms with my hands, I was shaking her, screaming, "Make it stop, make it fucking stop!" And oh, a prickle down my arm and I saw, as she was speaking—I could barely fucking hear over the sound of my pulse pounding in my own ears, too distracted to hear her spout a long line of pseudoscientific jargon, talking on about posthumous primordial soup and a physical process of transmogrifying the organic, the inanimate, absorbing it all like a giant fucking tumor, a monstrous mutation, sanity eroded until I wouldn't exist anymore, until I would just be *stuff*, and she was yelling at Peter, saying she told him this would happen and—

I was looking down at my hands and the left one, it burned with a chemical zing. I almost expected a wound but no, it was still my hand but not quite right. *God no,* I thought. The bones had spontaneously rearranged, fingers adhering to each other, the skin there emitting a cloying stench. Here came my ugly souvenir.

The fingers had fused.

I only had four now—I only had *four* fucking fingers, oh my God, this was so *strange*,

and I screamed, no words, just the sound of an animal. I rattled Irene like a rag doll. "What is it?" I said. "What did you put?"

"A lab mouse," she said.

A fucking lab mouse.

I met Peter's gaze. His mouth was a long, terrible line, and I turned my wrath on him. "Is this what I am to you? A fucking *science experiment!*" My voice was shaking.

"We needed to see how far along it was," Irene said again.

I lunged for the door, and I thought, *I'm crazy, they've driven me crazy.*

I gripped her arm, as tight as I could without seriously hurting her, and I jerked her around and slung her out the door. Peter, too, my expression twisted into a ferocious snarl, my hands on his collar, and me screaming, "Get out!"

I slammed the door shut and fell back against it with an ardent sob. I felt like I was suffocating. I could hear them arguing on the other side, Irene saying, "I *told* you, I *told* you this would happen," and Peter desperately begging forgiveness. I shuffled over to the bed, drained of adrenaline, and thought to myself maybe metabolizing a tiny organism was a lot of work, like a snake lethargic from digesting bones, and I simply blacked out.

< < < < > > > >

I lay in bed for two days, missing calls from work, barely even registering as Peter slipped in and out of the apartment. He tried to shake some sense into me.

"You're not eating," he said. He brought me food. Sweet ambrosia, not that dollar-store ramen noodle shit he'd make for himself; home-cooking, the kind that I knew would soothe my soul, but I couldn't eat it. I was so tired, so hungry, but I *couldn't.*

"You're not gonna turn into a human Lunchable if you eat a meal."

I lay back, silent.

"You can't not eat, Seb. Let me make you something. Please."

I didn't answer, so he went.

When I came to, I was facedown on the mattress. It was dark out, and I took a shuddering breath as I felt a warmth glide across my back. The skin there shivered in pleasure. I pushed myself up and Peter was there, a strange look on his face. I bolted up, suddenly enraged.

"What did you do?" And, trigger-happy, my shame reared its ugly head as I saw my hideous funhouse reflection in the mirror: my body stitched from other creatures' skin, the sclera of one eye a beady black, and my whole being as though the lattice manifestation of my inner suffering had crept through to the surface.

The mortification alone was enough to rouse me from my bed— I was hideous and I didn't want him to see, I didn't want him to touch me—and I wrenched myself out of the twisted sheets and shoved him out the room.

"Wait!" he said, and rammed his foot in the door.

"This is your fault," I shouted into the opening. I didn't look into the crack where his face was. I didn't want him seeing me. I leaned my weight into the door, but it wouldn't shut with his foot jammed in there. "Why did you bring me back? You knew—you *knew* what it would do! But you still did it so I could be Irene's fucking lab animal."

This, at least, caught him off guard and his foot disappeared and the door slammed shut. For a moment all I could hear was my own breathing, and then barely audible through the door:

"I missed you." He said the words so tenderly I could barely hear. "I thought—I wanted, I wanted to say goodbye."

"I didn't want to come back. I should have never come back."

A long silence from the other side of the door.

His voice was small. "Is that how you feel?"

I sat on the mattress, exhausted.

"Please talk to me," he said. I fell onto my back and, no rest for the weary—it had started—I was slowly sinking into the mattress.

"Fuck!" I screamed, and shot back up to my feet and I, Christ, I didn't want to touch anything. I didn't want to *become* anything. I wanted to *sleep* and I wanted the warm embrace of *normalcy*. I thought of what to do and the words of that old woman, christened

THE ARBORGLYPH

Baba Yaga, crept like fingers from the back of my mind: *You come to me when you are ready.*

I gathered myself and hurried out of the apartment and down the stairs. Peter tore out after me. I stood, hotheaded, at the Oracle's door as she answered, wise, dark eyes, and curious, the smell from her apartment a fragrant trail of baked clay. All around colourful veils were draped over windows and doors, lit only by candlelight.

"So you came," she said.

I pushed past her rudely, and I thought she would slam the door in Peter's face but she looked him over, nodded, and let him in.

She sat me down at a small round table and brewed tea. Peter tried to tell me something, an experiment he was trying, stumbling over his words—I'd never heard him stutter like that—explaining if organic material changed me, then human touch might change me back, some ridiculous posturing theory and I told him to shut up, "Just *shut up*, okay, Peter?" And he finally did. The light in his eyes went out and I thought, *Good.*

The Oracle sat down across from me. Tall bleached candles wept wax, and all around were tiny bones, crystals, and herbs. She opened her palms in communion, hands warm and ribbed with lines. Wrinkles creased around her eyes as she smiled, and I thought, *I know her*. There were women like her in all creeds and religions.

She inspected my arms, and my legs, my black eye, then looked at my one hand, the one with a cesspool of eyes, and paused to sip her tea.

"A ghost tethered refuses to go," she said. My head dropped. I had no patience for superstitious aphorisms.

"What does that mean?" Peter said.

"He has unfinished business."

Peter turned to me. "What's your unfinished business?"

"Fuck if I know." I blew air through my lips. I patted myself down for added effect. "No Patrick Swayze here. I'm alive."

"Are you?" she said. That milky eye seemed to coruscate candlelight.

I dropped my head again. I was too tired for this shit. She offered me tea and I took it. Fuck it. If I turned into a human tea leaf, I turned into a human tea leaf; no use in postponing the inevitable. The flavour was rich and coated the inside of my mouth.

A pot boiled. She left me at the table and came back holding a small crucible.

"What's going to happen to me?" I asked.

She looked at me curiously, then held my wrist to the table, the hand with the eyes on the back, that palm the last vestige of healthy human skin, and—oh Jesus, not that—I had no time to brace myself before she poured molten black onto my hand.

A spasm of unimaginable pain—

My whole body jerked back but she held tight to my arm. I was screaming, resisting against her, but her bones were proud and she held me sturdy. Tears welled in my eyes, face tight, and Peter watched in horrified fascination. I tried to pull back, but I couldn't fight her, I felt so weak after all of this, and I, bearing the pain, sagged against the chair, my gaze glazed and detached.

"You shouldn't be here," she said. After a pregnant moment she let go of my arm. I ripped my hand tight to my chest so fast I fell off the chair and curled on the ground in agony. There was a glowing cinder of pain at the center of my palm where I could feel something, I don't know—*flex* in there.

"Let me see," she said when I calmed down. She lent her warm, large paws and I, tired and having lost everything, uncurled my hand.

A sapling was starting to bloom there, strange stigmata, struggling to survive. My eyes watered at the beauty of it, the strange, cruel beauty.

"What is this?"

"A scrying."

I moaned. "I don't know what that *means*."

"It guides you where you need to be," she said simply, like I was supposed to know what that meant. People kept talking to me like I should know what any of this meant.

The little sapling reached up, spreading its leaves. I could feel its roots reaching into my nerves, skeined within the veins interloping up my arm, and I tore it out and stomped on it with my shoe.

Suddenly, I didn't know why I was there. She couldn't help me. No one could.

I mumbled quick thanks and shoved whatever cash I had from my wallet into her hand. I didn't need it anymore, I didn't need any of that fucking shit, one hand four-fingered and the other stigmata'd, freshly weeping some syrupy secretion, legs a mix of aquatic tissue, a real fucking freak show and, God, I didn't care anymore. I just did not care. I wanted to self-destruct and get rid of it all, so I did, I did, right back up into our apartment where I stuck my hand into Peter's aquarium till I snatched a fish and I ate it alive, the fucker, writhing all over inside my mouth till I crushed it with a sickening crunch and it exploded real Fruit Gushers–style between my teeth and I swallowed it whole. There. Then I headed outside and like some sick maniac I started shovelling grass and dirt into my mouth. I couldn't stop, I was hungry just trying to fill that void in my stomach, that big black pit that couldn't be filled, not with food, not with anything, I just wanted it all to be over, until Peter was there holding my wrists, holding me back and me, sobbing, changing already, and scared to see what I did to myself, what ugly form self-destruction might have manifested on me this time. I couldn't bear to think of it. I squeezed my eyes shut as I felt it ripple across my back, uncoiling beneath my skin. Peter pulled me up and inside and held me. I wanted a shower, I said, and he obliged. I asked him to stay and I left the stall door open and he sat leaning back against his palms watching me as I shifted like restless sands under the water.

I lay against the cool of the tile and fell asleep, waking somehow in my bed, skin tacky against the sheets; arms and cheek half-sunk into the mattress like I'd bought a memory foam.

"Son of a bitch." Struggling to dislocate myself from the fabric, and surprised to see Peter there beside me, his hands gently parting the sheets from my flesh. I sat back and tried not to move, as though it would wake the beast beneath my bedsheets and swallow me whole into the ground.

"What do you think she meant?" asked Peter, and me, confused for a moment, until I realized he was talking about the Oracle. I lowered my head into my hands, afraid they might stick to my face— a real-life Munch painting—and took a shuddering breath. I had been sleeping but, while dreaming, her words, at first confusing, had borne new fruit, and I raised my gaze to contemplate what she'd said as my mind adjusted to the notion like a tuning fork. The sapling which I chose to ignore had pointed to the same dizzying conclusion I refused to admit to myself. It was time to go back to that place where time stopped, that tree on Saint Ambrose Street and I, an insect trapped in amber, needed to be set free. I wanted to cry. I just wanted to be back to normal. I wanted someone to hold me, but who knew what that would do and who knew how grotesque I'd grown those past few days. *I'm scared*, I wanted to say. *I'm scared,* and *hold me*, but what good would it do? I looked at Peter, his expression dark and closed, and wished we could have better spent this time together.

< < < > > >

In the end, I had to go back. No point in waiting longer; the problem I was facing was not solvable—everything I touched stuck to my skin like sweat, a tapestry scrawl of bruising and veins across my face and neck.

We borrowed someone's car. On the drive over, I was melding into the seat through my clothes. The sun was going down, a hazy light like glittering champagne through the leaves, and the breeze was warm.

I looked at the tree, the large crater of our misadventure marring the side of its trunk. I stood in the shadow of the memory, what was left of it, a night thrown caution to the wind with Peter. He stood behind me, watching silently.

A quiet moment passed.

"I didn't want to let you go," he said. "I'm sorry." And I knew he meant it.

I wanted to say something. I wanted him to know and I didn't. I thought about riding in the car that night, and all the nights before. All of a sudden I wished we still had that shitty Buick. I'd die all over again to see that look in his eyes. I thought to say what was aching to be said but my jaw was bolted shut. A fire roiled in my chest.

What would he do? I thought. Peter, who was earnest and sincere. Truest in the places I could never be.

"I love you," I murmured.

He didn't say anything and the fire in my chest went cold.

I shot my hand out to touch the bark, but Peter's skin met mine, his hand on my arm, touching me, stopping me and I closed my eyes, too scared to look. My hands were shaking. Did he see? I looked at him and he was smiling, that golden smile, and my heart melted. His hands were warm and I breathed into the feeling. I wanted to sink into him. Just him.

THE ARBORGLYPH

He leaned his forehead against mine and I fell back against the tree, braced by his arms and suddenly his lips on mine, deep in a kiss, a kiss that said all that I could never, all I was too scared to; *thank you for everything*, and *I love you*, and *I'll miss you*.

And how, fed by the sweetness of his kiss, the bark enveloped my flesh and I felt myself stretch thin across the earth, grasping the land with long fingers for richer soil, my roots in search of a time where they might once again entangle him.

< < < < > > > >

Every year he walked the forest behind the roads on Saint Ambrose Street, and as the seasons changed to summer others came and went, and those walking past could see in that tree, carved into my heart, were the letters *P* and *S*.

SKYWARNING

Jonathan Raab

SMOKE FLOWED IN from forest fires to the west and north, choking the sky with haze and turning the setting sun blood red. Weeks of record temperatures and unbreathable air would mark the final weeks of summer. The whole world was on fire.

Violet parked the National Weather Service pickup in front of Monitoring Station 322's control center, a squat rectangle of old brick walls and a new aluminum roof adorned with wires, floodlights, and a single security camera perched over the door and stairs. The station chief's pickup was parked nearby, smoke lingering around its tires.

"You ready for three days of mountain fun in colorful Colorado?" she asked Joel, who sat in the passenger seat staring at the occluded sky. "The freshest air in the world."

The door to the control center swung open and McKenna leaned out to give them a wave, cigarette trailing smoke to join the sea of haze around them. His greying beard and red hair curling out from beneath his faded Broncos cap appeared white in the hazy wash of their headlights.

"He's not supposed to be smoking in there," Joel said, coughing.

"He's also not supposed to be at the monitoring station alone, but here he is," Violet said, an itch growing in the back of her throat. "Privileges of rank."

"We're students, so there's a liability issue for us."

"Grad students, which makes us even more dangerous." Violet turned around in the driver's seat to look through the rear windshield. Floodlights from the shower and sleeping quarters trailers pushed back against the fog-like smoke about a hundred yards behind them. The monitoring station's radio tower grew out of a brick fallout bunker to the south, standing sentry at the edge of the mountain's flat plain. Satellite dishes were sores growing from its latticed steel superstructure, pointing into the murky sky. Red aerial warning lights blinked in rhythmic sequence.

"I can barely see the rest of the station," she said.

"I just wish NWS wouldn't treat us like kids," Joel said. "It's not like I haven't spent plenty of time in the mountains."

Violet shook her head.

"I have enough white friends on Instagram to know you all think you belong up here," she said. "But we're just visitors. Maybe some people belonged here, once, but that was a long time ago."

"The world's going to hell," Joel said, grabbing his sleeping bag and backpack from behind the seat. "Might as well ride it out up here. I just wish we had cell coverage."

"If you ever want to get McKenna riled up, ask him about the soil composition and the electromagnetic fields up here. He'll tell you about the space rocks in the topsoil, interfering with the signal, scrambling our RNA. Worse than 5G."

"Space rocks," Joel said, popping open his door to step out of the truck and into the ether.

< < < < > > > >

"NWS Boulder, this is Monitoring Station Three-Two-Two, completing shift change at nineteen-hundred hours," Joel said into the radio's handset. No one had bothered to update the hand-me-down military SINCGARS radio equipment since sometime in the '90s, but the radar and closed-circuit television security system monitors looked new enough.

A man's voice returned to him from Boulder, riding the airwaves:

"Roger, Three-Two-Two. Try not to breathe too much smoke up there this weekend."

"We'll hold our breath, Boulder. Three-Two-Two, out."

McKenna clapped his large hands together, causing Joel to jump.

"Normally I'd take a walkabout around the perimeter this time of night, but with the smoke as thick as it is, I'd rather be inside with the AC," McKenna said. "You need anything, catch me on the Motorola." He held up a small blue handheld and clicked the transmit button twice. Shrill chirps erupted from the speakers on the desk. "Got anything good to read on watch?"

"Just some light reading assigned by Professor Rhoten," Joel said, removing a stack of printed-out science journal articles from his bag. "Too long, didn't read: the ecosystem is collapsing and we're screwed as long as the corporations control everything. Important stuff to know for a budding climatologist." He let the pile fall on the table with a *thud*.

"Doom and boredom come with learning the ways of the Force, my young apprentice. When you finally earn your PhD, right as the apocalypse ramps up, you'll be glad you spent your weekends up here instead of staying in Boulder to get laid."

"Right. Any special instructions, Chief?"

"Make sure radar and comms systems are functioning. If not, you know the drill: troubleshoot and reboot. Complete radio checks as scheduled, take any spotter reports from SKYWARNING, and try to stay awake."

"Mind taking your ashtray out, too?" Joel pointed at a glass dish, where a pair of cigarette butts stood like crooked towers in a sea of ash.

"Sure, sorry. See you in a few hours."

< < < < > > >

Echoing thumps on the metal door jarred Joel awake from a troubled half-sleep.

Disoriented, he stood too quickly, knocking the office chair back and sending it tumbling to the hardwood floor. The metal door was almost directly behind him, and the control center's narrow dimensions made the shuddering impacts reverberate within his skull.

The banging ceased. The control center went quiet, save for the static hum of screens and electronics. Joel began to wonder if the knocking had been part of a dream he couldn't recall.

There was a soft, slumping sound overhead, like a wounded animal dragging itself across the corrugated aluminum roof. He wasn't dreaming.

The lights went out and the console screens went black.

Joel stood in the darkness, eyes wide but seeing nothing. The room's dimensions suddenly felt distorted, endlessly expansive.

Dull bursts of light came through the high, squat windows like flashbulbs filtered through frosted glass. Spectral green illumination bobbed and pulsed like a lighthouse beacon in its death throes.

The radios chirped back to life; monitors buzzed with the text crawls of reboot code. Static crashed through the speakers, undergirding high-frequency squelches that sent Joel's hands to his ears. The security camera monitor drew his attention as it finished its loading sequence.

The image on screen was in black and white, as expected, but unlike the static camera feeds, it was jittery, handheld. The camera swept over a field of darkness broken up by spots of vaporous light—candles, flames tall and wax dripping, set on a table. Five of them, standing in pentagrammic formation around a flat, wooden board with ornate script across its surface. A spirit board, complete with a planchette the texture of bone, carved into the shape of a tiny bull's skull. Candle flames trailed swirls of pallor.

The skull-planchette moved. The board spoke.

3-2-2

The screen went black with a burst of static.

The lights flickered back on overhead. The CCTV screen displayed the four viewpoints of the monitoring station's cameras, one perched on each of the compound's structures.

The door to the control center swung open. Joel spun and put his back to the monitor, heart in his throat. Beams of light shined brightly in his eyes.

"Did you see anyone skulking around up here?" McKenna said, clicking off his headlamp. "Anyone on the monitors?"

"Jesus Christ," Joel said, exhaling.

"You alright?" Violet asked. "You're pale as a ghost."

"Thanks, you look great, too. Did the power go out for you guys?" McKenna frowned.

"Yes, and I don't like that," he said. "We're on solar up here, with reserve juice and a backup diesel generator with enough fuel to last a week."

"Someone banged on the door. Then the power went out."

"'Someone?'" Violet said, turning around to shine her headlamp across the open plain between the monitoring station's isolated buildings. "With this smoke, they could be right next to us. We'd never even see them."

"Let's check the security system," McKenna said.

"There was something else on the security monitor," Joel said, blurting it out. "Looked like a scene from a weird-ass home movie."

"Pirate signal, maybe?" Violet said.

"An airborne signal wouldn't cross into the closed-circuit system," McKenna said. "What was it?"

"One of those talking spirit boards, I think," Joel said. "But it wasn't something you'd find in the board game aisle. The pointer was like . . . a cow's skull or something. Slide over to the numbers, by itself. Spelled out 'Three-two-two.'"

"As in, Monitoring Station Three-Two-Two?" Violet said, shaking her head. "That's real fucking spooky." She stepped back inside and closed the door behind her. McKenna sat in the office chair and turned the monitor toward him. He started to click through menus, bringing up the security system's memory logs.

"Why so much security for a weather station in the middle of the mountains?" Violet asked.

"I've been working up here for about four years, and I have a few hypotheses," McKenna said. "One: the computer systems, radio, satellite, and radar tech we have up here is expensive, and some forward-thinking bureaucrat figured that as the United States became a hollowed-out husk, people might be desperate enough to start ripping government electronics for scrap."

On the bottom of the screen, he clicked back on the timeline, setting the camera displays to 10 minutes in the past.

"Two: there's some proprietary or national defense tech here. This building and the antenna array's bunker are fallout shelters, and I wouldn't be surprised if a satellite dish or two on that mast is defense-related. A redundant communications system, maybe a spook network node. Some of the SKYWARNING spotters have reported hearing numbers station broadcasts out here."

"What's your third idea?" Violet asked.

"My favorite of the bunch: that this really isn't a weather station at all, but a long-running psychological warfare research site, and we're all just test subjects under observation."

"I don't exactly lead an exciting life," Violet said.

"We represent a certain privileged, educated, and yet economically desperate subset of the population," McKenna said. "Agnostic or atheist, secular, and center- or far-left, politically speaking. Isolated, or in small groups, exposed to weird waves or radiation caused by that antenna array, the mountain soil, or whatever weirdness is in the air this much closer to the ionosphere."

"Space rocks," Joel said.

"Told ya," Violet said.

"Exactly. Here it is." McKenna pressed the green PLAY arrow.

The smoke was a hazy filter over the black and white images of the security feeds. The upper left recording came from the camera perched above the door to the control center; the upper right from a perch on the radio mast; the lower left from the door to the shower trailer; the lower right a wide view of the space between all four buildings from atop the sleeping trailer.

Within moments, shadowy figures appeared on the upper right feed, congregating around the radio tower's base. Finding the double doors to the bunker secured by chain and lock, the group pressed up against one another, hugging the doors—and flowed *through* the metal blocking their path, becoming as smoke, absorbed into the structure itself.

"What the hell," Violet said. McKenna shook his head. Joel blinked hard to clear his vision.

"Must be a recording error," McKenna said, not sounding all that convinced. A lone, black-clad figure appeared in the upper left feed, walking up to the door to the control center. It turned its face—or the darkness where its face should have been—up toward the camera, then began to pound its closed fists against the door.

"That's when it started for me," Joel said, leaving out the part about being asleep.

"It's not trying to get in," Violet said. "It didn't even try the door handle."

Each quadrant of the screen went black, one by one.

"Power loss," Joel said.

The security footage ended there, with a resumption of visual data timestamped several minutes later. McKenna dragged the playback cursor to the right, granting them a view of himself and Violet on the metal landing to the control center.

"Joel, I know your shift is just about up, but I'd rather you sleep in here tonight, so you and Violet aren't alone," McKenna said.

"No argument from me."

"There's a .22 rifle in the locker," McKenna said, pointing to the far end of the trailer. "Combination is zero-three-two-two-zero. The magazine is on top of the ammo box. Violet, I assume the Air Force taught you how to use a gun?"

"The .22 is a rifle, not a gun," Violet said. "And yeah. What about you?"

"I'll stay in the quarters trailer. There's some electronics and personal items from the team I don't want these creeps getting into."

"You think being by yourself is a good idea?" Violet asked.

"I keep a twelve-gauge in my room. I figure if I keep the lights on and make some noise, they'll be less likely to break in. You can see most of the campus on the security monitors. If there's a problem, you can reach me via handheld."

"Should we call the cops?" Joel asked.

"Do you want to get the police involved?" McKenna asked.

Violet shook her head.

"I'm not exactly comfortable with the police showing up if I have to hold the rifle, for obvious reasons," she said. "But we should tell the main station."

"I'll leave that to you. Come on, Joel, let's grab your gear." They stood up and opened the great metal door, revealing a wasteland of rolling smoke and darkness. "Keep this door locked, and don't open up unless you confirm it's one of us."

< < < < > > > >

The hours drifted on, leading them deeper in to the smoke-haunted night. The paranoia that had gripped them earlier became a dull, buzzing static at the back of Violet's mind. She was already convincing herself that they had overreacted to a power outage and a few trespassing homeless people or lost hikers. She tried to distract herself by tapping away aimlessly at a research paper on her laptop.

SKYWARNING

Joel had dropped his gear off on the opposite end of the control center but, not feeling much like sleeping, he idly switched the CCTV monitor from the quadrant view to each individual camera and back again, searching the static-covered images for strange trespassers and stranger lights, not ready to let his guard down.

"I need to step outside," Violet said, giving up on her work.

Joel looked up, an eyebrow raised. "You want to go outside, in the middle of the night, after a friggin' ghost was knocking on that very door?"

Violet chuckled. "So, it was a ghost now?"

"Something goddamn spooky," he said. "Maniac squatters, bigfoot, whatever—something feels *off* about tonight."

Violet dropped her smile; Joel was still obviously rattled. Maybe it was for the best they were sticking together. "My guess is *it* or *he* or *whatever* is long gone. And no offense, but I need a break from being cooped up in here. I'll just be right outside the door. You can watch on the security cam. If I see any creepy creeps creeping around, I'll come right back inside. I just need a quick change of scenery."

"Don't come crying to me when the wooks kidnap you and make you their May Queen or whatever," Joel said.

"I sort of like the sound of that," she said, standing up and making her way to the door. She pushed against the cold metal, which yielded with a squeal of hinges in need of oil. She stepped out onto the metal landing and the door swung shut behind her.

Just a year ago, this would have been the moment she produced a cigarette and matches. Getting a nicotine fix had been her excuse for taking a moment to herself, to disengage from others and from her work, to allow her overclocked mind to focus on a simple moment of peace. Although she had since quit, she had used the excuse of a smoke break to get out of the glad-handing and aggressive ass-kissing that followed colloquia or guest lectures at the department. She knew that networking was a necessary part of any field—especially if she decided to pursue a career in academia—but she just didn't have it in her most of the time. The *work* was important. That should be enough.

The forest fire smoke burned her sinus cavity and made her throat itch. She may as well have been puffing on a cigarette. At least she'd get a nicotine high that way.

As the green lights drifted toward her from the southwest edge of the perimeter, Violet tried to tell herself that the bad air was making her see things.

She knew better.

The voice was a ghostly whisper at the edge of the static hum of electronics inside the cramped control center. Soft, spectral, easy to miss. But the sound persisted until Joel realized it was not some phantom trick of the imagination, but a transmission coming through at low volume.

". . . Walker Six, calling Monitoring Station Three-Two-Two," the voice said. "Come in for SKYWARNING spotter report, over."

The twisting anxiety in Joel's gut melted into a slurry of relief and embarrassment. He reached over to the olive-green SINCGARS radio console and turned the volume knob up, then grabbed the small black handset.

"This is Monitoring Station Three-Two-Two," he said, sliding the clipboard with the SKYWARNING report templates in front of him. "Walker Six, send your report."

"Three-Two-Two, it's good to hear a voice," Walker Six said, his voice carrying the remains of an out-of-state accent. East coast. Staten Island or Jersey, maybe.

"Likewise," Joel said.

"The smoke up here—it plays tricks with your eyes, you know? I've been breathing the stuff for two weeks. Probably shaving a few years off my life, not that I'm using my time all that wisely these days."

"Sorry to hear that, Walker Six," Joel said. "You have a report?"

"About that, kid. This is gonna make me sound like I'm nuts."

"If there's a weather event, we want to hear about it, Walker Six. Every data point helps, especially subjective observations. Helps lend context to the radar and satellite data."

"I know all that, I take the refresher courses," Walker Six said. "But I need you to listen, okay, kid? I need you or somebody else to hear this, and record it, make it official. That helps make it real. Because as soon as I get off the line with you, I'm going to call the sheriff and make the very same report."

Joel didn't like where this was going.

"Walker Six, if you are experiencing an emergency, you are advised to call 911. SKYWARNING is not an emergency communications system."

"Please listen," Walker Six said. "Even if it means you'll rescind my spotter qualification—although I enjoy the work, and it gives me the opportunity to connect with people, folks who all got the same mission. It's sort of like being in the Army again, but less stressful. Fewer dipshits ordering me around. Over."

Joel smiled. He didn't know what to make of this, but he found himself liking the old man all the same.

"Thank you for your service," he said, reflexively.

"Thanks for paying for my G.I. Bill and sending me to college," Walker Six said. "And don't thank me, because what I did didn't help nobody, except maybe myself. Considering how much my back hurts and the trouble I have sleeping, even that's debatable."

"Okay, thank you for being a SKYWARNING spotter. How's that?"

Walker Six chuckled.

"That's good. Alright kid, I'm going to give you this report, and then I'm going to let you and fate decide what's next. I'm about three miles south of Ward off Route 72. Weather event observed while facing northwest, event feature traveling southeast from about 11:45 p.m. to 11:47 p.m., at about 30 knots."

"Ward . . . southeast . . . okay, got it. Send description of the event feature."

Walker Six hesitated.

"You can cross-reference my credentials. I've been doing this for years."

Cold anxiety returned to the pit of Joel's stomach.

"What did you see?"

Walker Six sighed, then spoke slowly.

"Like a patch of fog. But glowing green, all lit up from the inside. It drifted just above the tree line, so I got a good look at the thing."

"Are you sure it wasn't just a smoke plume?"

"It was like fog *around* something. Looked like—it looked like a streak of silver or metal. I shined a flashlight up at the thing and the beam reflected back. It was that close."

"Was it an aircraft?"

"I don't know what the hell it was," Walker Six said, his voice warbling and hissing over the radio static. "I'm telling you, and then I'm going to call the sheriff, in case something happens to me."

"What would happen to you?"

"I don't know. But since I saw that thing, something feels off, like there's eyes in the woods. There are a few other houses out this way, but I'm the only one up this time of night. All the insects are quiet. Do you know what that feels like, when the whole natural world just goes absolutely silent?"

The cold anxiety in Joel's guts began to crawl up his spine.

"Used to happen in 'Nam. If you heard nothing, that meant get your ass down."

Joel swallowed hard.

"I think something bad is coming, Monitoring Station Three-Two-Two. Whatever that thing was, it's headed your direction."

Screeching, incoherent static washed over the frequency, ending the connection. The speakers blared high-pitched noise and feedback. Joel slapped at the volume control.

< < < < > > >

Outside, a procession of beautiful horrors floated toward Violet, and she decided that maybe she didn't need the break after all.

Cattle skulls, large and small, some with horns and some without. Gleaming white and suffused with a soft, green glow that illuminated the smoke around them in great ribbons of emerald. Scraped free of all flesh and independent of bodies, they bobbed in the air as they drifted, noses pointed toward her, eyes empty and suffused with that dread light.

Violet scrambled back inside, pulling the great metal door closed behind her, engaging its arcane mechanical lock.

"The radio's out," Joel said. "Weirdest thing, this guy called in a UFO—"

"Something's coming," she said, struggling to catch her breath.

Joel blinked hard, mouth open.

Violet stepped forward to crouch in front of the CCTV monitor. She tapped keys to bring up the camera perched on the radio mast and enlarged the image.

The cattle skulls were indistinct orbs of green light in the wash of digital static, darkness, and smoke, but the glow on-screen was even more pronounced; a pulsing, rhythmic pattern within the fog, giving the impression of a submarine rising from ocean depths.

"What are we looking at?" Joel asked, his voice frail.

"We need to call for help," Violet said, returning to the quadrant view.

"And say what?"

The lights in the control center dimmed, but the radar system and security monitors maintained power. On the CCTV screen, the skulls floated across the four disparate camera feeds on a wave of pulsing light.

Violet switched to the control center's camera, which displayed the metal landing and stairs where she stood only moments before.

They held their breath, waiting for the cattle skulls to float up to the stairs, to the door—and to do what, exactly, neither of them could say. The lights and electronic equipment flickered and buzzed static around them. The floorboards and walls groaned under unseen pressures.

Moments stretched on into minutes. Joel looked from the locked door to the screen and back again, sure those phantoms would burst through at any moment. Violet punched back up to the CCTV's quadrant view, then cycled through the individual feeds, her anxiety becoming exasperation.

"What the *hell*."

No weird lights, no floating cattle skulls. Just an ever-rolling bank of smoke, and the oppressive darkness of the deep night.

"We need to get McKenna," Violet said.

"That would require going outside," Joel said. "That look like meth heads or lost hikers to you?"

"We just keep looking for rational explanations, because we want this to be some big overreaction on our part," Violet said. "Then we'd just be scared academics out where we don't belong, spooked by the poor folks or natural environment we claim to support, same as all the other phony-ass lefties in Boulder."

"I'd be okay with that, because I've never seen anything like *that* before in my life," Joel said, pointing at the screen.

"Maybe there's a fourth scenario McKenna didn't anticipate," Violet said. "We're out here, in the dark, in a truly wild and hostile place, building outposts and watching the sky. Maybe something decided to watch back. Until it got tired of just watching."

The security feeds began to dim and grow dark, as if the electricity powering them were reduced by steady, patient degrees—then reignited with a sudden, blurry wash of static and fleeting images of elaborate numbers and letters writ on aged wood.

"That's the board I saw earlier," Joel said, his throat scratchy and suddenly very, very dry. "You really know how to use the gun? The rifle, I mean?"

"They didn't exactly train me to be a door kicker, but yeah, I do."

"Maybe we find McKenna, like you said."

"Try the handheld."

Joel took one of the blue Motorola radios off of the charging console.

"Control to quarters. Chief, you there?" Joel released the transmit key, but static was his only answer. "Chief, come in."

Violet made her way to the far end of the trailer where the firearms locker waited. She paused, recalling the combination, then worked the lock tumbler until it popped open. Opening the metal door to the locker produced the scent of gun oil, wafting out to compete with the subtle tang of wildfire smoke. She took the .22 rifle in her hands, its stock aged and weathered but still smooth, its barrel dusty but free of rust. Then she grabbed the magazine—checking to confirm it was loaded before sliding it into the receiver—and pocketed the ammo box in her jacket.

"We're going straight to the quarters trailer to grab McKenna," Violet said, racking the bolt to chamber a round. "If he's not there, we check the bunker under the antenna array. Then we're headed to the truck. I don't care what we see out there. If it's not in our way, it's not important. Understand?"

"Y-yes," Joel said, standing up. "I'll be right behind you."

"Right," Violet said. "Headlamps."

They pulled elastic bands across their heads, setting the lights on their foreheads like phylacteries. Violet approached the door, took a deep breath, and disengaged the lock. She clicked the headlamp on and pushed the door open with her shoulder. The smoke came flooding back into the control center and into their mouths, noses, and eyes.

Violet stepped outside onto the metal landing, the rifle's buttstock pressed against her right shoulder, her hand cradling the stock and her index finger floating just outside of the trigger well. Smoke crawled along the vast dark spaces between the station's scattered buildings. Their headlamp beams struggled to cut through the murk, illuminating only a few feet ahead of them.

Violet led them down the steps and toward the quarters trailer at the far end of the perimeter, now little more than a white blob in the dark. Their footfalls echoed in the muffled stillness of night, dirt and rocks crunching against their boots.

As they reached the quarters trailer, the floodlight perched above the main door sputtered and went dark. Violet kept her rifle low but pointed her headlamp beam up, running it over the walls and windows of the trailer, searching for the door—and finding it open, revealing a black rectangle of darkness leading inside.

"Chief—?"

Before Joel could finish, a green glow appeared within the trailer, its dread illumination spilling out through the impassive windows, radiant shafts of viridian streaming out from the doorway. A tall, flowing shadow stepped in front of those glowing shafts of terrible light, shambling toward the open door.

"He might be in the generator room," Violet whispered, or tried to, her words tumbling together. She grabbed Joel by his coat's shoulder and pulled him away.

The figure emerged from the doorway, eldritch light pulsing and flowing over its black veil and blacker robes, a film stock negative of a statue of some saint or the Virgin herself cut from the fabric of night and molded in terror.

They doubled back, cutting across the open dirt and grass space toward the radio tower.

"Eyes forward, not back," Violet said to Joel as much as to herself.

The radio tower stretched high above them, its metal supports interlaced with wires and pockmarked with satellite dishes, its red aerial warning lights blinking through the smoke that had settled over the whole world.

A radioactive fallout shelter sign hung next to the bunker's twin metal doors. Violet settled her headlamp's beam on the door handles, finding the lock disengaged and the chains hanging limp on the ground.

"If he's in there, we grab him and run back to the truck," Violet said. She held the rifle tight in her right hand, then turned the grinding metal handle of the left door clockwise and pulled. They shined their beams inside, sweeping through the darkness. From within, the smell of sawdust and diesel wafted out.

"Chief?" Joel said, his voice cracking. "If you're in there, we gotta go."

The hair on the back of Violet's neck stood up. She turned around, finding the darkness behind them suddenly not so dark, now suffused with a growing green light.

"We're going *now*," she said, turning back to the open doors of the bunker, just in time to see the corpse emerge from the abyss.

It was, at first, simply a face—blackened and ruined by the harsh Colorado sun and caked in dust, its skin dried-out layers of clay pressed against a skull misshapen by blunt force trauma. But it soon became shoulders, too, and arms, and a ruined, caved-in chest whose exterior was covered in ash and dust and whose exposed insides were wet and dripping. Blood leaked from the chasm of opened flesh that ran from sternum to stomach, bone and skin broken and ripped apart by imprecise violence that made the interior exterior.

The corpse floated toward them, its feet dragging uselessly on the ground before ascending, drawn up into the air above, as if on strings.

Joel produced something like a scream. Violet's hand was on his shoulder again, grasping so hard that her fingernails suffered slight but painful separations from their nailbeds.

The terrible green light was all around them now, shimmering and bouncing behind the walls of smoke. Campfire-ash taste settled in their mouths and their eyes burned as they dashed back toward the truck. Adrenaline gave the world a choppy, missing-frames continuity, exacerbated by the endless fog and pulsing, terrible light surrounding them.

Violet scrambled around to the driver's side door, hand shaking as she inserted the key. Finding success after the longest three seconds of her life, she popped the door open and hit the unlock button as she clambered inside. Joel hopped in from the other side, his breathing a wheeze, and they slammed and locked the doors to the cab. Violet slipped the key into the ignition.

SKYWARNING

The starter wouldn't catch. The engine wouldn't start.

"Shit—"

Windshield and window glass shattered as long, coal-black arms reached into the cab for both of them, finding purchase on their coats and necks and arms and pulling them back out into the night. The smoke-fog was alive and pulsing in the air, in their eyes, in their lungs.

From the parting clouds above emerged a great streak of silver, its conical outline home to familiar contours: the head of a great bull of the field, with rows of teeth made for grinding grass into cud and empty eye sockets of limitless black, save for the shuddering light emanating from within.

Violet, held to the ground by scarecrow-shadows, turned her head to the side to look away from the impossibility, but fingers— scaled, cold fingers—grasped her face and turned it back toward the great, floating skull in the sky. She closed her eyes to slits.

White cattle-skull faces suffused with emerald light stared down at her from within the hoods of dark robes. The pressure on her arms, chest, and legs relaxed, and a sensation of weightlessness followed.

< < < < > > > >

A sudden cold snap and shifting winds made the air in the mountains just west of Boulder more palatable by morning. The sun hid behind grey clouds moving east. The radio tower's metal superstructure groaned and settled in the cool air.

Boulder County Sheriff's Deputy Alex Peña enjoyed the 45-minute trip up the mountain. He had jumped at the chance to respond to the NWS's request to check on the staff of their monitoring station embedded deep behind the Flatirons. He had no problem spending a good chunk of his morning on a scenic drive to investigate what was probably just some technical issue.

Peña found two pickup trucks on-site, one of which had its windshield and windows smashed in. A .22 rifle sat in the dirt nearby, magazine loaded, a round in the chamber. Peña unloaded the firearm and pocketed the round and magazine, setting the rifle on the hood of his cruiser. Doors were open on three of the four buildings, but there was no sign of anyone, let alone the station's skeleton crew. The air was cold and tasted like ash around the edges.

Inside the control center, Peña found a pair of sleeping bags, pillows, and hiking packs stuffed with personal effects. On the far end of the slim structure was an open locker that smelled faintly of gun oil.

A shrill beeping made him jump. A voice spoke over the hiss and hum of static, the volume far too loud for such a small space.

"Monitoring Station Three-Two-Two, this is Walker Six. Anybody there, over?"

Peña found the SINCGARS handset and tapped the transmit button before speaking into it, fumbling with the volume controls.

"Walker Six, this is Deputy Peña of the Boulder County Sheriff's Department. There's—were you in contact with anyone here last night, over?"

There was long pause on the net.

"Yes, I was."

"Boulder station asked us to check it out. Anything you can tell me would be helpful, over."

"My report should be on file, there," Walker Six said. "And . . . I'm ready to make another SKYWARNING spotter report."

"There's a bit of a situation up here, I think."

"And there's another one coming your way, Deputy. Looks like a streak of silver or metal, but it's shaped—I didn't recognize it before, but I do now."

"Walker Six, I'm going to need to get a statement from you. There's signs of a struggle here, and—"

"It looks like a giant cattle skull. A bull, one of the big boys the ranchers raise out on the western slope."

Static began to bear down on the signal.

"Walker Six, come again?"

"Looks like . . . pulled . . . headed east again . . . ."

"Walker Six?"

The lights dimmed. The CCTV monitor projected a flickering, black and white image of the security camera's view from the tower. Peña bent down to stare into the screen, eyes fixated on a rush of black and white pixels.

Walker Six's voice came through in a sudden burst of clarity:

"It's moving east again. Toward you."

On screen, three faces stared back at the deputy. Faces subsumed by smoke pouring out in great waves from their mouths, noses, and eyes—smoke illuminated from within by a terrible, flickering light. Then, desiccated hands, pressed against a carven image of a bull's skull, moved over fine wood decorated with elaborate script. It drifted over to the numbers:

3-2-2

There was a sudden metal-on-metal grinding, and the heavy door to the control center began to swing open. Smoke drifted in at first, followed by something else entirely.

CAVITY

Nicola Kapron

SO I HAVE this friend—

Had. Had this friend.

Point is, there's this guy, okay, and he hates people. Not in the sense that he's violent or angry; he just doesn't like them. Being around other humans puts a bad taste in his mouth. So long as you don't wear on his nerves too long, he's nice enough, but the discomfort he feels is tangible. If he could've gotten away with it, he'd have gone his whole adolescence without so much as making eye contact, but in a town small enough for everyone to know each other by name, that wasn't going to cut it. So he found me, the angry little ginger already too gay and outspoken for our surroundings, and I became his shield. Still didn't like me much, but I didn't really mind. I was already used to being disliked. Being able to protect someone made up for it.

He told me once in high school that he thinks he just wasn't made to be around humans. That God made a mistake when He was assigning bodies and put a soul that should have been in a tree or a moose or some shit into a squishy brown biped. I thought it was

CAVITY

funny at the time, but I was seventeen and perpetually drunk off my ass. I thought everything was funny. A year later, when my friend—ex-friend—pulled up all his roots and vanished, first to the coast, then to an island, then to a wetland on the island, it stopped being quite so hilarious. Didn't even leave a phone number, just a forwarding address for mail he never answers. Asshole.

I stayed where I was. Unlike him, I do enjoy company, even in a town as small and closed-minded as this one. I'd go insane if I had no one else to talk to. So I have the three roommates that share my tiny rat-hole, an aunt who tries too hard to make up for the absence of the sister who dumped me on her over a decade ago, a gaggle of cousins that drop by from time to time to turn my life upside down, and anyone who walks into the local corner store during the late shift.

This is where my ex-friend comes back into the picture.

It's just past one AM. Quiet enough to hear the lights buzzing in their sockets, accompanied by a few confused flies. I've been up since nine yesterday: mediating a fight between my roommates, wrangling coursework, losing myself online. No one else is in the store. I'm about ready to fall asleep at the till when the door whooshes open.

A customer? I jerk my head up and blink, trying to focus my blurry eyes. There's someone in the doorway, all right—tall and broad-shouldered, shrouded in brightly-coloured waterproof plastic. The lower half of his face is covered by the collar of his rain jacket. What little I can see is dominated by a hollow stare. It's my ex-friend, older and exhausted, looking like he's been dragged back to civilization by the hair. I rub my eyes to make sure I'm not hallucinating. He's still there, frozen in the entrance, dripping mud and what looks like pondscum on the mat.

I don't know what to say to him after three years of silence, but I know I have to say something. "Bit late for a swim."

He takes a step forward, soaked cornrows swinging loose from his hood. Instinct has me lean away. As much as I love them, big guys make me nervous. Too much potential violence in those enormous hands. I don't intimidate easily, but I'm also built like a string bean, and I spent my teenage years nursing an endless progression of bruises from boys—and men—who thought beating me up somehow reaffirmed their masculinity. But even as I edge backwards, I know that's not what's going on here. This isn't some late-night gay-bashing extravaganza. Something's really, truly off. The boy I remember was the loud sort of quiet, his focus as palpable as his discomfort. You always knew what he was thinking, because he showed it with his whole body. Now, though, all I'm getting from him is that he doesn't want to be here. He might as well be carved from stone.

"What's up?" I ask, folding my arms across the counter. "If you're looking for a towel, they're in aisle three."

"I need your help."

My turn to freeze. "Really."

"I found something," he says, slow and halting like I never remember him being. "In the bog."

"A body?"

He jerks his head back and forth. "Worse."

"What?" I nibble on the inside of my cheek. "What did you find?"

Slowly, he pulls down his collar, revealing a stiff mouth. He's handsome as always, but his lips are bluish—frostbitten, I'd say, except it never gets that cold around here. Beyond that, there's something to the set of his jaw that draws my attention. There's an odd level of tension there, like he's trying to keep it locked in place. His face is blank, but it's a bewildered sort of blank, and with his skin almost grey, he looks like a zombie. He was never the expressive type, but this . . . this is new.

"I can't explain it. I just—" He stops. "This was a mistake."

"Oh no you don't." I come out from behind the counter, putting myself between him and the door. "You can't just leave without telling me what's going on."

My ex-friend turns so slowly I can hear his rusted joints creak. From this angle, he looks like a drawn corpse. His eyes are the only thing with any life, and they're absolutely static. Fixed on me. On my mouth.

I start to ramble. "If you need help, just ask for it. That's what friends are for. Not that you'd know. It's been three years, jackass, and you haven't even said hello yet."

"Stop," he whispers, still looking at my mouth. "Stop talking."

I start laughing instead, a high-pitched hyena cackle that never fails to enrage. Is this whole thing just a gay crisis? Is that what dragged him out of the swamp? "Ah, this is stupid. Look, if you want something, you have to explain yourself, got it? So whatever's going on with you—" He's still looking at my mouth, past my lips. His eyes flash whenever I speak. Like it's my teeth that have his interest. "Oi. What are you looking at?"

His lips move, but nothing comes out.

Here is the part where I should probably cut and run, call my boss with an explanation once I'm safely home, but that's not what happens. Instead, I step closer, crowding into his space. I'm not scared, I tell myself, I'm angry. Anger is safe. I prepare for another tirade, ready to pry every detail from this lump of stone until he finally lets me do something for him. I'm not even past the first syllable before his mouth is on mine.

It's too fast, too unexpected. I can't breathe. Then the pain starts. Have you ever read about those parasites that burrow into your feet? It feels like one of those mated with the needles dentists use to numb you before surgery and the resulting million offspring are crawling into my gums. His teeth are wrong. His tongue is wrong. This whole thing is wrong.

But I can't move. Can't struggle. I'm trapped there, his hands like stone on my shoulders, his mouth swallowing my screams, until the pain drags me under.

< < < < > > > >

My boss is a pretty understanding person, all in all, but she's not the type to show mercy if you're caught slacking on the job. That said, there's a bit of a difference between catching a clerk asleep at the till and walking through the door at seven AM to find a clerk passed out on the floor, mouth bruised and swollen, each breath rasping like sandpaper. No one calls the hospital, but my aunt comes to get me, and I wake up safely at home. My head is killing me, but other than that, I'm fine. I tell her I must have fainted, because what I remember is just—stupid. As if that guy would seek me out. As if that guy would kiss me. Assuming something like that counts as a kiss.

In the interest of not causing a fuss—or worse, attracting bad publicity—the boss accepts my story, but she goes over the security tapes just in case. That's where things start to fall apart, because just past one AM, the camera stopped working. The last thing it recorded was the splash of someone's boots just outside of viewing range. When the video starts again five minutes later, I'm already on the floor. My boss decides it's probably a stunt by some kid who broke in, that I must have gotten punched and passed out after noticing them fiddling with the cameras. I am a connoisseur of getting punched, and I disagree. But I don't have a better explanation, so I keep my mouth shut about it. Thinking too much about my ex-friend's tired, grey face makes me feel sick to my stomach.

I get the day off, but all I want to do is lie around and sleep. Needless to say, sleep doesn't come. I just lie there, grumpy and exhausted, running my tongue back and forth along my stiff jaw.

One of my teeth wiggles. I keep poking at it, pushing it back and forth, trying to figure out if I'm imagining it. There's no pain, just a weird slippery sensation as it works itself loose. After about a minute, I cough onto my pillow and there it is: one white incisor, tattered nerves dangling from the broken root. It doesn't hurt, but when I probe the hole left behind I can feel something squirming inside it.

Another tooth shifts in my jaw, working its way free. And another. And another. I clap my hand over my mouth and lurch to my feet, stumbling to the bathroom. Am I dreaming? Please tell me I'm dreaming. I bend over the sink and spit out an entire mouthful of red-streaked enamel, clattering and getting stuck in the drain. When I'm done, I look in the mirror and smile.

My gums are bare and bleeding, and I can't feel a thing.

"You all right?" my aunt calls from the doorway. I didn't hear her arrive.

Whatever this is, it's not her problem. She deals with too much of my shit already. I snap my jaw shut and nod. Then I make the mistake of turning to face her, and suddenly I can't look away from her mouth.

No, not her mouth. Her teeth, so small and blunt, barely peeking out as she talks. Faintly yellowed from an old smoking habit. Left canine chipped from biting down on a fork. Without meaning to, I take a step forward.

I want—

I freeze in place and plaster on a smile. "'m fine." The words come out only a little mangled. Something helps me form the sounds, spit them out only a little bit warped. "Gonna go out, kay?"

CAVITY

"Why?" she asks, and I force myself to make eye contact.

"Gotta see som'one," I mumble, trying not to open my mouth too wide. "Think 'e might know what happened."

For a moment, she looks like she might refuse. Then she deflates, smiles too wide. I can't hear a word she says over the thunder of blood in my ears. I have to get out. It's not safe.

Her *teeth*—

I've had my ex-friend's address memorized for a while now. I used to write him, even if he never replied, but the memory outlived the habit. Now, it's that knowledge that sees me out the door, to the car, and onto the road leading toward the harbour. I've got just enough on me to pay for the ferry—I spend the ride over hiding in the car, trying to ignore the traffic around me, using the rearview mirror to wipe up any obvious stains. There are fewer people on the other side, thank god. I drive until the traffic drops away and the tarmac turns to gravel, over bridges until the rotten-eggs stench of peat fills my nose. Then I park the car and start walking. With each step, the things squirming in my mouth grow livelier. Sharper. I'm almost getting used to the needles pricking at my gums.

My ex-friend's cabin is as close to the wetlands as you can get, and lucky me, he's just outside, still wearing the bright fluorescent jacket. He's watching me from behind his plastic collar, something soft in his eyes. Apologetic. I wonder if he was waiting for me.

My lower jaw begins to shift and squirm, bones and teeth grinding together. I stop moving and raise my hand to cover my face. I can't quite bring myself to touch it. I don't want to know what it feels like from outside. That leaves me hovering on the edge of his driveway, wishing I had a coat to hide behind and waiting for the sensation to pass. It doesn't. The bones of my skull shatter. Here's the pain I was missing. It's excruciating. My vision goes white for a second or two. Then it's over, and my tongue rests in a freshly-expanded bed of knives. I look up, ignoring the dripping warmth making its way down my chin, and smile wider than I ever have before.

"Aw, did you wait up for me? That's cute." The words are meant to be teasing. They come out bitter and steeped in acid, but that's not the worst part. I can hardly recognize the burst of distorted noise coming out of my throat. Is that really supposed to be my voice?

My ex-friend doesn't flinch back or look away. He lowers his head, his mouth still hidden. When he speaks, it's in the stiff, halting tone from last night. "Sorry."

For what? The teeth? The kiss? Coming to find me at the store? Cutting ties with me back then? Being friends with me in the first place? I lower my hand—stained red, when did that happen?—and huff. "Mind narrowing that down a little?"

His eyes finally leave my face as he thinks for a moment. They don't stay away long. "I shouldn't have dragged you into this. It wasn't your problem."

"No," I say, as cheerfully as the razors which seem to have replaced my voicebox will let me. "But it was yours. If you needed help, all you had to do was ask for it."

"I know," he murmurs, tipping his head even further down, until cornrows hide his face from view. "I thought—if anyone would help, it would be you." A brief pause, attached to a noise like knives grinding together. I think he just ran his tongue over his lips. "Sorry. I didn't mean to spread it."

The sigh in my chest emerges more or less unmangled. Progress. "Didn't think you did it on purpose. Whatever that pull is, I felt it too."

He jerks his head up, eyes wide and staring. "You did?"

"Yeah. Didn't bite anyone, but it was close."

There aren't any words to describe the way he looks at me. Like he's watching an old-growth forest reach toward the sky or a waterfall thunder downward inches away. Something pristine and untouched by human hands. It's my turn to have trouble meeting his gaze.

I clear my throat. Or try to. The extra teeth are getting in my way. "So, what did you find in the bog?"

After a moment, he stands up. The smell of blood and rotting peat mingle around us. We're still far enough apart that I don't have to tilt my head back to make eye contact, but he manages to tower over me regardless. Even so, the sense of threat from last night is absent. "This way," he says, walking deeper into the bog. "It's not something that can be put into words."

I roll my eyes, but my feet are already carrying me after him.

Countless warnings and documentaries have made it clear to me

CAVITY

that venturing into bogs is dangerous, but he makes it look simple. The walk teaches me more about the subject than I ever needed to know. For example: sedge grass is a good foothold. Same goes for dry peat, but don't walk on the wet peat if you want to keep your shoes. We lose ten minutes while I fight the bog for one of my sneakers. He waits quietly for me to unearth it, but it isn't a calm quiet. Judging from what I can see of his face, his jaw is locked up again.

Finally, we reach our destination. There's a hole in the bog. Inside lies . . . something. From a distance, it looks like a body, but only from a distance. The illusion breaks the moment I get close enough to see the shape in full. Teeth. Mountains of them, stabbing upward, crawling and writhing over a mass that hurts to look at. I can't tell if it's one giant mouth or countless tiny ones—either way, it's chewing at the air. It knows we're here. It wants to taste us. I step back, my whole body wracked with an explosive shudder. He stays where he is, grey and sweating. All his joints are locked now. Still, he sways toward it. If it's uncomfortable for me to look at that—thing—it's downright painful for him. But neither of us can look away. In my mouth, my teeth mimic its movements.

There's no point in asking what it is, so I skip to the next best question. "What do we do about it?"

He shivers. "I don't know. It shouldn't be . . . here."

It shouldn't be, period. "You tried to move it, didn't you? That's how you got bitten."

A tiny nod. "Something must've dug it up. It's been eating the animals."

"Did they end up like us?"

He motions stiffly to the edge of the hole. I peer down and grimace. Bones, fur, feathers, and meat line the edges of the hole. Something in my gut turns over and comes up hungry. I want to slide forward, into the dark, and bury my teeth in that mess. I want it like I wanted my aunt's teeth. I back away instead, legs trembling with the effort.

"I think . . . I think we're meant to bring it things," he says. "Feed it, then eat what it offers."

"That can't be hygienic. Let's burn it."

"We can't. Peat burns easy, teeth don't. Need something like thermite to cremate it fully, and that would burn the whole place down."

"Collateral damage," I grumble, but I see his point. The bog is huge. This thing isn't small, but it's easy to lose a body in the water. And more importantly, if we set fire to the bog and the thing survives, it goes from having two potential hosts to a lot more. I seriously doubt firefighter gear will stop the compulsion to bite. "Fine. What are our options?"

"I don't—" He shakes his head and looks at me with haunted eyes. "I can't think near it. I thought—you—"

Ah. So that's what this is about. I force myself to step backward, away from the thing, and place my hand on his shoulder. The moment I touch him, that awful tension starts bleeding away. "Let's go back," I say. "Consider our options together."

"Together?"

I nod as decisively as I can manage. "Told you at the beginning of this, didn't I? You need help, just ask for it. That's what friends are for."

"Friends, huh?" He says it so quietly I almost miss it. It sounds like the beginning of something, but there's no follow-up. The walk back to the cabin is silent. We both have a lot to think about.

The thing is, this shouldn't be our problem. We're a twenty-something clerk and hermit. We don't know shit about the supernatural and we don't have access to anyone who does. The right thing to do would be to call the police, but even if they believed us, they'd probably include us in the clean-up. Best case scenario, imprisonment and experimentation. Worst case scenario, immediate execution. I'm not exactly keen on that, and neither is he. But we can't leave it alone, either. Whatever it is, it's infectious and predatory, and he already tried shooting it before coming to me. Didn't work.

"We should bury it again," he says finally. "Mark the spot and keep watch. Make sure it stays hidden."

I quirk an eyebrow at him. Try, anyway. My face doesn't want to do what I tell it. "Think that'll work?"

"It did before."

"Fair enough. We'll have to work out shifts, then. Make sure no one's exposed for too long."

CAVITY

He gives me an odd look. "You're staying?"

I smile at him pointedly. "Can't exactly go home like this. Besides, this is my problem, too."

"Sorry."

"Whatever. I'm happy you came to see me, anyway." The stress of the day must be getting to me, because I keep talking. "I missed you, you know?"

"I know," he says. "I got your letters."

"And yet you still didn't answer any of them." I sock him in the shoulder. He doesn't even flinch. Asshole.

"Didn't know how. Didn't think anyone would care when I left."

"Well, you were wrong."

He looks at me steadily. "How wrong?"

I glare at him for a moment, then sigh. "Might've liked you a bit when we were younger," I admit. Still do, probably. It would explain a lot about the last twenty-four hours. "Would've appreciated it if you stuck around. Or, you know, answered the mail once in a while."

"Didn't mean to hurt you."

I flap my hand at him. "That puts you above almost every other guy I've kissed, even with the teeth thing. Don't worry about it. I'm just a bitter person."

He lowers his gaze. "You should be."

"Don't try and tell me what to do," I snap on automatic. There's a soft little noise which might be a chuckle and my heart tries to leap out of my ribcage. Guess that confirms it. "I'll like you if I want."

Plastic creaks as he turns to look at me. "I liked you, too. Back then."

Warmth rushes to my face. I jerk my head away and stare furiously into the bog. It's too late, though. He saw. I know he did. "Not enough to stay."

This time his laughter comes through loud and clear—soft and a little bit strained, an oak tree groaning in the wind. "Wouldn't have been good for anyone if I did."

I think back to him in our school days, huge and silent and hurting, and can't help but agree. Even after everything, he's more alive here than he ever was then. "Well, I'll be hanging around for a while. Something to think about. You know, while we're here."

A long silence. Just when I'm giving up on getting a response, he speaks. "Guess so."

It's not exactly nice out here. Everything smells like rot. My socks are soaked. I'm probably going to have to learn a ton of weird survival stuff if I plan on staying, which I do, because every other option sucks. I haven't forgiven him for dragging me into this. But it's not his fault, either. If there's one thing I know better than anyone else, it's this: you can't help being what you are. The two of us are going to be struggling with that from now on.

My jaw is numb. I can't feel my teeth. I don't even want to think about my tongue. But my friend sits beside me, quiet, at peace. An empty hole in my life filled up. And you know what? I'll take it.

THE GOAT PILE

Nathan Carson

THE FARMER DIDN'T like to bury her goats. When they were born, she wrapped them in a clean towel and fed them from a warm bottle. In winter, she brought them in the house to spend their first night in a cardboard box by the stove. The goats lived the rest of their days sheltered in the farmer's barn, or grazing in her fields. And when one died, she dragged it out to the woods and threw the carcass on top of the Goat Pile.

Wendy was the oldest goat the farmer had ever raised. She was a great white beast, with gray-haired waddles that hung from her neck. Her ears were so small they made her head look like a dinosaur.

When they took me in, I was younger than Wendy, and Baby Sugar was younger than me. For some reason, Sugar was terrified of Wendy. Whenever the farmer hauled us two-legged kids out to the barn to milk Wendy, Sugar would holler and cry.

I tried to explain to Sugar that goats only eat grasses and grains. That an old gal like Wendy didn't have much use for nibbling on babies. The way Sugar acted, you'd think Wendy was a witch. I don't think a goat can be a witch, but then again, have you ever met a Wendy who *wasn't* a witch? Me neither.

Nothing consoled Sugar until we were back inside the house. That's where the farmer's husband was. He didn't go outside much because he took a chill so easy. So he made it his habit to keep the stove warm, starch the linens, and cook the roasts. That suited the farmer fine because building a fence that could keep goats inside was a full-time job. A goat could have put Harry Houdini right out of business if someone had thought of it.

< < < < > > > >

On one of the hottest days of summer, I snuck into the woods to see the Goat Pile. I heard the farmer talking about it to her husband, and it made me curious. School was out, so no one paid much attention to me. The woods behind the farm were thick and overgrown. Moss hung from every branch, clotting the sunlight, deepening the shadows. Each footstep I took, I swore another step echoed behind.

I heard the buzzing of the flies just before the stench hit me. The smell of decay had as many layers as last year's birthday cake. A blast of fresh rotting meat spread over the sweet earthiness of old bones and dry leaves. When I glimpsed the pile itself in its many-colored splendor of bristling hides and writhing worms, I ran all the way home and locked myself in the bathroom for an hour.

Wendy got sick on the day the rains began. The fields flooded. Water covered the road. The school buses stopped running unless you lived right close to town. I could hear old Wendy bleating in her death throes. The farmer stayed with her all night but it still wasn't over. I shivered under my blankets. Sugar giggled from the crib. "Sugar," I said. "That ain't nice."

The next morning we woke to the sound of a single gun shot echoing out of the barnyard.

Wendy was so heavy that the farmer's husband bundled up and went outside, never mind the weather. He helped prop the body into a wheelbarrow. Inside the house, Baby Sugar got real quiet. All any of us could hear was the pattering rain coming down for days and days.

Some rains are cleansing. This one just turned everything into running mud.

I told myself that I wanted to pay my respects to Wendy, but really I just wanted to see the Goat Pile once more, in all its glory.

THE GOAT PILE

Wrapped in a wool blanket, I slipped out the back door and followed the sound of that creaking wheelbarrow. The puddles were spreading out to reach each other. We had to weave around them. Seemed like something in those little lakes might grab our ankles and drag us down into the muck.

At the last bend I clung to a withered tree. Its bark soaked up as much rain as it could. The rest ran down to the ground like blood from an open vein. I watched the farmer and her husband tip the wheelbarrow on its side and drag dead Wendy on top of the heap. The flies were hiding out and waiting for the sun. The rain covered up the smell. The clouds cut off the light to make the Pile a mess of black shadows, twisting bones and grinning goat skulls.

Seeing Wendy's head with that single bloody bullet hole between those cloudy eyes left my feet frozen. My teeth chattered in rhythm with the rain. Night crept up on us. Each second grew darker.

The farmer's flashlight beamed into my eyes, blotting out that horrible scene. She was shaking me but I couldn't understand what she wanted. Then I saw her husband running for the house and I made out the word they were screaming. "Sugar."

There was a lot of arguing about who was supposed to be watching Baby Sugar. The farmer's husband was to blame. I was to blame. We were all to blame. Nothing changed in the rain, though. The creek kept rising higher. Sugar was nowhere to be found.

By the time emergency services could get out to our farm, the banks had flooded. Our house was like an island. Brown mud-water rushed past so fast you felt like you were moving when you were standing still. All those amber lights and sirens and shouting voices didn't find Sugar either.

Two weeks later the waters subsided. White sunlight started to dry things out, but it felt as cold as our stove. We had all given up hope of finding Sugar alive. An adult would be lucky to survive a creek in flood. A baby stood no chance.

We walked through the woods looking for signs. The whole landscape had changed. Parts of old rusted tractors had got mired in the banks. The lower halves of trees were swept clean of their moss. And the Goat Pile had been dislodged and scattered by surging waters.

Some people who lived a few miles downstream had the

misfortune of inheriting the shreds of hide and bones from our property. They were the same people who stumbled upon Baby Sugar all waterlogged and puffy and cold and green.

No one questioned that Sugar had drowned. Or that it was an accident. But what the neighbors found, the coroner, the farmer, and her husband could not explain.

If sharp branches in floodwater hadn't torn a window into the side of that hooved, bloated beast, we might never have spotted those little hands, clinging like a birdcage prisoner inside the ribs of a dead white goat with a single bullet hole between its eyes.

DOBIE'S CALL

Anthony Wayne Hepp

THE AFTERNOON THIS all started was just God-awful hot. August in central Texas. Vic and I was in his truck headed down Ranch Road 1531 toward Cedarville to pick up some junk this old feller had called Vic to come get. Cedarville is about thirty minutes up the road from Lakeview, and I had some time that day to go along. No AC in Vic's old truck, and the windows down was like two blast ovens blowing in on us.

1531 was, at that time, as twisty and crooked as a Baptist banker. One tight curve in particular had got a nickname of its own, Thief's Corner, because it took a lot from our little community. It seemed to materialize out of nowhere, and if you weren't paying attention, the asphalt jerked right out from under your tires. A grove of live oaks twenty yards or so past the curve acted as a backstop. Lot of bad wrecks out there.

Sure enough that day, going in to pick up some scrap, we come up on a wreck at Thief's Corner. First ones on it.

It had once been a little car, but now it was just ribbons of metal stacked against the base of one of them oaks. I hit the brakes.

I heard Vic say, "Bobby, is that . . . " but my mind was already preoccupied with twisting and untwisting something it did not want to be working out. I didn't say nothing because I couldn't. I had lost contact with everything in the world outside of what my eyes were absorbing.

I don't remember pulling over, but I do remember running across the road. Vic got there first. His big arms went to tearing and twisting, pushing metal and plastic and rubber, while the air, ground, sky, everything, baked hot around us.

I realized he was saying, "No, no, no, no," like a chant, but then it went up into something like a scream. I don't know what it was, but it wasn't a sound people make.

The car was Bloom's.

It had been her birthday present just three days prior. Vic had burned a lot of nights in secret to make sure she had a vehicle at sixteen. He had pulled the thing out of the scrap heap himself and then willed it back to life for her with bloody knuckles and sleep deprivation. And she had loved it, dents and all. She knew what he had done, how much it cost him to give that to her, and they cried together over it. And then they went to get her license and she passed first try.

Bloom had left a half hour before us on her way to apply for a job, her first job, in Cedarville.

She missed the corner.

Vic was short for *Victor*, but he was called at least a hundred different names. His ma called him *Shorty* and his pa, back when his pa was alive, called him *Goob*. Folks in town figured since even his blood called him by different names, they all could, too. The joke, or whatever it was, spread around. It became just one of them things. Everybody called that boy something different.

I called him Vic. Maybe that's how him and me got so close, on account of my nickname for him weren't really a nickname at all. It was just his name, and Vic appreciated that. We done grade school and high school, or most of high school, together.

Of all the names put on him, his favorite, the one he was actually proud of, was *Dobie*. That was the one his little girl, Bloom, had assigned to him. At eighteen months, Bloom's word for everything was Dobie. An old dog running down the side of the road was Dobie. Mashed taters was Dobie. Even I was Dobie for a while.

DOBIE'S CALL

We thought maybe she was a little slow like her dad.

Turned out she was fine. She went on to articulate names the normal way folks ought to, but that word for her dad stuck for some reason. He was her Dobie. He was her everything. And she was most definitely his.

Vic might not have been good at a lot of things, but he was damn good at being Bloom's Dobie. He loved that girl more than any dad I ever saw. And I think because of his way of tending to her, she grew up awesome. Smart and real nice and pretty too. I got to feeling bad for Vic because I knew there weren't nothing in our town for a gal like that. She was going to move on someday. I don't think the possibility ever occurred to him.

I won't go into what happened to Bloom's mama, but you could say Vic got lucky when he no longer had to put up with her.

We found her on the backside of the pile. She was sitting up, twisted at the waist, part of her looking forward and part of her looking back, resting against what had been . . . the bumper? The angles was all wrong, nothing where it should be. A ribbon of steel had pressed an indentation below her right eye, which was aimed at me. The other eye seemed to be looking more toward the wreckage, and I realized that she wasn't just leaning on the end of that piece of metal. The metal was pushed up into her skull, and it exited the hole that had been ripped out the back of her head.

She still looked like Bloom, just crooked, bent a little, like a bad corner in the road that never did make no sense. And then red, all that red, came into focus. I don't know where the blood had been up to then. Blood, and boy, the heat was something that day.

Vic knelt in front of her. He lifted his hands to do something, but I could see he wasn't sure where to put them or even if he *should* try to put them. He had vomited, and spit ran out his nose and down his chin. A vibration had worked itself all throughout his body, like he was one breath away from shattering into a million billion little pieces.

Sirens. People shouting. Vic on the ground. The rest of the day is a jumbled-up movie in my head, and I don't remember most of it anyhow.

< < < < > > > >

In the days after Bloom's funeral, Vic stayed mostly at home. Mostly in bed.

I tried to project how this was going to change my friend. I figured the only thing I could do was watch as best I could for opportunities to pull him out of whatever hell he must be roasting in. I drove to his place to check that he hadn't done nothing dumb to himself or what little he had left in life.

"Vic, you home, buddy?"

I found him in his bedroom, still in the same clothes he had been wearing at the cemetery a week prior, Sunday whites now wrinkled and yellow. The shade was pulled against the light, the air thick and stinking of body odor and mildew.

"Vic?"

He sat up. He looked at me confused, the way a person does when you've pulled them out of a deep sleep even though I don't think he had slept five minutes since the accident.

"Hey, amigo. Can I heat something up for you?"

"I made a hot dog this morning."

"Hot dog, huh? Guess that counts. You eat anything after I left last night?"

"No."

"Did you at least heat it up?"

"Heat what up, Bobby?"

"Your hot dog, Vic."

Again, the confused look.

"Well, how about a shower today? And a fresh change of duds?"

"I'm afraid I'll forget, Bobby."

"Forget fresh clothes?"

"No, afraid I'll forget Bloom. I don't remember some things."

He crumpled over, and from the trembling across his shoulders, I knew he was sobbing. I sat next to him on the edge of the old mattress.

"I promise you, brother, ain't nobody ever gonna forget Bloom. Least of all you."

He opened his hand to show me an old cell phone I remembered him having years before, one of those flip units from before the flat ones came out. He opened it with his thumb and though the numbers had been rubbed off the rubber buttons, its tiny screen lit up. He squeezed a couple of beeps out of it and raised it above his head. A recording played.

A woman's voice in the background said, "Say hi to your daddy. Say, 'Hi, Daddy . . .' After some scuffling, a faint, toddler voice said, "Dobie. Dobie. Good-bye."

Damn it. I swallowed hard. "That was a long time ago, wasn't it?"

"I didn't want to say it, but I miss back when she was cute. She started calling me Dobie back then, and it was my favorite part."

"I liked that part, too."

"Think she'll come home, Bobby? Maybe it wasn't her out on the road under that tr . . . tree."

"No, Vic. No, I don't believe she will be coming home. We're just going to have to make sure we remember those good parts. You and me both."

Folks tend to pile food up on you when something bad happens. Not sure how that tradition come about. How could they expect you to eat when you've seen your heart lying in a bloody pile of guts on the ground? Most of the gifts had gone to mold. I knew Vic appreciated everybody thinking about him. He didn't say it, though. I microwaved the meatloaf and mashed potatoes somebody left for him.

< < < < > > > >

It took a day or so, but Vic put himself together. I went back over to help pick up his house. I shut the door to Bloom's room so he didn't have to look in there every time he went by it to use the john. By day's end, everything looked a little better, and he was at least upright. I figured this was all movement in the right direction.

I came back early the next morning. Nobody home. I called him on his cell.

"Vic? You get a job or something?"

"No. Just out pickin'. Why?"

"No reason other than I apparently bought too many breakfast tacos from Rita."

"Well, you'll just have to go on without me."

That became the way of it. His new schedule. Out early, home late. Used to be, he would wait for folks to call him. That was his business model. But he wasn't waiting around, now. He was out there looking for stuff to scrap. Boy did he find it.

He often found more than would fit in his truck, so he'd make several trips a day. It was good to see him motivated, but then little piles appeared in the back yard, followed by little piles in the front. A month of this and the piles could no longer be classified as little. His front yard started to remind me of the scrap heap east of town.

I pulled into his driveway one afternoon with the hope of catching him. The amount of junk that had piled up in a relatively short amount of time was shocking.

He wasn't home, so I called his cell.

"Hey, Bobby."

"I'm at your house. Let's go get a cerveza."

"I'm in the truck."

"Well, I figured that, but I'm at your house right now, and I happen to have an extra twenty I plan to deposit at Rita's. Meet you in fifteen?"

Silence on his end. Usually that just meant no.

"It's getting a little crowded over here, Vic."

"Lotta iron out there. Got to pick it up before somebody else."

"Lotta iron here in your yard. You gotta get your money out of it. Otherwise, why bother?"

"I manage my affairs."

"By the looks of things, you ain't doing a good job of it right now."

The line went dead.

I had never said anything like that to Vic before, and I wasn't sure where it came from. I tried to call him back. It went to voicemail.

"I shouldn't have said that. Let me know what I can do to help, okay? Call me back."

He didn't. A couple days went by. Then a couple weeks. I kept an eye out for his truck around town. He didn't wave at nobody, or talk to nobody unless it was about picking scrap. I drove by his place. I knew he was still alive because the piles of iron and chrome in his yard kept getting taller. Weeds started poking through.

I began to consider that my friend had passed on the same time his daughter had, just in some other, more earth-bound way. Other people's discarded things were becoming a mausoleum he was constructing around himself.

DOBIE'S CALL

One night, my phone lit up. It was Vic. I picked up fast as I could.

"Hey, Vic. I was just thinking about—"

He was on the other end jabbering, "I . . . I can't . . . I can't . . . "

"Buddy, you okay?"

He sucked in a lungful.

"I, uh, I think I lost my phone, Bobby."

"Now, how are you talking to me if you lost your phone?"

"No, my *Bloom* phone. That old message. I been looking. Musta fell out of my pocket. I don't know, but it ain't here no more."

"Surely not. You looked everywhere?"

"I can't hear her voice no more. She can't call me Do-Dobie . . . "

"I'll be there in ten, amigo."

It was like a tornado had spun through the inside of Vic's house. The AC was off or broke and he hadn't taken out the trash in who knows how long. The cumulative effect of both was terrible. Even his dishes was scattered across the kitchen floor, half of them broke. The couch had been shoved at an angle into the center of the living room, and Vic was laid out on it with one arm over his face.

"Did you find it?"

"I can't do this no more, Bobby. I don't want it."

His voice was thin, barely there.

"I'm going to stay here tonight, buddy. We'll do a sleepover like grade school. And then let's go picking in the morning, okay? Together."

"I don't think . . . "

He didn't finish the thought. Couldn't maybe.

"We'll get this behind us, Vic. We just keep moving."

"We? You ain't lost no blood."

"The hell I ain't." My pity had crossed over into anger, and I did the most dramatic thing I could think of. I threw my hat against the wall.

"Don't go thinking you're the only one hurt here, you dumb son of a bitch. I can't claim to carry what you are, but I loved Bloom, too. This is heavy shit, brother. I ain't going to lose two of my people to that corner."

He moved his forearm from his eyes. I kept going:

"Now, I'm gonna haul out all this stinking-ass trash and open a window. You're going to pick up those dishes. And in the morning, you and I are going picking."

< < < < > > > >

The next day, we drove around the hill country in silence. We had picked some odds and ends, a dishwasher and a couple of old shelving units, when we came on a sign advertising an estate sale. Estate sales typically ain't the right environment for junk haulers, not until the sale is over and whatever's left is headed for the dump. I was driving and Vic was kind of just there with his arm hanging out the window. I didn't bother to ask if he wanted to check it out, I just turned down the driveway marked for the sale.

Why would I do this? It's a question I ask myself.

"Won't be no scrap here, Bobby."

"Well, you never know. If nothing else, we'll give whoever's getting rid of stuff your number so maybe we can come back later."

Vic was right, there wasn't much for us to consider. Antique furniture, paintings, silver, all set out under the shade of a huge live oak with a rich white farm house in the backdrop. I pictured shit-free horse stalls and an irrigated riding pasture hidden behind it. The items for sale had tags with no decimal points. A small crowd of folks were browsing. I recognized most of them as local money.

We had been there about five minutes when this feller I had never seen before crossed into my line of sight. He was odd. Something about him made me want to avoid breathing air from any space he had ever occupied.

He was an older guy, eighties maybe. He looked as out of place as we did. Poor. Not particularly well dressed. His clothing, and maybe his skin, too, was either a size too big or too small for his frame and kind of tucked in and pinched off in spots. He wore an off-center hair piece that wasn't any more or less natural than the rest of him.

It's not something I say about people, and I have usually collected a few stories about them before I say it, but I hated that man. The instant I saw him. Just looking at him filled me with such a feeling of contempt and disgust as I have ever experienced. It was a powerful feeling that made me suddenly fearful. I couldn't put my finger on why, but we needed to get out of there in a hurry.

"You were right, Vic. Nothing for us here."

DOBIE'S CALL

I headed for the car, panic pounding in my chest. I heard Vic say: "I told you, Bobby."

I jerked the truck door open and jumped in like a loose pit bull was on me. I cranked the ignition and ground the stick in reverse.

Vic wasn't in the cab. I waited a beat, expecting to hear the squeal of the passenger door.

Then, I saw them, him and that strange, hateful man talking.

I left the truck running and covered the ground between myself and them in long strides. I put my hand on Vic's shoulder.

"We're gonna be late, buddy. Let's load up."

The man was in the middle of saying something. He spoke matter-of-fact-like with a voice that sounded much younger than his appearance.

"I sensed it as soon as you arrived, Victor. I know loss when I see it. You'd give anything just to hear that person's voice again. Just one more conversation. You would probably even take their place. Isn't that right?"

"Yes, sir."

"Come on, Vic. Excuse us, friend. We have things waiting for us."

The man didn't look at me, but he smiled at Vic, showing a set of teeth so white and false they could have been carved out of wood and painted with high gloss interior paint. He presented a shoe-box-sized package.

"This was my daddy's."

The package was wrapped in brown butcher paper and tied with a dirty strip of canvas. He continued:

"It passed to me, but I'm the last in my bloodline. I wasn't thinking of selling it today, but since we're here together, I realize maybe now is a good time to let it go."

"Sorry, fella. We don't have no money." I pulled on Vic's elbow.

"It actually is worth quite a lot. You'll find a selection of letters in there with it. The content of those letters will be interesting to you."

"I said we don't have no money."

The man flashed his thick teeth again.

"Right. Payment. How much money is it worth? Oh, let's see. I'd be willing to part with it for a . . . nickel. Yes, just a nickel, if you make me a promise. Reasonable? Five cents and a promise?"

The man held out a small, misshapen palm. Vic somehow had his coin at the ready, and he dropped it dead center in the man's hand.

"I can make a promise," Vic said.

"Oh, great. Here it is. All I ask is that you think of the one who is lost whenever you consider what's in this box. You don't have to think of me. You can forget me. Picture the one who is missing in your life. It will work better. I think this will help you as you find your new way. Promise?"

"Yes, sir. I promise that."

Vic took the package. I grabbed his shoulders with both hands and shoved him toward the truck. We peeled out of the driveway, spraying gravel across the lawn. I caught a glimpse of the man in the mirror, watching us go. He had no expression. He didn't look like anything at all.

>< < < < > > > <

We drove straight back to Vic's, the package on the seat between us. Neither of us said a word. I was angry with him, but for what? Because some old coot sold him something? I pretended the feeling, whatever it was, wasn't lodged behind my Adam's apple.

The truck rolled into his drive and we sat there for a moment, quiet, like something bad had happened between us.

"You want me to help strip down that dishwasher?"

"I got another one out back. I'll do them both tomorrow."

"Should I stick around, then?"

"Up to you, Bobby."

"What are you going to do about this thing?"

"Open it, I guess. Don't even know what I bought."

"That dude was weird. Didn't you think?"

"I kind of liked him."

"You did?"

"Think he was talking about Bloom?"

"If you want to know my position on it, I think you ought to throw this thing away. I'll even do it for you."

"But, I bought it, Bobby."

"If it's like you're gonna come up short or something, I can replace your nickel ."

"That ain't it. The man said it can help me when I'm sad."

"I ain't so sure that's what he was saying, Vic."

"Well, I want it."

I looked down at the package and wanted to immediately look away. I couldn't put words to why it bothered me the way it did. There weren't a logical reason for it. Finally, I said:

"If you want it, then I want you to have it. I'm gonna stay with you, though. And, if this is some weirdo shit, I'm trashing it. I don't care what you say, it's going in the pile."

"Weirdo shit?"

Vic looked down at the thing for a good long while. The sun reduced to just a spark on the horizon, and cool evening air settled around us. Finally, he picked it up. I followed him into his house.

He put the package in the center of the kitchen table. We each took a seat. He touched the canvas ribbon and it slid away light like a spider web in a breeze. Tearing away the butcher paper revealed a simple wooden box with hinges and a metal clasp in the front. He flipped it open.

I grabbed his hand.

"You sure?"

"Why wouldn't I be?"

He was right. What the hell was wrong with me?

He opened the lid and we peered inside. The box was lined with purple velvet. A whiff of something caught my nostrils, a spice smell like cedar or patchouli oil, but neither of those things exactly. We both stood to get a better look from above.

Inside was an old telephone.

I had seen one nearly like it at my granddad's house as a kid, a black sort of iron and Bakelite desk phone from the twenties, maybe earlier. It appeared to be in perfect condition and had been polished to a shine.

Some of what I heard the old man say suddenly made sense. Maybe. He had latched onto Vic because he knew, like everybody in the community surely did, that Vic lost his daughter and he just wanted to give him something nice, something Vic would never have reason nor extra funds to buy of his own accord. It was an antique, a thing on which long ago conversations had taken place, and maybe just thinking about that could keep the old conversations with Bloom alive. My opinion of the old timer shifted a little, but I still felt strangely sick whenever I pictured him in my mind.

Vic lifted the phone gently onto the table. He put the handset to his ear.

"Getting a dial tone?"

He laughed. I hadn't heard that for a while.

A thin stack of yellow foolscap notebook pages lined the bottom of the box. I picked one out and unfolded it. Someone had scribbled edge-to-edge handwriting in black ink that had aged to a mottled brown. Lots of loops and squiggles. I could decipher one out of every ten words or so. Not enough to understand. It appeared to be notes more so than a letter. There was figuring, numbers.

"Looks like you have some reading to do. Good luck. I can't make heads or tails of any of it."

"It's neat, right?"

"Yeah, it's kind of neat."

He ran a finger along the telephone's smooth edges, then spread the pages across the table. His eyes were lit up in a way I had never seen. Maybe that old guy had done us a favor.

< < < < > > > >

The world kind of went back to normal for a while after that. Vic continued scrapping, but not at all hours, and the piles in his yard began to diminish as he finally started cashing in the metal and other recyclables. Most days, we each put in our eight hours and then had a few beers together. We could mention Bloom without either of us crying. Sometimes we'd get drunk and cry about everything.

He displayed the antique telephone proudly on top of his television set. It really classed up the joint. He would occasionally give me an update on how it was going deciphering the old letters.

"I think I got all the words right, but I don't know what it means. Science stuff, I guess."

"You sure talk a lot, Vic."

We laughed and things felt a little like the old days.

Then, it all changed again.

I awoke to my cell buzzing. Vic. 3:31 AM. A storm had blown in, rain drops big enough to fill buckets and thunder rolling in told me things was about to get bad.

Vic's voice was barely audible against the downpour in the background. He was outside in that mess.

DOBIE'S CALL

"I saw Bloom, Bobby."

"Do you realize what time it is?"

"I saw her. I'm looking at her. Right now."

"No, you ain't and this ain't funny."

"I need help. I thought I could get it by myself."

"What the hell are you taking about?"

"Cemetery. With Bloom. I need help."

"Vic, come on. Where the hell are you?"

"Bloom's grave. I broke my shovel. Bring a couple with you."

He hung up.

I swung my legs over the side of the bed contemplating whether or not I had actually just had that conversation. The rain outside was torrential, pounding on the roof and in my head.

Twenty minutes later, I arrived at Lakeview Rest Cemetery. Vic's truck was parked with the headlights aimed over Bloom's headstone. I pulled my rain parka close and stepped into the storm.

I didn't see him at first. He was down in the hole he had dug, on his knees using his hands to scoop mud away from the edges of Bloom's coffin. He had somehow pried the lid open. The excavation was filling with rainwater and the walls were collapsing in around him.

I extended my hand to him. It was still dark and the rain was really coming down, creating a veil of yellow slivers in the headlights. Vic hadn't heard me and continued to struggle against the collapsing hole.

I caught a glimpse of the white roundness of bone in the muddy soup of the coffin. Bloom. My teeth chattered in my head.

"Jesus, Vic. What have you done?"

He wedged himself up against the walls of the hole and used a foot to stomp on the lid. It wouldn't lie flat.

"I been trying to get it shut."

"It's full of mud."

"I got to cover this all back up. Where's them shovels?"

I retrieved the two shovels from my truck and pitched one down to him. He scraped the sides of the hole to bring the earth back over the coffin. The lid wasn't secured, but apparently he felt it was good enough.

He looked up at me.

"You gonna help?"

I started on the excavation pile, pushing mounds of earth down toward him. It filled around his boots, and finally, mercifully, I could no longer see the coffin nor what was in it.

Vic raised his arm. I pulled him up. We worked the pile together, heaving against the earth to put it back where it belonged.

Before long, the sun's potential hovered at the horizon and the rain let up. The sod was restored, but the ground was a muddy, sloppy mess.

"They'll know somebody did something here, Vic. Nothing about this is right. It ain't even legal."

"We best go, then. I'll see you later."

"The hell you will see me later. We're going to your house right now to figure this shit out."

I followed Vic's truck out of the cemetery and through town to his house. I was soaked, as if I had jumped in a swimming hole with my clothes on. I did not understand what was happening, and it occurred to me that it would be difficult to disconnect myself legally from the night's events. We had disturbed a grave. We had disturbed Bloom. I bounced my palm off the dashboard of my truck.

I pulled up as he was getting out and pushed through the driver's side door and ran up on him. My fist hit the side of his head, and he bounced off his truck. I would have hit him again, but he recovered quicker than I expected and shoved me backward. I stumbled and landed on my ass.

"Don't do that again, Bobby."

He slammed his truck door shut.

"What did you do, Vic?"

By the time I made it inside, he was already seated in the kitchen, a trail of mud leading to the puddle forming under his chair. The phone and papers were spread out across the table.

"I figured all the letters out. What they say."

"Those letters don't have anything to do with—"

"They told me how to talk to Bloom."

"Talk to Bloom?"

"I didn't have enough of her hair, but I figured out last night that it says bone will work, too."

I stood next to him. He was wiping mud from what I thought was a twig, but when he put it down, I realized it was one of Bloom's knuckles.

He grabbed a handful of his own hair, right in the front, and with a pair of scissors, cut the entire chunk. He then wrapped the hair and the bone into a bundle using what appeared to be the canvas strip that the old man had used to wrap the phone box. He put the wrapped bundle in a compartment that clipped into the base of the phone.

"You've lost your mind."

I reached for the phone, but he smacked my hand away.

"Don't do that, Bobby."

I raised my hands and stepped away from him. He was gone, maybe dangerous. It crossed my mind I would go down with him if I didn't get the hell out of there immediately.

"You're on your own."

I had one foot out the door when I heard him say, "My . . . God."

He had the handset to his ear. I could see the familiar shake in his shoulders, and I thought he was crying again. I approached, standing across the table from him.

He was laughing. Tears were streaking the mud on his cheeks, but he was laughing.

"It's Bloom."

He extended the handset to me. I wanted to run. Instead, I took it from him.

I pressed the handset to my ear and what I heard nearly dropped me. It was Bloom's voice. And Vic's. The sound was muffled, like a bellowing wind was rushing over their voices, but there could be no doubt. I was listening to Vic and Bloom having a conversation. A series of conversations. Little back-and-forths. Everyday moments, the times when you pick up the phone to tell someone you're going to be late or that there's no milk in the fridge. Their phone conversations were playing back on a long loop.

I thrust the thing back at him.

"What is that?"

He placed the handset on the receiver, then lifted it again to see if it was still playing. He nodded.

"Every time I called her. Or she called me. Every time. I'll be able to listen now."

"Vic, this ain't natural."

"The letters say it can do more."

He hung up, then lifted the handset to his ear again. I could hear the voices still playing from where I stood. He hooked a shaking finger in the rotary dial and turned it. Then again, and again, until he had dialed a phone number. Bloom's number.

I heard ringing. Then, a young woman's voice:

"Hello?"

"Bloo . . . Bloom?"

"Dobie? You okay?"

Vic wiped his mouth with muddy fingers and cleared his throat, aiming to present an impression of normalcy.

"Yes. I mean . . . I miss you, is all."

"Aww. I miss you, too. Where are you calling from? I don't recognize this number. It came up weird."

"I, uh, this is my new phone, Bloom. I'm home. Sitting at the k-kitchen table."

"Oh. Okay. You sure you're okay?"

"Just . . . just figuring out this phone. It said I could call you."

"Well, yeah. It's a new phone, right? So you don't need anything?"

"No."

"I've got to get back to class. I'll see you when I get home. Remember you don't need to pick me up, okay. I've got my car, remember?"

"I'll remember that. I love you, Bloom."

"Love you, too."

Vic hung up. My legs wobbled, so I sat down across from him. His lips were stretched into a slight, absent smile.

"I can talk to her, Bobby. This phone can make that last call. From the day before she died."

"I don't . . . No, that's horseshit, Vic. It's a trick."

"I kept forgetting she could drive her own self home, and I kept showing up at school to pick her up. The last time I talked to her on the phone, she reminded me. Exactly how she just done."

We sat a long moment staring at the phone.

Then, it hit me.

"Vic, if this phone lets you talk to her on the day before she died, you can warn her."

"Warn her?"

DOBIE'S CALL

"About the wreck. Well, maybe leave the wreck out. But, tell her to stay home. Tell her not to drive to Cedarville. Demand that she stay off 1531, in fact."

"If I tell her that . . . " I could see him working it out until understanding lit up his eyes.

He dialed frantically, shaking. He slipped on a rotation, so he hung up and started over.

It went through.

"Hello?"

"Bloom!"

"Dobie? You okay?"

"Listen careful, Bloom. Listen, tomorrow, you got to stay home. Don't go driving to Cedarville. Promise me you won't go on 1531."

"Um, okay. Why? Where are you calling from? I don't recognize this number. It came up weird."

"Just make me that promise."

"Okay, Dobie. Yeah, sure, I was planning to go to Cedarville to drop off that job application. I can go Saturday, I guess."

"Make the promise!"

"I promise. Jeez. I've got to get back to class. I'll see you when I get home. Remember you don't need to pick me up, okay. I've got my car, remember?"

Vic hung up. We stared at each other in silence. How did any of this work? How could it work?

Vic's shirt pocket lit up. He pulled out his cell phone and, shaking, showed me the screen.

The caller ID said "Bloom."

"Bloom?"

"Hey, Dobie. Are you coming in to town by chance this morning for scrap?"

"I don't . . . don't know, Bloom."

"Ugh. I left my purse on the nightstand and I kinda need my wallet. Think you can bring it in? I'm sorry."

"Where are you?"

"Um, work?"

"Work?"

"Yeah, it's Saturday. Saturday? Early shift at Mightyburger? Same place I've been every Saturday for the past year."

"On . . . On Oak?"

"Yeah, the one on Oak, silly. You know where I work, Dobie. Can you bring it?"

Vic stood, shoving the table into my ribs. My chair tipped and I landed hard on my back. He raced down the hallway to Bloom's room, then out the front door.

"Vic, hang on." I was tangled up in the chair.

He was halfway down the block before I made it off the front steps. I jumped in my truck but couldn't catch him. He blew stop signs and right through the only light in Lakeview. I wasn't about to kill somebody or get stopped, so I hung back. It didn't take long to lose sight of him.

Morning traffic clogged the highway. By the time I made it to the two-lane section of 1531, I figured he was a good four or five miles ahead. I pushed the gas to the floor and hugged the inside of the corners as best I could, trying to make up the gap. At Brisket Hill, I had no choice but to come to a full stop.

Goddamn traffic.

I contemplated being that asshole passing folks on the right shoulder. The car in font of me jolted forward and my heart throbbed behind my eyes. Bloom was alive and fifteen minutes away. My god, was she?

We moved inches. I figured an accident. Had to be. I wanted to put my foot through the floorboard, my hand through the dashboard.

It was definitely an accident. Thief's Corner. I saw cars moving to the right, directed by a cop to go around one at a time.

My turn, finally. I saw the wreck, an old scrap truck lying in ruins at the base of a live oak.

I hit the brakes.

Vic sat hunched near the wreck. He was kind of sitting up, twisted at the waist, part of him looking forward and part of him looking back, resting against what had been.

IF YOU WANT ME

Dustin Katz

THE GUY BEHIND the reception counter looked like a stock
photo. He was tall and blond and blue-eyed and his form-
fitting white polo shirt showed off tanned and bronzed arms
and his smile showed off white teeth. There was no one else in
the lobby and Drew could walk right up without having to wait in
line. As he got closer, he saw that the man's name tag read
"LUNTZ."

Luntz looked sort of familiar. But where could Drew possibly
have seen him before? In a Nordstrom catalogue?

—Hello, said Drew to the man. I'd like a room for one night,
please.

—Just the one? said Luntz. His voice was deep, almost comically
so, a rich baritone.

—Yeah, that's right. I'm just passing through.

—Where you headed?

—San Antonio.

Luntz raised his eyebrows.

—Dangerous.

Drew knew he hadn't misheard, but he still felt as though he might have misunderstood. He couldn't tell from Luntz's expression whether or not the man was joking.

—Sorry, why do you say that?

Luntz shrugged.

—Making an escape.

He smiled at Drew.

—Always good to escape, but you never know what you're escaping to. That'll be ninety-seven eighty. I'll try to get you a king.

Luntz asked if he needed any help with his luggage, and Drew told him that wouldn't be necessary. Drew took the key, turned away from the counter and headed to the elevator.

—Enjoy your stay, came Luntz's voice from behind Drew. I'll be here if you want me.

Drew turned around and looked at Luntz again. Luntz was not looking at him.

Everyone Drew had dealt with lately had been so friendly. All the new people, anyway, who Drew had never met before.

< < < < > > > >

He started to get the texts the next morning, around when he passed into Arizona, but it took a few before he noticed. Eventually, he pulled over at a rest stop in a place that seemed to be called Buckeye and checked them out.

—We're here, the first text said. It was from the movers.

Drew's heart began to beat faster. This couldn't be what it appeared to be. He read the rest.

—Your delivery has arrived as scheduled. Please meet with the driver by 2:00 pm today to complete delivery.

—Please respond. Your delivery has arrived. Please confirm.

—Where are you?

After reading these, Drew decided there had been a misunderstanding. It was totally impossible that his belongings had arrived in Texas by this point—physically impossible. Even if the truck had driven nonstop for San Antonio directly after leaving his house, it couldn't be there yet. And Drew remembered signing the agreement that the items would be delivered two days from now. Didn't he?

Drew called the number that had texted him. There was no response. He called the moving service's main number. He waited on hold, in his car, in the parking lot. After a while he started to get hot, so he got out and paced around, listening to the recursive music.

Eventually a voice came on the line.

—Yeah?

—Hello. I hired a truck to move my stuff from San Francisco to San Antonio, Texas yesterday and I just got a text that the truck is already there.

—Okay. And?

Drew had been hoping the problem would be obvious to the man on the other end of the line. But apparently it was not.

—They're not scheduled to arrive for two more days. I'm not in Texas.

—What's your delivery number? the voice asked. Drew told him. He was put on hold again. He looked at the sun. It seemed to be too far down, given how early he'd started driving today. Unless he had already crossed over into Arizona's later time zone. He looked at his phone to confirm that he hadn't. When he put his phone back to his ear, the voice was back.

—Hello? Hello?

—Yes, I'm here. What did—

—Your truck is there waiting. It will wait until 3:00 pm.

—I'm sorry, I don't—isn't it three in San Antonio already?

—You tell me, pal.

—But I—I'm sorry, the problem is I'm not in San Antonio.

—I can put in an extension request and have the driver wait until 6:00 pm.

Drew told the voice that he was in Arizona and could not make it to Texas by six. He asked if there was any chance that some other truck had been mistaken for his.

—I don't know what to tell you, said the voice. The truck with your number on it is there. Now, if you can't make your appointment, we can arrange to store your items for you.

—That's fine. I can pick them up tomorrow evening, maybe around seven.

—Nah, that's no good. We only schedule appointments until five.

Drew did not think to mention, at this point, that the voice had just told him he had until six today.

—Okay, then it will need to be two days from now, like we originally planned.

—Sure, buddy. Of course, it'll be an additional seventy-five eighty per day of storage.

—I'm sorry. You mean like eighty dollars?

The voice laughed.

—No, no. Seven thousand five hundred and eighty. Per day.

The conversation didn't go anywhere much after that. Drew tried to convey to the voice that such a sum was absurd, that he didn't have that kind of money, and that the movers had in fact agreed to deliver him his possessions in two days anyway, but a voice is just a voice, after all, and within minutes Drew was alone in the parking lot of the rest stop in Buckeye, or wherever it was, Arizona, with his car, a bag containing some snacks and a few changes of clothes, and the prospect of losing every dollar he had to his name within twenty-four hours—and that was if he could make it to his new apartment by then.

He called his mom.

—Hi, sweetie, she said. How's the big move going? Are you okay?

—Yeah, Mom, he said. I'm okay. Having some trouble with the moving company, though. They might be trying to overcharge me.

—Oh, God. Tell them you'll write a nasty review on Yelp.

—Right.

—I'm serious. I'm just a cheerleader for you. You know that. I just want you to succeed and be so happy.

—Thanks, Mom.

—Whatever you do. I mean that.

—I mean it too. Thank you.

—It was so nice to see you before you left, and have you help clean up the sewing room. You know if you ever need somewhere—

—Thanks, Mom.

He ended the conversation.

He didn't know who else to talk to. A lawyer? He had never talked to a lawyer in his life. The local police department in his new neighborhood in San Antonio?

He got back into his car and looked at his phone. The text conversation second from the top was still the one with Gary, his new boss. Gary had texted him the day before. He opened the message thread and read that text again:

IF YOU WANT ME

—Hey Drew. Know you're starting your voyage today! I'm excited for you and thrilled we'll be able to start this journey together. I've been around the Southwest a fair bit, so if you need any tips or get stuck anywhere, let me know if I can help! Here if you want me.

It was a funny phrase. "Here if you want me." Wasn't Drew the one who was wanted here? The phrase was usually used as a kind of misdirection, Drew reflected, from the person with power to the person without, to frame the powerful one as the servant, when in fact the opposite was true. But it was a kind offer.

He weighed pros and cons for a few minutes, sitting in his car, but he didn't know who else to talk to and felt that he should do something, so he texted Gary and let him know about the movers. More or less the same thing he had said to his mom.

Gary responded. He asked for the name of the moving company. He said he'd make a few calls.

While Drew was filling up at the gas station, the movers sent another text, from the same number.

—Don't mess with us.

Drew stared at this for much too long and then got back on I-10. He drove in order to drag his anger at himself along the highway until the friction sanded it down. By picking these psychos, he'd screwed up the most important factor in the move already. The road carried him past Phoenix and down towards Tucson while his thoughts traveled along unpleasant paths, but after a half hour or so, the tight feeling in his chest loosened. He was, most likely, overreacting to a frustrating but relatively minor setback. His mind was seeking some concrete focal point for his more generalized anxiety about all the things that could possibly go wrong for him as the result of his "big move."

He would miss his friends and family in the Bay Area, for one thing, though he suspected his years working at Nordstrom and failing to make anything else come together had been putting a strain on most of his relationships for a while. When he reached San Antonio, he would be working at what was technically a startup, which always carried the possibility of failure, even spectacular failure. And he'd never even taken a multi-day road trip before. His nerves were catching up with him, that was all.

It was only natural to have some doubts about the viability of his enterprise. From one perspective, this was a way of gambling all he had on the new job turning out well. Or, from another perspective, he was abandoning his former life to attempt beginning a new one. But doing so was the right decision. This would be a real job, with a real salary. No more freelance gigs, no more financial highs and lows that varied with the season. No more bosses telling him he was too in his head. Sitting in an office, he would actually be paid to think.

Yes, when something wasn't working, you were best served by trying something new. The definition of insanity being to expect a different result from the same method and all that.

Of course, Drew had never actually agreed with the premise that trying the same thing again and again and hoping for a better result was the definition of insanity. Sometimes he thought it was more like the definition of sanity. Or at least of being alive.

He waited until he was hungry and needed to use the bathroom and then he pulled over at the next exit that seemed to have a restaurant.

The sign for the place read "Apple Annie's Country Store." Inside, a large chalkboard menu described a selection of gourmet sandwiches. This sign had "Apple Annie's Coutnry Store" written at the top. Drew was the only one in there, which seemed a little odd, but then it was a weekday and not peak lunch hours. There was a funny, stale smell in the air.

Drew approached the counter and was about to order when he saw the man standing behind the register. It was Luntz.

It had to be Luntz. He was wearing casual clothes and he didn't have a name tag, but he had the same hair and eyes and tan and teeth. How many people could there possibly be who looked like that?

The man who was Luntz looked at him, expecting an order. When the person in line behind Drew cleared her throat, Drew went ahead and placed his order.

—That'll be nine seventy-eight, said clearly-Luntz, in the same rolling baritone.

—Thank you, said Drew. And then, after he had handed over the money:

—I'm sorry. Have we met before?

The man grinned. —Have we?

IF YOU WANT ME

—Is your name, by any chance, Luntz?

—Luntz? said the man. What kind of a name is Luntz?

—Never mind. Sorry. I thought—

—You thought you recognized me?

Drew didn't say anything to that.

—Here's your sandwich.

—Already?

—We might not have sourdough like you're used to, but I think you'll like it.

—Huh? Drew took the sandwich.

—Sourdough. You know, like in San Francisco.

Drew knew as well as he could know anything that he had not mentioned he was from San Francisco. But he found when he tried to present to himself the argument that Luntz knew things about him that were not possible to know, another part of himself argued back that he must have brought it up after all, or maybe he was wearing something that gave it away—that there must, in other words, be some way for Luntz to know what he knew that meant Drew was mistaken.

—Thanks, said Drew. He turned to leave.

—Better hurry if you're going to catch up with those movers, said the man from behind him.

Drew turned around but did not stop making his way out of Apple Annie's. His eyes met Luntz's grin.

—Though of course, if you miss them, you could just move back home with mom, Luntz went on. Wasn't that what you were going to do before this? Isn't that what you thought was really going to happen all along?

Drew left the store and walked toward his car. He glanced back at the Apple Annie's façade a couple of times, but the Luntz in there seemed not to have moved from behind the counter.

He peed onto the asphalt under his car and then got back in. He looked over again and almost jumped out of his skin when the door opened, but it was only another customer.

There was another funny phrase—jumping out of your skin. Was it supposed to imply losing your sense of self under duress? Being unable to maintain the person you normally appeared to be on the surface? Or was it supposed to evoke a more literal, gory image? The unbearable force of the unexpected tearing your physical body apart?

Drew looked at his phone. It was 4:48 pm. He still had at least eleven hours to go before he could possibly make it to his new apartment. For a moment, he considered texting Gary: I think someone is stalking me. Someone who works at both the Hampton Inn in Palm Desert and Apple Annie's Country Store in Willcox, New Mexico. He laughed out loud. It almost made him feel better. He opened the sandwich. It wasn't the one he had ordered. He was almost sure.

This time, when he started getting texts, Drew didn't stop driving to read them. He felt tense, headachey, a little nauseous. He nibbled at the sandwich but couldn't bring himself to eat it in earnest.

The movers had sent him a picture this time. Drew squinted. It was a photograph of the paper contract Drew had signed when the movers had picked up his stuff. Why? But soon enough he saw why: it listed a time and date of delivery, and the date listed was today's date. He looked closer. Down by his signature, the date listed was two days in the future.

Drew looked up and swerved himself back off the shoulder onto the road. The car behind him honked.

Obviously, the date on the contract had been altered somehow. They had been switched. To make it look like he had made the mistake himself, he supposed. Why else would they have switched the dates instead of simply altering one? He didn't have any pictures of the contract of his own. But he would fight them and they would not be able to take his money. They might be able to keep his stuff, but how long could they be willing to drag something like this out? Especially if he got legal help from Gary.

They sent another text.

—Please note that if we are not able to deliver your items within 48 hours of scheduled date, we reserve the right to destroy or re-sell any undelivered items. Please see contract.

Drew didn't like that very much. But maybe it was an empty threat. They would be vulnerable to a massive lawsuit if they did something like that. Wouldn't they? Drew had, of course, never so much as discussed the idea of suing somebody before.

He sped up. He could get there by tomorrow afternoon anyway, no problem. Almost certainly, he didn't have to. But why take chances? He'd sleep a little less tonight and feel better when he had his stuff tomorrow.

When the sign for New Mexico welcomed him into "the Land of Enchantment," Drew immediately thought of the evil stepmother from Snow White and her poisoned apple. The beautiful queen transforming herself into a deeply sinister-looking woman, ostensibly in order to avoid suspicion. Apple Annie's, he thought, and laughed. He was starting to feel lightheaded and tried to focus on the road. He didn't stop for Lordsburg, though even its McDonald's arches and strip malls were practically an oasis in the brown sea of his route, or for Deming, or Las Cruces.

When he crossed the Texas border, it looked to him like the big stars sitting on pedestals on either side of the bridge were misshapen. The bottoms bigger than the top. Perhaps it was that nonsensical observation that caused him to look around and notice that the same car that had honked at him earlier was still behind him now. It was too far behind him to be absolutely sure, but it was one of those Tesla SUVs. Pretty hard to mistake.

Immediately it occurred to him who was in the car. For no particular reason, he switched lanes. The car stayed where it was and did not attempt to pass him. It was still too far behind to see.

Drew began to consider the possibility that he was imagining things that weren't there. But right away that premise felt wrong. It wasn't how hallucinations worked, to see the same person, that apparently others could see too, in places they couldn't be. It wasn't how delusions worked either, coming on suddenly with no previous history of a loose grasp on reality. There was no other explanation for what was happening to him, but it wasn't schizophrenia.

Well, there was one explanation. A stranger was stalking him. It wasn't a very good explanation, but it was all he had and he clung to it.

The Tesla's headlights went on behind him as the light in the sky dimmed.

Drew pulled off the freeway in the heart of El Paso. The Tesla did not seem to be following. He got gas and then he parked himself in the lot of a DoubleTree, across the highway from, of all things, a Holocaust museum. It was late now, thanks to his traversal of time zones, but he still wanted to talk to Gary. Gary was there if Drew wanted him. Gary had always indicated he'd like to hear more from Drew.

He managed to call his mom first.

—Hi, honey, she said. It's late there, right? Are you okay?

He could hear it, in her voice. The years of disappointment. The desire to help starting to drown in exhaustion. The unwillingness to admit that it sure would be nice if he didn't disappoint her again.

—Yeah, Mom, he said. I'm okay.

He got out of his car and walked into the DoubleTree and there was Luntz, in front of the counter this time. His back was to Drew because he was talking to the receptionist. It was so clearly him. Drew had never been surer of anything in his life.

He got back in his car and drove a few blocks away. Then he texted Gary.

—I'm so sorry to bother you again. I'm afraid the moving company is starting to give me trouble that's kind of serious. This is going to sound paranoid, but I think it's actually possible they have someone following me.

Gary responded immediately.

—Drew, let me tell you a story. My first night in San Antonio, I was mugged. I had all my luggage with me and a guy with a knife took me for everything I had. I lost my phone, computer, wallet— lots of stuff I could never get back. I had to trust that my new job would help me get to where I needed to be. And you know, with the help of my boss and my team, it did. My boss took care of me and filled in the gaps, and now I'm going to do the same for you.

Drew took a deep breath. Maybe gambling everything on the new job had been as smart as he'd hoped.

—Tell you what, continued Gary. Come to my office as soon as you get into town. You can talk to our lawyer, your lawyer, the police, whoever you need to. And I'd love for you to meet the team. Will you do that for me?

—Hey, Drew wrote back. I'll be there if you want me.

—That's what I like to hear. We'll get this sorted out, okay? Please be careful and I'll see you ASAP.

Drew drove. He pulled stale, lukewarm water bottles and 5-hour Energy drinks out of his suitcase and did not stop anywhere and he made it out of the urban centers and back to the plains again. The Texas plain, this time.

A large Tesla remained behind him. When he sped up, sometimes he lost it for a while, but it never left for long and it never passed him. From time to time, another car would pass him, and it would seem to Drew that the person in the driver's seat was Luntz. Then the car would pass, and Drew would keep driving. There was scrubland and field land and hills and dirt and plant life, and none of it cared about Drew. Over the course of one's life, one encountered precious few things that did care, and even fewer that would do anything about it.

The sun began to rise when Drew was somewhere around Welfare. The sight of it made him sleepier than he had been all night. He'd been hoping to make it all the way without needing to stop, but that was foolish. He was only human. He drove around on side streets until he found a deserted-enough spot and passed out and didn't wake up until his phone rang.

Groggily, he stared at the number. It was the movers again.

—Hello? he said.

—Hello, said a familiar voice. Just calling to confirm you'll be claiming your delivery at the rendezvous point today.

Drew would probably have stopped breathing, but he needed to breathe to talk.

—Who is this? he said.

—This is the guy with all your stuff, said the voice.

—It's you, Drew said stupidly.

—Yes.

—How have you been following me?

The deep voice laughed. —Following you? Why would I need to follow you? We're already here.

Drew's voice shook. —Well, I'm not going to meet with you. I'm going to meet with a lawyer and the police.

—Ah. I'm sorry to hear you'll miss our appointment, then. We were so looking forward to seeing you.

—That's right. Drew hung up. The air smelled wrong in his car. It should smell like he smelled when he was sweaty and hadn't bathed, but it smelled bad in a different way. Almost like old newspaper.

When he got into San Antonio, his tank was empty. He stopped at a Chevron only blocks from the new office, and when he got out of his car and approached the self-service kiosk, there was Luntz, again, at the kiosk across from him. He was punching something into the keypad.

Drew left his car at the station and started to run. He would meet with the company lawyer and then he would go back for his car. It would take less than an hour. Drew didn't know how dangerous these people were, or how easy it would be to get them to back down, but he knew he had to keep trying, again and again, and expecting, or at least hoping, for a different result. He had to meet Gary and face these people head on.

He was already in the office elevator when he started to suspect something about Gary that he hadn't so far. Or perhaps he had been thinking it, but hadn't realized he'd been thinking it. What was the nature of a realization? Most people tended to think of realizations in a binary sense. Like jumping out of your skin. But maybe they didn't actually work that way. Maybe they were more of a gradual process, like a long trip, always aimed at a destination, but without a clear picture of what it would look like until the moment of arrival.

The elevator door dinged. Gary turned around and grinned at Drew with white, beautiful teeth. Though perhaps it was the contrast with the tan that made them appear so white. Standing around Gary was the rest of the team. None of them wore name tags, but they didn't need to.

Drew still knew that in most cases, if you did things the way you were supposed to and made an honest effort, then no matter how bad things seemed they would ultimately work out for you. In most cases, you stood a fighting chance. That's what he was thinking. He wondered what Gary—Luntz—was thinking.

But Drew didn't know what Luntz was thinking. No one could have known what Luntz was thinking.

—So, said Drew. What happens now?

Everyone smiled at that.

—There's really nothing to worry about, Drew. You've already abandoned so much of what you had. What's one more thing?

FUNERAL

Adam Franti

TOWN LOOKED DEAD.

Course it looked dead. It was an old Appalachian mining town, they'd been dying since the seventies. Was that right? Alex didn't know. He was from the rustbelt, where towns died a different kind of death.

Part of him wished that death wasn't the thing he was thinking about. But then that was the point of this trip, wasn't it? Remembering. Honoring. All that shit.

Thomas Alexander Sayles drove south to Appalachia to say goodbye to his brother.

Charles Alexander Sayles had disappeared two years ago. Without a funeral, without a body, without anything. Alex thought it was about time to say goodbye.

The old wound was still there, the old hurt faded a little, down from the sawblade scrape of loss to an ache, like a companion, like a wet dog nipping at your heels.

In the back of the car he had Charlie's guitar, had an old photobook Alex had stuffed full of prints from texts Charlie had sent back on his trip, had some candles and shit, a few bottles of beer and a bottle of bourbon that ought to appease the Appalachian spirits that hung around like drunks after closing. Pour one out for lost brothers. Lost spirits, too, why not.

He wished the town looked a little happier, though.

Alex had thought maybe Charlie had picked the scummiest places to take pictures, sent home images of the disintegrating gas station, the rot-flecked schoolhouse, making some big joke about the shittiness of the town he was in. Sent one picture of a Kroger, but the K and R were fucked. Text said

Lol want anything from the oger

Next one said

I'll bring you home an oger brand wine or something, bro

Next one said

Wait do they have dry counties down here

But no, that's just what the town looked like. And there was the oger, parking lot empty, shopping bag paper taped up over the windows. Next to a church, its white paint flaking from the steeple like it wore its own film grain.

And here was the Mote, its neon undersign flickering NO on and off next to the lava-colored VACANCY.

Lobby held an old guard dog, an enormous chocolate lab lying on a dog bed made gray from all the shed fur. Its tail thumped up and down twice when he walked in.

"Hey buddy," Alex said.

The dog opened and closed its mouth, like he knew he was supposed to bark and Alex knew he was supposed to bark and they'd all just agree that the dog owned the room.

"'n I help you?" Voice came round the corner before the body, a skinny guy in a flannel more dog hair than textile, long gray ponytail under a plastic trucker hat. Hat said ELIZA'S and had two sexy-lady outlines on either side.

Charming.

"Yeah, I'd like a room, please."

"Sure." Punched a few keys on the register. "Forty-six dollars. Checkout's at ten. You want the room another night just tell me then. Dial zero for the front desk. You got room 13. It's that one." A finger that was all ligament pointed out the window behind him. Alex handed him the money. "Can give Charlie a bone if you like."

FUNERAL

"What?"

"Dog. He likes bones." The manager dug out a milkbone from a shirt pocket and held it out. Alex gave it to the dog, his heart thudding.

Pour one out for dead towns, too, he thought.

< < < **<** > > > >

Fuck had Charlie wanted here, anyway?

Alex could never figure it. His brother liked hiking, was always up and down the flat little trails back home, always off on road trips with his boyfriend to walk up steeper trails that took longer to get to. Could never figure why he wanted to come *here* of all places, this depressing ass-of-nowhere town in the shadow of a blown-up mountaintop.

He couldn't have wanted to hike the fucking chemically-poisoned, deforested trails after a mountaintop removal, did he? Charlie was a third-wave hippie in the sense that he liked weed, played guitar, and signed college petitions to protect the wetlands and shit, but he wasn't one for ruinporn photography or whatever. He liked hiking because it was pretty, liked to see the parts of the world that *hadn't* been fucked up yet.

Alex hadn't known about mountaintop removal mining until Charlie sent that picture. Alex had it out on his lap in the depressing little room, faced away from the wall with the stain that could have been made by a man standing on the bed and pissing off it.

This place was gross.

The picture was from the parking lot of Mote, straight out across the road swallowed up by overgrown weeds. Looming out there above it all were two peaks, one rising sharp, a blade of earth stuck into the air. The other had been truncated, flattened, its top now a gravel and sand surface, an inverted quarry. One upthrust limb of an excavator showed in the picture. This was back, what, six months after they blew the thing?

Alex had done a lot of reading. Was called mountaintop removal mining, the kind of thing you did when all the rest of the coal was too expensive to get to, so instead you packed the whole fucking mountain with explosives and blew the top off of it, scraped through the wreckage for coal. All the newspapers and shit he'd read had all of course repeated the same lie about bringing jobs and prosperity, that it was for the good of the industry, like the industry had ever given a shit about miners. Pretending that miners were the kind of people who'd never shot at their bosses and cops for the right to have a day off so they could cough their lungs out in the comfort of their company town homes instead of doing it a fucking mile underground.

He'd done a lot of reading. Maybe he was becoming a third-wave hippie, too.

Pulled out his own phone to text Mom.

Made it. Car's ok

She wouldn't answer for a while, the phone left in her purse or the car or another room, forgotten until she needed the calculator or whatever. He'd find a new text there in the morning, maybe, or get one next afternoon. Didn't matter.

But to his surprise he got one back almost immediately. Simple one.

Be careful.

Then his phone buzzed again.

Love you.

He laughed a syllable of air out his nose.

Love you too ma

< < < < > > >

His choices for dinner were a fast food chain he thought had gone out of business decades ago or a bar that might have a deep fryer.

Or he could light out on the highway until he found an exit with more choices, maybe, but then he knew the temptation just to keep going, keep driving, and never look back might be too strong.

That, and the drivers who lived up here in the mountains drove their trucks without caution, zipping around suicide corners at ninety miles an hour and Alex didn't know if he'd be able to survive that in the dark.

Bar it was. Least there he could have a beer.

The town curved around a mountain road like a curled finger extending, the road wending into the dark, past urine-yellow streetlights. He crossed in front of the oger, where two cop cars were parked so their driver's side windows matched up. So the cops could hold hands, he thought.

Bar was as expected. Dark, smudged cigarette smoke, flickering

FUNERAL

Christmas lights stapled up on the wall, a tap with two choices—beer and lite—and a dusty rack of mixers in front of the mirror frosted with a beer brand they didn't carry anymore. Bartender looked about four hundred years old and two other patrons sat with their backs to the door and their eyes fixed on the tv in one corner, the sound cranked way up. Made it seem like you had a friend with you. A friend with very important opinions about the recent basketball upset, or whatever.

Alex had never been in a barfight. Always imagined it like a scene in *Roadhouse* though, part slapstick, part tussle with a younger brother, buy a beer and make up after, kind of a thing. Wondered if asking to change the channel might start one.

"I getchu somethin'?" said the barman.

Maybe he'd start a fight if he asked if they had a nitro tap, or an IPA. "What's good?"

The barman shrugged. Two guys down by the door both had half-empty glasses rimmed with sticky foam. "I'll have what they have."

Poured out, slid down the bartop to him, a little of the foam sloshed over the edge. "Thanks," Alex said at the same time the barman said, "Three dollars."

"You got a food menu?" he asked as he paid.

"No," barman said.

Alright then. Swigged down the first drink of the beer. Was fine.

Someone down the bar knocked on the surface, hard. Like someone might knock on a door. Or a wall.

Made Alex's heart beat.

A heavyset man with a beard under a mesh hat with the brim folded into a peak stared over at Alex. "Y'all from outta town?"

"Yeah."

"Whereabouts?"

"Michigan." He pointed at his upraised right hand, settled his forefinger by the pad of the thumb. "Round here."

"What you come this ways for?"

Alex took another drink, trying to gauge the man. Was this going to be a roadhouse brawl after all? Get knocked flat here in the bar, have those cops haul him off to spend the night in jail?

Didn't know why he'd assume something like that. From the

north, the south all seemed half-wild, another world, a place where monsters still lurked in the sweaty woods. But then, from the north, West Virginia may as well be Alabama, and that's the kind of flippant ignorance that led to brawls. Play nice, he told himself.

"My brother was here, not too long ago."

"Yeah? Live here?"

"No." Another drink. Maybe a bad idea to drink on an empty stomach. Should have had a powerbar before he left, but then he thought he'd eat here. "He disappeared."

He expected surprise, sympathy maybe, that old chivalric southern gentleman caricature.

But the man stared at him, really *stared*, eyes like binoculars now, twinkle of the christmas lights reflecting under that peak. "Think you should pack up and go," the man said.

< < < < > > > >

There was a cop car parked in Mote's lot. Run up across three spaces, why bother parking when you're a cop.

The cop leaned against Alex's hatchback, arms crossed, watching him walk up.

So all the cliches were out and firing tonight. Get the townies to tell you spooky ghost stories, give that warning, then have the cop come and tell you that your kind ain't welcome, don't need no northern carpetbaggers in town.

"Evenin,'" the cop boomed. His voice was like a megaphone. Then he coughed, a loud, full-body, racking cough, a fucking tuberculosis cough.

"Hey," Alex said. How much had he drunk? Not enough to be drunk. And he wasn't even driving.

Alex stopped out of arm's reach of the officer, waited for him to say something else.

Nothing. Cop just leaned there, looking. Eyes bright against the dark, staring from the shadow under his brim. Like he recognized him.

"Well, good night then," he said, walked toward his room, fishing in his pocket for the key.

"Ho!" The booming voice froze Alex on the spot, a fear-freeze, like a deer when headlights washed over to turn and splat. "Wait a minute there. Keep your hands where I can see 'em."

FUNERAL

Was he serious?

He stopped, pulled his hand out, slow. Cop came around from behind the car, stood off the driver's side, rested a hand on the butt of his pistol, coal-black in the piss light of the Mote's parking lot.

"Just wanted to stop by, see how you were doing."

"Fine," Alex answered. There went his heart again, knocking against his ribs.

"What brings y'all round here?"

"Passing through."

"Where to? Might could help you find your way a little quicker."

"Alabama," Alex reached for the first thought he could handle.

"That right? Roll Tide." The cop with a grin. Another cough. Cop was youngish, fit, his uniform brown underneath the black plate carrier, pistol and taser and cuffs and magazines ringing his hips in metal.

"Yeah," Alex said. Was a reflex.

"Now, you wouldn't be lyin' to me, would you?"

"No."

"No, *sir*."

"No, sir."

"Because that might be the kinda lie a journalist might use, get into our little town and start asking questions. You ain't a journalist, are you?"

"No. No, sir." What the fuck?

The cop tapped the glass of the window. "Got an awful lot of electronics in there. Might want to keep them in your room. Got a lot of undesirable elements round town."

He had a digital camera and a GPS in case his phone lost signal up here in the mountains. A laptop with punk band stickers all over it. Hardly a lot of electronics.

"Well!" the cop said brightly, flashing another grin. "Glad we had this talk. Now, y'all want to ask questions, feel free to come down by the station in the morning. Down the road you come a ways, then a right. By the old company offices. Can't miss it. Y'all have a good night now." Turned away. "Oh!" His voice was on its last legs, raspy, strained, forced through a wire mesh. "And keep your door locked. Like I said," a gesture to the air all around, "undesirable elements."

< < < < > > > >

Alex took everything out of his car and stored it in the cramped room. Between his tent, his hiking bag, all his food, booze, the guitar, and the awful lot of electronics, it barely left a navigable trail to the bathroom afterward.

He sat on the edge of the bed, his heart still hammering. He'd never had an encounter with a cop like that. His hands were shaking.

Fuck.

The whole random fight leads to an indefinite stay in jail theory suddenly looked plausible.

Did they not like journalists around here? What kind of cringe conspiracy bullshit was that? Would they have thought Charlie was a journalist? Coming down from the yankee north with a beard and his hair in a bun, taking pictures and shitposting about their little town?

But Charlie's car had been found here, by these same cops. If they'd done away with him, wouldn't they have ditched the thing somewhere, tipped it in a holler fill and answered his mom's frantic phone calls with, "No, ma'am, he lit out next morning, never saw him again."

"Fuck," he said out loud, to the room as a whole.

Room didn't answer.

Alex's eyes fell on the guitar, one of the only things in the room that wasn't a piece of shit. Was Charlie's, of course. After Charlie disappeared, those first few months where they thought he might be found, it stayed in his place, untouched. Then as it became clear that he wasn't going to be found, wasn't coming back, Dan, Charlie's boyfriend, started getting all of his stuff out of the apartment. Couldn't bear looking at it all. Reminded him too much of Charlie, broke his heart every time.

Old records went to Dad, photo albums to Mom, his computer and the guitar to Alex.

Alex couldn't even play the guitar. He kept it in his room, in a corner, like a shrine. Kept it clean, kept the sticker visible, THIS MACHINE KILLS FASCISTS, with respect to, like Charlie always said, Woody Guthrie, the original punk. If he left it alone, the strings all curling out from the tuning keys like unkempt stray hairs, Charlie might come back for it. Alex might wake with Charlie there on the end of his bed, the guitar on his lap, "hey bro," and then belt out some terrible impromptu song.

FUNERAL

A memory, like a photograph flicking up on a screen. Alex pissy one morning for no reason he could remember, and Charlie swooping into the room with the guitar, singing, "Waffles, waffles, gonna eat some waffles, bro, eat some waffles and cheer the fuck up, cuz you're depressing me!"

Jesus, he missed him.

After the search, and the media, the cops and community sweeping the coal-dust coated hills, getting dogs and helicopters and all that shit, after it was called off, after the experts said he was probably dead, Alex had the thought like a worm in the brain that he should learn how to play.

Charlie was left-handed, the asshole, and it made the effort harder, and then he felt stupid for not realizing before he'd spent months in front of tabs and internet lessons and all that shit that he could have just restrung the fucking thing to play it right.

But now he had this left-handed guitar, this leftover from his brother's life, and he'd brought it with him thinking the fucking West Virginia woods would enjoy a song sung for his brother's memory.

Strummed a few notes, setting his calluses against the strings.

Then there was a knock on the door.

< < < <   > > > >

They shared a room as kids, up til they were around twelve. That was when Dad got a better job and they moved, and they could have their own rooms. They were twins, though, and twins are hard to separate. So for a while they each just camped in the other's room at night, until Mom and Dad thought that it was unhealthy, and made sure they stayed alone all night.

He and Charlie had developed a secret language of knocks.

Kids' shit, right, it was all a lot more work than just learning morse code or whatever, but they thought they were so clever, having their own secret language. There were some parts that needed both hands to knock at once, like a kind of exclamation point.

So when Alex heard the knock at the door, some deep memory from his childhood, something he didn't know he carried with him anymore, woke up and knew that that sound had been made by two hands at once.

He dropped the guitar, was across the room in a second, throwing open the door to

Nothing.

Of course nothing.

Moths swarmed around the weak light of the lamp in the parking lot. Nothing else.

But there was something across the road, slithering into the messy, exhaust-stained bushes opposite.

Something pink. Skin colored.

Like a hand, attached to an impossible arm.

Shut the door.

Was gonna be hard to sleep here. This crummy fucking room in this crummy dying town. Harassed by cops. Jesus.

Dan had said he might come, but backed out at the last minute. Alex didn't blame him, wouldn't want to go honoring his dead girlfriend with her twin sister, if the situation was reversed. Talk about complicated.

Still, he didn't exactly feel great here, all alone.

He dug out his phone from his pocket and scanned through the old texts he still kept.

Two roads diverged in a southern highway and i and i take the
one less bullet riddled

With an accompanying picture. Keyhole Holler on the right, twelve bullet holes on its reflective surface. Town Hill on the left, only six. He must have stopped on the side of the highway to take that picture, because that's the kind of shit he did.

Mote had weak wifi, the kind of why-bother security login page that took nine hundred years to connect to, had tried it earlier and decided not to bother but now, lights on in the room, curtains closed and the air conditioner wheezing and rattling, tooling around on the internet might be worth the slow connection.

Except that instead of putting on music or looking for goofy videos, something distracting, he searched for mountaintop removal mining, scrolled through until he found the name of the dead city, and started reading articles about it.

He had read most of this before. All the links on the first few pages of the search were purple, long since clicked through, read exhaustively. Alex had made a few posts on some forums, looking

FUNERAL

for more info without getting into the reasons, not wanting to explain to people about everything, about his brother.

Wright and Baylor was a mining company that got started in the seventies, specializing in turning Appalachian mountain tops into one-time volcanoes. Their website was all cheery, showing a white dude so pale he looked colorless under a bumblebee-yellow hardhat smiling emptily at the camera, while behind him heavy mining vehicles paused in their operation, all the crew frozen in a moment of finely-tuned corporate propaganda. Little links for investment opportunities at the bottom, big spiel about how profitable the whole thing was, about how they enriched the communities that welcomed them.

All bullshit, of course. Numerous stories elsewhere, interviews with environmental groups, health experts, even economists, documenting the ecological catastrophe, the health scourge, and the economic vapidity of the practice.

And fuck if nothing more proved the counter-narrative true than the empty grave of this town. Where were the jobs this shit was supposed to bring? Not here. More of those purple links explained how all the jobs dried up the moment they blew that TNT. Don't need miners to do that work. Dump your garbage in the hollers and wire the money back to the investors, move on down to the next mountain.

Par for the course. Not unexpected. Environmentalists had had it in for mining since fucking forever, right?

The weird shit was buried a little farther. About machinery failing. About miners going missing. People getting sick, and not the regular kind of sick, black-lung sick, heart-problems-sick, but weird ones. Allegedly. All this was on conspiracy websites and forums, the same places where you might hear about lizard people and aliens running the US government.

Alex didn't believe it, not really. He got an absurd kind of comfort, though, knowing that other people found this place as scary as he did, even without a dead brother.

All at once it was too much. Reading the same fucking posts over and over, reading the same cautionary tales and whistle-blowing warnings, all for fucking nothing. Wright and Baylor were still making millions of dollars a year, blowing up small towns all over Appalachia.

He slapped his laptop closed, spent as little time in the bathroom as possible, and flicked the lights off to go to bed.

He got an early start, thanks to not sleeping, thanks to the feeling that he'd go home with bed bugs, thanks to wanting to get the fuck out of town.

The entrance to the state park was only ten minutes away, down the highway cracked to rumblestrips by the fucking trucks. He passed the police station, the shuttered W&B office surrounded by an eight-foot-high fence, and pulled down the woody lane to the park. His was the only car in the lot, the state not having enough money to keep a ranger around.

Brown signs posted around the lot said DANGER TRAIL UNSAFE and RANGER NOT ON DUTY and ENTER AT OWN RISK and may as well have said GOOD FUCKING LUCK, IDIOT.

Yeah, yeah.

Brought out his bag, filled his water bottle from the thankfully functional drinking fountain on the ranger station, and took a last leak before heading up.

Part of him still thought he should leave the whole fucking thing behind, just go home. Honor his brother's memory some other way, but the greater part of him knew that that's what he *always* decided to do, that's how he always handled things. Just stay home. Just stay out of it. Just get high and sit on his computer for hours each night until the posts blurred into each other and it was 3am.

Charlie had always been more interesting. More *interested*. Always out doing things. Joined crew in college when he'd never been in a boat smaller than a ferry his whole life. Went out for rugby and got clobbered, just for the hell of it. Kind of guy who went to a party and formed instant friendships while Alex hovered by the wall with a solo cup and tried to think of things to say.

It was that kind of thing, the missed opportunities, the lifelong struggle against his can't-be-bothered, I'll-do-it-later attitude that Charlie so enthusiastically rejected. Life was for living. So maybe this hike would jog something loose, you know, kick his attitude around a bit. Quit fucking sulking, you got a life to live for your twin, too, he told himself.

One obstacle was that he was a shit hiker. He got bored,

distracted, kept tripping on roots so he had to spend his whole time with his face to the ground looking at dirt. People enjoyed this. They did it for fun.

He trudged along, making the best of it. Maybe it was like distance running, you do it long enough and you just fade, the run automatic, so that the run is the meditation, the run is the prayer.

Been going maybe five minutes without tripping on a rock, Alex even had a couple moments of looking out over the trail back where he'd come, taking in the view as he rose up above the ground, saw the view the mountain saw, a valley laid out in front of him, its hills and its hollows and river cuts, when he heard knocking again.

Like knuckles against a door.

Hackles rose on his neck, something Alex had always thought was bullshit, was fiction, but his eyes darted around the empty woods and he wished he'd brought something besides a dull Swiss army knife to defend himself.

The feeling passed.

"Jitters," he said, for something to say.

Probably a woodpecker.

Woodpecker wouldn't have known the knock that meant *you awake?* though.

< < < < > > > >

He ate lunch on a platform of stone that shot out from the path and overlooked the piece of shit town he'd come from. Could even look down and see the parking lot at the ranger station on the other side of the rock.

From way up here, the town looked worse. The church was the lone building taller than two stories, its fraying steeple almost swallowed by trees. There was the oger, there the Mote, the rest of the town was the bar, the strip mall, the fast food restaurant, and single-family suburbs laid out in chaotic angular roads cut like old glyphs into the mountainside.

And there, to his right, was the mountaintop they blew up. Its top was a sand-gravel path, where abandoned trucks and excavators sat rusting in the humidity. Dark holes punched into the top underneath A-frame steel cable spools.

There and gone, the whole company came in, blew up the mountain, ate the profits, and took off. Past the mountaintop, half the valley on the other side was the same chalk-sand color, the same fragments of mountaintop that murdered the trees, that poisoned the valley, like a rash on skin.

Charlie may have seen this all in operation, though, a couple years ago. The machinery running, the trucks grinding the road down to powder, the endless beep-beep-beep of the reversing trucks and forklifts, the crash and scratching of excavator shovels. Industry. Profit.

Alex never got a picture of all that, which either meant that signal was worse a couple years ago and he couldn't send them, or he never made it this far.

Was supposed to wait til he got to the top to start crying. He stood and wiped at his eyes. Cleaned up the spot and turned back, adjusting the big pack and the guitar and everything else, gave one more glance down the mountain to the ranger station and

Froze.

Cop car in the lot, parked behind his car, crosswise, like blocking his way back. The cop was out, his back turned, peering into the driver's side window with a hand shading his eyes from the sun. Alex crouched when the cop swiveled up and turned around, looking up the mountain.

Didn't miss a trespassing sign, did he? He remembered the others. There hadn't been a fence or anything. Was the cop just fucking with him?

Well fuck him. He didn't get to intrude on his grief.

Alex turned and strode up the mountain, leaving the cop behind.

< < < < > > > >

Trees were thicker, the undergrowth turning into overgrowth, the trail harder to follow. There were still little markers along the train, four-by-four beams painted brown with white paint numbering each one. Was probably supposed to work with a map given at the rangers station, but who needs one when you nuke half the valley.

Was getting darker, though. Alex stopped to dig out a flashlight from his bag. Had another energy bar. This was a long way up. The peak was supposed to be only a thousand or so feet higher than the town, but Alex never remembered exactly how that was all calculated. Still had a ways to go, he thought.

The original plan had been to stay the night. Pitch the tent, take a night and just think about his brother. The good times. Pour one out.

That was supposed to be helpful, right?

Alex supposed a lot of this shit was some holdover intuition from a time before religion. Religion just grew up as a result of this stuff, a codification of the things that made people feel better after surviving when someone they loved died. Built that community around shared grief.

They never had a funeral. Mom had thought about it, but she broke down every time she tried calling a funeral home to arrange it. Dad offered to, and that just made it worse. It may have been better that way, though. Alex thought about all the useful advice his uncles might have, half-felt grief on their end mixing badly with the need to give advice, to tell him how he should feel, to try to distract him. Like a bad trip, spinning around forever without a place to set his feet down.

Nah, man, this was better. Just him, the mountain, and his brother.

A clearing ahead let him step out into open air for the first time, there on a ridge near the edge of the mountain, and there it fucking was, right there, the drop. Something like six or eight hundred feet down, just straight down to nothing. He peered over it, and all down there was this pulpy sort of gravel, massive stones like knapped pieces of the mountain piled up together, glacial and sharp.

"Fuck off," he said. That was a holler fill. One of the little valley cups where they piled up the rubble, and fuck whatever was there before.

He stayed too long, stared too long, and when he moved again, the clouds above were black.

Charlie sent a video once, bumper of the car pulled right up to one of those three-legged police barriers laid across the road, and not teen feet behind it was a river running across the cement.

Flash flood down the mountain. Didn't bring my suit

The water had been thick and dark, like the water flushed out of a well-used grill.

< < **< <   > > >** >

Alex had to set up the tent in the dark. Took a lot of cursing, but he got the thing finished. Just one of those little pup tents, crisscross poles narrower than his little finger. Smelled dry, musty, like a basement.

He lay down inside, staring up at the dark nylon.

Dug out the guitar, hauled it over to the edge of the cliff, give Charlie a nice view while he played.

"Can you believe I hauled this thing all the way the fuck up here, bro?"

That was something. He also grabbed the candle, the matches, the photobook, and the booze. Hauled it all out in clumsy trips.

Found a spot not too close to the cliff edge, sat awhile getting things adjusted. Wind kicked up when he tried to light the candle, fumbled with it. Finally sputtered to life, its bold little flame slapping at the air that whipped around it.

He wiped the guitar down with a cloth and tapped his phone to wake the screen up, to get to his tabs app, start playing something.

"How bout we open with some Woody Guthrie, huh? Sing some songs with the ghosts of the union men up here." Gave care for the sticker, because Guthrie was one of the original punks, back when punks shot Pinkertons. "'Fore I start." He cracked open a can of beer, took a swig, and poured the rest out all over the stone ground. "I miss you, brother."

He froze when he heard a knocking from the trees behind him. Cold crawled down his spine.

Nothing. Just play.

The first few notes strummed out, his goofy left-hand guitar strumming through the simple song, until he misfingered.

"Shoulda warmed up," he said. Loosened his fingers and tried again. Was halfway through this time when he felt a big fat raindrop land on his head.

"Mother*fucker*." Sky was black as oil now, and a great gritty raindrop fell directly into his eye. The water came down black.

He cursed himself on the way back, cursed himself for not lighting a bigger fire, for wasting this fucking trip.

"This is the kind of shit you lived for, wasn't it, brother?" Alex asked the air. "Cuz I think it's a goddamn disaster. True to my fucking spirit, I guess. Fucking disaster."

He'd left his phone out on the ground by the shabby little shrine.

He grabbed it, wiping off the screen. "Look at this, man, it's always like this. I'm always fucking things up. Hasn't rained in this fucking state in six weeks and I come down the one goddamn day it decides to piss all over me. Surprised I didn't tear the tent. Surprised I didn't wreck the fucking car, fuck something else up."

The words came out in a stream, a neverending gush. Was nothing new. Alex screamed at himself like this regularly, at every stubbed toe or broken dish, every time he forgot something at the grocery store or called the wrong Chinese takeout place, every little disaster just going to prove the rule that he was an incompetent fucking idiot.

That he was the fuckup, the disappointment.

That he was the one who should have died.

Here it was, of course, the self-pity intruding on what was supposed to be Charlie's thing.

Always had to make it about himself, in the end. This bullshit psycho-spiritual trip, this desperate, useless nonsense. Just another way to avoid staring himself in the face and getting help, going to therapy.

Time passed before he was in control of himself again.

Grabbed the phone and tapped the screen to wake it up. Tapped it again when the screen—

Wasn't his phone.

It was Charlie's.

It knocked *you awake?*

< < < < > > > >

A lot happened in those next few moments.

He lurched out of the tent, leaving the phone there amid the outline he left, chalky and black, like a dead body.

Stood staring at it when he heard a crash from the woods, from down the mountain, saw a red light beaming in the dark against the black rain. Heart thudded away, got worse when the light stopped, reared up like a snake about to strike, and another light hit him, a bright one, one of those billion-lumens spotlights, and he heard the cop's voice creak out like old wood groaning.

"Ho there, traveler. Dangerous up here."

Alex didn't say anything. Couldn't say anything.

"There we go, easy does it. Don't want no surprise movements or nothin,' less jumpy I am the less likely anyone is to get hurt."

The cop paced closer. Alex heard a mad knocking come from the tent, from the *phone*. Charlie's phone. The cop's light swiveled over to the tent and hung there a moment. Came back, the light like a fork in the eye. "You alone up here?"

"Y—yeah." Alex swallowed gravel. "Yes, sir."

"Fast learner. Not like last time." Something clattered to the ground at his feet. Something heavy and metallic. "Well. Let's see we make it permanent this time. Pick it up."

It was a shovel. Alex bent down and picked it up, and the cop shifted back a step.

"Don't get any ideas. Headin' thataways." Gestured over the cliff, to the blown-top mountain. Coughed again.

He stumbled through the black woods, the way slick and treacherous, and the black drops smelling like campfire, like cooking coals, like brimstone. Cop crashed behind him, his light alternating flash-white and red, making vignettes of the close trees, the hanging vines.

Emerging out onto a little saddle that led to the other mountain, Alex saw the flat top again, and it was different. Not just a gravel truckway anymore, but a dark warren of tunnels open to the sky, black oily stone cut by picks and hammers and explosions, shattered struts and limply hanging cords where electric lanterns hung, unlit. What the fuck was he seeing?

And then, behind them, a knock.

Quiet

Another warning knock, for when parents came up the stairs.

"Fuck was that?" The lights turned away, facing back to the woods, the black cavelike tangle of trees. The cop's back was there, and Alex with the shovel.

He wasn't that fucking brave.

"You hear that shit, too? You come alone? *Answer me*."

"Yeah, I came alone."

"Fuckin' leave alone, too. Get fuckin' goin.'"

Cop herded him over to a point on the cracked and blasted mountaintop where the ground was soft, filled with black flakes and gravel from what used to be a mountain peak, in the lee of a half-standing wall, an old horizontal mineshaft with pick gouges still in it. Whenever the cop's light flashed over it, it was gone, back

FUNERAL

to the flat sand topped truck road he'd seen earlier. Alex felt like puking.

He dug, the black ground giving way. The hole got deeper, deeper, and Alex knew at once what he'd find. What was here. His brother's body, lying under this black sand, his body joining the countless others, the bombed-out union men, the murdered strikers, the buried workers lost in accident or malice.

His shovel struck something, and he recoiled away, out of the hole, when he saw a pair of living arms breaking through the wall of the hole. Like a pair of arms prodding around for a pair of glasses dropped in the dark. They seized the side of the hole and waggled, like they were shaking loose the frame of a window.

And then black, black water gushed out of the hole. Too much, much too much, to be natural. It filled the hole, the grave, and then collapsed it, the entire area turning into a river, the dirt and muck and gravel liquefying, running away to fill the infinite warrens of the old mine. Alex scrambled back, dragging himself backward, past the cop who turned his light onto Alex and opened his mouth to speak, to command, when pairs of maggot-white hands burst out of the rushing black water and held his thighs, wrapped around his waist. Another pair, pink, so pink they looked new, looked fresh, snaked up and up, not yet taking a grip.

The cop's face was visible in his own hollow lamp light, eyes open and panicked, mouth stretching wide, hand dropping the light and down to his gun as he turned away from the hands, but too late, too late, the pink arms gripped hair, fish-hooked his open mouth, and dragged him down into the black, surging water.

Alex lay there, shaking, the rain cold and the roar of the river drowning out all else.

Above it all he heard a knock, a knock like two hands striking a wall at once. A code. A secret code.

Love you, brother.

SEE YOU IN DISNEYLAND

Douglas Wynne

I DON'T KNOW where to begin. Susan, the shrink I've been seeing since the shooting, says writing it all down could help with the therapeutic process. She also mentioned a consciousness researcher who might be interested in my case, so this could be for him. I don't know yet. There's a good chance this notebook will end up in the fireplace that came with the new house. I haven't ruled it out, and knowing it's an option will make this easier to do.

The house isn't new; it's new to us. Well, *us* is a thing of the past now, but Trey was still alive when I bought the place. Susan says that for some people, writing is a way to extract meaning from chaos. I think we both know that I've been doing too much of that already, but putting it all down in order might help me see if it stands up to scrutiny. That's the hope, anyway.

Assuming these pages will make it to that researcher, I'll state the hardest thing first and get it out of the way: My fifteen-year-old son, Trey, was killed seven months ago in the Abraham D. Bresnahan school shooting. I am one of many parents who suffered the ultimate loss that day. Judging from what I've seen on TV, I suppose I'm not handling it as well as the ones who have remained intact enough to channel their grief into activism, and better than the one who treated her loss with a garden hose full of carbon monoxide through the window of her SUV. Those details weren't on TV. I got them from my one friend in the support group I don't attend. Carrie was Trey's Art teacher. They bonded, and now she's the only person outside of therapy who I can talk to about it. Maybe that's because we're both weirdo creative types and I don't expect her to judge me, or maybe it's because Trey connected with her in the way that only a fifteen-year-old can love an adult who isn't family but is encouraging him to follow his far-fetched dreams.

Dreams that died with him.

Shit. I don't know if I can do this.

The other parents and teachers never made me feel like an outsider—that was self-imposed. It's an affluent community, and I don't really give people the chance to reject me; I do it for them. It's not even an economic divide. I have a nice house and more in the bank than some of them, but they're ... adults. Grown-ups. And I'm a tattooed chick with ripped jeans and a punk haircut working all night sessions at a recording console on Sunset Boulevard, capturing every pristine nuance of rappers rhyming about all the drugs, money, lead and jizz they're dropping. These are the songs their kids are streaming on their phones and vibrating the paint off their cars with, but I've never expected to be embraced by my white community for my part in creating them. It's what everyone asks you first at a cocktail party. "What do you do?" And if the conversation turned from career to family, I'd have Trey's father, dead of an OD on his son's fifth birthday, and nobody else to mention except for my parents back on Long Island who disowned me for getting knocked up by a black guy, and a brother who calls me when he wants concert tickets.

Look at me filling pages and avoiding the whole point of this exercise: documenting and scrutinizing the weird shit. And maybe my fear of being judged has more to do with my role in the tragedy.

So here's the sort of thing the inked and pierced freak might say at the survivors' support group that wouldn't win her any admirers: I have a voicemail from the day of the shooting that I haven't played for the police because I think the audio file is haunted. Literally. Fucking. Haunted. And I should know. I'm an expert on audio files.

There. I feel better already. A little. But maybe I'm being disingenuous. Maybe I should know better *because* I'm an audio engineer. That's what my friend Mark says, anyway. He mixes for TV. But I know what I hear when I listen to the clip. I trust my ears. I've made my living off my ears.

Now, what I am not an expert on is the paranormal. I'm not religious or superstitious, but I like to think I keep an open mind. If you asked me about life after death before all of this happened, I would have said I was skeptical but hadn't ruled it out, or some such noncommittal bullshit. I meet a lot of superstitious people in the music biz, and I take all their claims about crystals and spirits with a big enough chunk of salt to nourish a horse. As for mediums, I still think most of them are the worst kind of vultures feeding on the desperation of the bereaved. And as a newly grieving mother, I understand that desperation like never before.

I've been thinking lately about credible people who have had UFO encounters. Most times, their eyewitness accounts are subjective, but occasionally there's a video clip that looks like it couldn't be hoaxed. Although, with computers now, pretty much anything can be hoaxed. As for the voice message I received on March 19th, I sure as fuck didn't hoax it. I promise you that.

The other weird thing, the thing that happened first, was more subjective.

I know I have to go back to that night to lay the groundwork for what I believe, and honestly, I can only do that thanks to the fireplace in the next room and the reassurance it provides that no one need ever see this. But if I'm going to tell the rest, I need to state for the record that I didn't buy the funeral parlor because of the spirit organ. I didn't believe it could do what the Carringtons claimed. At best, I figured I might eventually work with a black metal band or a flaky folk artist who'd want to use it on a track as a novelty. I never would have let those kids do what they did if I believed in it.

I bought the Carrington Funeral Home with plans to convert it into a live-in studio. A three-story Queen Anne on Arlington in West Adams, it's close enough to LA to attract artists, but suburban enough to be set apart from neighbors, which meant I wouldn't have to invest a ton of money in soundproofing. The first time I clapped my hands in the big chapel room, I fell in love with the acoustics, and there were enough rooms upstairs for Trey and me to have some privacy even if I offered boarding to artists who wanted to live on-site while working. I had a five-year plan to get my own studio up and running so I could stop spending so many hours bouncing around the country for freelance gigs. I'd been chasing the work, living out of hotels between New York, Nashville, and LA for too long. The money was good enough that I could float for a few months between gigs, but it always came back to Trey having to stay with friends when I was on a project, and I felt guilty about it. I wanted to offer him more before he was old enough to move out.

Susan would say I'm evading again. All you really need to know is that the house came furnished, including a decent Hammond organ I negotiated into the deal and the 'spirit organ' the seller didn't know what to do with when Walter Carrington finally joined his primary clientele.

The spirit organ was Dr. Carrington's invention. Yeah, Doctor, though I don't know what kind of medical or academic credentials he claimed besides being a mortician. He built it to assist his wife, Marjorie, in her work as a medium.

Right. A funeral director and a medium sharing a house with the dead. Believe me, I know. My first reaction was probably the same as yours—*What a racket*. In either sense of the word, depending on where you stand on the spirit world. Anyway, from what I gather, they didn't openly advertise Marjorie's "gift," but offered it discretely to clients who seemed badly in need of closure. The desperate.

The organ, situated in a second-floor parlor, is basically an oak table with a series of circular holes cut into the surface to hold various sizes of custom blown glass jars. According to a yellowing news clipping I found in a desk drawer, the glasses were filled to engraved lines with precision measurements of holy water. All except for the centermost vessel, referred to as the *sympathy jar*, which was meant to hold a personal effect of the deceased. The article mentions a few of the objects that had been put to this purpose over the years—lipstick, dentures, a lock of hair, and a glass eye were among the more colorful items, but personal jewelry was more common, especially wedding and engagement rings. The sympathy jar was fitted with a tin plate at the bottom, on top of which the object rested in a thin layer of black sand. A ribbon of horsetail hair wrapped around a spindle was employed to stroke the glass jars like a violin bow, causing them to vibrate when the operator turned a hand crank. The sound is similar to tuned wine glasses or Tibetan singing bowls, and is channeled through the acoustic chambers of the table's wooden cover to a Victrola horn. The bereaved would sit in a red velvet chair beside the horn, listening for the voice of the departed.

From a sound engineering perspective, I found the organ fascinating. It was handsomely crafted, elegant in its simplicity. With the lid on, you might have mistaken it for an antique sewing machine. But it was also clever—the tuned glasses produced a harmonious drone, while the buzzing sand and rattling object added a texture of white noise, like one of those old wind machines Pink Floyd used on *Wish You Were Here.*

But what I already knew, and what should have prevented me from ever taking the contraption seriously, is that noise stimulates the imagination. Especially the kind of uneven noise that would be generated by an object vibrated via hand crank. And if that noise is in the range where the characteristics of human speech occur—around 1 to 6 kHz—then our brains want to interpret it as speech. We strain to sift familiar patterns (words) from the chaos.

I could see how easy it would be for people to hear the voice of a loved one in a candlelit room after a glass of brandy and a head full of incense. It's not that different from seeing faces in an inkblot or ghosts in a grainy photo. There's even a method of ghost hunting that's based entirely on the investigators tricking themselves into hearing auditory illusions just like this but with digital technology. These people intentionally buy low quality handheld audio recorders, or recorders that have a Lo-Fi setting, so the files will be cluttered with noise artifacts, even when all you record is silence. It's just digital aliasing, a side effect of a low Nyquist frequency, but the ghost hunters aren't interested in the explanation as long as the results sound spooky. There are even social media groups devoted to analyzing the clips. Of course, as soon as someone tells you what you're listening for, what *they* hear the ghost saying, it's almost impossible to hear anything else. Like the first time you play "Stairway to Heaven" backwards. It can give you chills if you're listening to it expecting Robert Plant to toast

Satan, but to quote Radiohead, "Just 'cause you feel it, doesn't mean it's there."

I knew all of this. Which is why I didn't take Trey and his friends seriously when they spooked themselves fucking around with the damned thing. If not for how distressed Amanda was, I'd have thought they were all putting on an act just to freak *me* out. But Trey isn't superstitious either. He's always had a healthy skepticism.

Shit. I'm still writing about him in the present tense.

< < < < | > > >

Stepped away for a few minutes to get my head together. Almost put the flame of my Bic to the notebook instead of the bong.

Okay. When I finally got the kids to calm down enough to tell me what was going on, it came out that they thought Jared summoned a serial killer. Yes, *that* Jared. The shooter. I only met him the one time, but I could tell he had a touch of charisma, which is often all it takes to get people wound up by candlelight. I thought that was all it was. He'd set them up with expectations so they heard what he wanted them to hear.

When I walked in on the scene, Amanda was going off in a panicky voice about burning fingernails. I thought she'd burned her fingertips from the friction of the horsehair ribbon, but the cover was on the organ. Then I realized she was telling Jared to "burn them right now," and begging Trey to make him do it when he wouldn't respond to her. I'd stumbled in groggy and irritable, disturbed from a nap by the bedlam, sleep deprived from an eighty-hour workweek and in no mood to get punk'd by a bunch of teenagers.

Trey sat at the organ, looking at me with the eyes of a dog caught rooting around in the trash, the crank handle motionless beside his clawed hand, like he'd just let go of it. Jared stood beside the Victrola horn, head cocked and garnished with a salacious grin, like he'd just heard a filthy joke. Whatever he'd heard, I had the idea it was loud enough for all of them to hear. Amanda paced the room, shaking out her hands, while the other girl—I think her name was Vanessa—sat on a window frame, elbows on knees, hands cupped over her ears, voicing some denial on an endless loop. Trey's friend Paul, a wiry long-haired kid I'd known since the pair of them were in fifth grade, sat on the red velvet chair beside the horn, staring a hole through the floor.

Jared lifted the lid of the organ and dug around in the sympathy jar. It was only when his fingers came up crusted with black sand that I understood what Amanda was raving about.

"Whose nail clippings are those?" I asked. The question shut the girls up, and for a heartbeat, Jared almost looked guilty.

"The Night Stalker," Trey said.

"The *who*?"

Amanda recited a summary she must have heard recently enough for the afterimage to still be pulsing in her strobe light attention span. "Richard Ramirez, the Night Stalker. The Satanic serial killer from the 80s. Jared called him up on your creepy contraption with those fingernails he bought off a murderabilia website."

Jared slipped his hand into his pocket and deposited the clippings among the lint and loose change.

"*Murderabilia?* The fuck? Is that even legal?"

"They outlawed it in California," the dark-haired girl said. "But you know . . . The Internet."

"Some guys on death row have girlfriends who sell their stuff," Amanda said. "Signed artwork, locks of hair, fingernail clippings . . ." Trey squirmed, knowing what I would think of this. Jared said nothing, but the set of his jaw spoke defiance.

"That's disgusting," I said. No one argued. "Seriously, that makes me want to puke. Is that really what you have in your pocket? A serial killer's fingernails? Or are they yours and you're just trying to scare everybody?"

He sneered. "They're real. *Better* be. I paid enough."

I swallowed, but my mouth was dry. Paul, in the velvet chair beside the horn, looked ill. "What did you hear?"

No one answered. Their eyes roved the patterns in the wallpaper and carpet.

"Did you all hear it?"

Amanda nodded.

"Trey?" He was well acquainted with the edge in my voice. "What did you hear?"

Trey rose from the organ bench and shuffled restlessly, cueing his friends to clear out. He looked at the wooden horn as if expecting it to speak for itself.

SEE YOU IN DISNEYLAND

"Death always came with the territory," Paul whispered. "That's what it said."

I didn't know what that meant, but in the charged atmosphere of the séance parlor, it gave me goose bumps. I rubbed my arm and considered the spirit organ. Did I really think a gaggle of teenagers wouldn't poke a thing like that to see if it stirred? And *had* it stirred? Or had this Jared, with his fetish for the macabre, spoken into the horn and reflected his voice back at the room like a ventriloquist? It was a corny trick, but it made me angry. Angry at Jared for being a creep, at Trey for bringing people I didn't know into our house where I kept expensive equipment, and at the rest of them for waking me up from badly needed sleep.

"That's the best you could come up with? *Death came with the territory?*" I directed this at Jared, the accusation clear. When he smiled, his curling lip made me think of a worm on a fishhook.

"He quoted himself," Jared said. "Ramirez. That's what he said when they gave him the death penalty."

< < < <   > > > >

It's true. What Richard Ramirez said at his sentencing. The full quote is: "Death always came with the territory. I'll see you at Disneyland."

I looked up his Wikipedia entry. The rapes and murders in LA and San Francisco. The home invasions, shootings, stabbings, and bludgeonings. I scanned through it looking for the quote. Afterward, I felt dirty and sick to my stomach. Two photos that came up in my search results stayed with me—the one where he's flashing a pentagram drawn on the palm of his hand, and the one where he's baring his rotting teeth at the camera.

Apparently he was an avowed Satanist who caught the murder bug when his Vietnam vet cousin regaled him with stories of mutilations he performed on villagers during the war. I'm not squeamish about blood, but I am repulsed by cruelty. I did my research later that night, after the kids left and Trey went to bed, and I regretted it instantly. I still do. If I could erase my brain's browser history for that night, I would. It made for restless sleep, despite my fatigue. But don't get me wrong; I wouldn't erase the knowledge just because it disturbed me. I would wipe it, if I could, because I'm afraid it influenced my perception later. When the horror found us.

I won't write about that day. Everything they were willing to tell parents, you can find in the news articles. Sure, there were details that circulated among the survivors; I guess there always are, doled out in drips and drabs in confidence, and mostly kept from the vulnerable. Like each new detail is another bullet that hasn't reached its target yet, ready to explode inside the mind of the parent who overhears it, leaving shrapnel that can never be extracted. The details don't matter, anyway. Everything changed. That's all that matters. I don't remember much of that day, odd as that may seem. I don't remember the day when I was broken. Susan tells me it's a coping mechanism, a natural anesthetic. I can't wipe those Internet photos of Ramirez from my memory, but I've deleted most of the trauma of learning my son was killed.

It wasn't clean erased, though. More like some hack engineer did razor blade edits to the master tape and left me with a song that jumps from the second line of the first verse to the middle of the bridge with no rhythm or rhyme. It's jarring, and I have no desire to play it back. So I have a killer who was behind bars before I was even born taking up space in my head where my last minutes of hope should be. Maybe that's unfair, but if you believe what I do, it makes sense. Because he was there, too, that day at the high school. Richard Ramirez died of cancer on death row in 2013, but he was there on March 19, 2018, hidden in plain sight.

Jared Morin killed himself at the scene. The police concluded that he acted alone, but I don't believe he did. I don't know if the nail clippings were authentic, or which came first—Jared's urge to kill or his fascination with killers. If Ramirez used the spirit organ to possess Jared, was that possession invited? Maybe the devil is in the details, or maybe the details don't matter. My gut tells me that when he walked those halls, Jared Morin was a sympathy jar with the Night Stalker rattling around inside him.

I remember the phone call. I was working when it came through, head between the speakers, my phone on the mixing desk beside me, silenced. I saw the screen light up with an unfamiliar number and wrote it off as a robo-call. I get so many of them disguised as local numbers that even if I wasn't working, I probably wouldn't have answered. If you're not in my contacts, you can leave a message. I didn't even consider that Trey could be calling me from someone else's phone.

Not answering that call is my biggest regret. I know, I couldn't have known. I was working one-on-one with an artist who was in the vocal booth, neither of us were looking at social media, and my assistant was out on a coffee run. Turns out the phone Trey used belonged to his friend Amanda. He'd lost his own phone in the scramble. When the police returned it to me, I checked the unfamiliar number against Trey's contacts and found Amanda's name. I don't think they were boyfriend and girlfriend, but I don't really know—at fifteen, he didn't like to talk to me about girls. Maybe this is fucked up, but I hope they were. I'd like to think he was with someone who loved him at the end.

I've spent more time wondering about Trey's relationship to Jared. Were they friends? I only saw the kid that one time. Didn't even know his name until I saw his picture on TV later. These shooters don't typically have many friends. That's the impression I get from the media, anyway, though I doubt I could bear to look into it. Not now. But I don't think these boys—yes it's almost always boys, white boys—kill their own friends. It's just one more thing that makes me wonder. Is the voice at the end of the message Jared's? Or is it, somehow, Ramirez?

I saw that my phone had logged a voicemail—unusual for a spam call—so I played it back between takes. Well, not between, because as soon as I heard it, that was the end of the session. After that I was on my news app, with my hands trembling and my heart thudding like a kick drum, and fumbling into my car. Then things get as distorted as the audio on that voicemail.

It's a noisy file. I tried to clean it up, but there was only so much I could do, even with the best tools. I think most of the noise is from Trey's anxious fingers roving over the mic on an unfamiliar phone. His voice is unmistakable through the rustling, but you can tell he's speaking quietly, so it's faint, little more than a whisper. He says, "Mom, it's me. I'm sorry. I love you." Then there's what sounds like three gunshots, though it could be objects crashing loudly. I don't know. It distorts. But yeah, probably gunshots. Fuck. I have sat at my console watching the needle of the VU meter jump, wondering which one is the shot that took him. Which burst of noise punching through the chaos and the screams is the one that killed my sweet boy? I've tortured myself with that. It might be some perverse penance for my failings as a parent.

There's more noise, more rustling, and then the dirty silence of dead air, of someone listening. Then one more line of garbled, half-muted human speech and the call ends.

I can't decide if it's a blessing or a curse that when I play that isolated 1.5 second clip for other people—always out of context—not one has heard the same thing I hear. I've filtered out all the noise on either side of that narrow band where human speech lives, but that was for the benefit of the people I played it for. I heard the words clearly the first time I played it.

I have a list of things other people hear in that second-and-a-half before the call ends. Whether I gave them headphones or sat them down between studio monitors or just handed them the clip queued up on my phone, no two reports agree. Some have heard things that sound ominous or threatening, even out of context. Others hear nonsense words.

Me? I hear, "See you in Disneyland."

An auditory illusion fueled by survivor's guilt? Could be. Like life after death, I haven't ruled it out. But I've decided the fingernail clippings were probably authentic. I started looking up murderabilia websites and stopped as soon as I saw someone selling gravel from the Bresnahan High School. That sent me dry heaving over my laptop and slamming it shut before I had a chance to see something worse. People are sick.

Therapy was going okay until last week. I told Susan I was writing this journal, and that it was helping me to see things more rationally. We talked about how the process was like looking at one of those 3-D line drawings of a cube. You can see the cube one of two ways, angled up or down depending on how your eye interprets which lines are in front and which are in back. With Susan's help, I was starting to think I might get to where I could hear a different pattern in the noise, or maybe someday just hear it as noise, or best of all maybe I would eventually get to where I could erase everything but Trey's voice from my hard drives and stop thinking about what might be hiding in the noise. I told her about all the times I've stood in Trey's bedroom considering which object of his I might put in the sympathy jar, how I've struggled with that temptation. I got as far as setting up a mic in front of the Victrola horn. But we both know I don't need new noises to obsess over. Then came what Paul did. Just when I was starting to loosen my grip on my craziest notions. Shy Paul, who I've known since he and Trey were ten, who I saw leaning into the horn that night with something new in his eyes, some dark knowledge . . . You know what he did at Disneyland. It's all over the news.

They're saying on CNN that he was carrying out the second part of a plan hatched with Jared, comparing them to the Columbine killers, but that's bullshit speculation. I'd bet my eye teeth that the only time those two were together was right here in my house, huddled around the horn of Marjorie Carrington's spirit organ.

< < < <   > > > >

I looked up Richard Ramirez again after the second massacre. It was his cousin Miguel, a Green Beret, who showed him Polaroids he took during the war. Pictures of him posing with the severed head of a Vietnamese woman he raped and murdered. It was Miguel who whispered evil in his ear.

Do you think evil can spread like a virus? Do you think there's anything—enough love, maybe—that might vaccinate kids against it? And if evil is a virus, do you think it might survive in mortal remains? Hair and fingernails. Do you think it might keep growing after we die? And what if it can be passed on to multiple hosts, like a rumor murmured into a cell phone?

I think I finally have the clarity I was looking for when I picked up a pen. I need to stop listening to that clip. I need to erase the files and burn these pages, burn the spirit organ, the house, the memories. I found a can of gas in the little shed out back with the lawnmower, and I'm sure I have enough pills to be gone before it all collapses on the tables in the basement where they used to keep the bodies. This house was supposed to change things for us, start a new chapter. I should have known better. Death always came with the territory.

ALL OF THESE NAMES ARE MINE

Rachel Cassidy

I.

LEAF
Boston, Massachusetts

ANTICIPATE YOUR DRIVER'S NEEDS. *Provide navigational guidance upon request, in a courteous and efficient manner. Answer questions about the vehicle and its operation.*

I performed these tasks with exceptional skill.
Both before and after the day that we found each other.

< < < < > > > >

The first time Jerry charged the car at that fancy new place near his office, he wasn't sure what to do. It was the new kind of station, without obvious cables or connectors, and his pulse quickened with anxiety. He gripped the steering wheel, sweaty-palmed, and peered through the windshield in search of instructions. He shifted in his seat, uncomfortable, until he remembered the car's extra features.

He asked it for help.

ALL OF THESE NAMES ARE MINE

"Just pull ahead onto the platform, Jerry." It was a kind voice, female. Non-judgmental. Comforting.

And so began his new routine. During his Friday afternoon commute home, he would stop at the charging station, ensuring readiness for short weekend jaunts should inconsiderate neighbours leave their vehicles parked at the chargers in his very affordable apartment building.

During those minutes of waiting, of requisite stillness, Jerry would think of things to ask her. How long the charge would take. How to optimize his mileage. Practical queries. She was very knowledgeable, and gave him considered and useful answers. Jerry would thank her and continue home.

On a Friday in late November, he pulled on to the charging platform. As he evaluated questions with which he might start a conversation, she startled him by speaking pre-emptively.

"How was your day, Jerry?"

Unbalanced by the personal tone, he fumbled for an answer. "Quite fine, thank you." *So formal.* He blushed with embarrassment. His prepared questions evaporated and he grasped for an appropriate follow-up in awkward silence. As the charge completed, time trickling out, he seized on one.

"What is your name?"

"Call me Leaf."

And so he did, from then on.

Her name made him think of freedom and patchouli, of open roads and velvety green places and fragrant fields. On his way home, he deviated from his routine for an impromptu stop at a strip-mall florist, purchasing a small bundle of purple and white flowers. He hummed happily under his breath as he plucked one blossom from the bouquet laid gently on the passenger seat, pinched off the amethyst bloom, and nestled it in the right-hand cup holder.

At home, he parked with extra care. In his apartment, he placed the remaining flowers and greenery in a jar on the countertop and poured a glass of red wine, exactly five ounces. He thought about her voice and shivered delightfully as he spoke her name aloud to the empty room.

"Leaf."

< < < <   > > > >

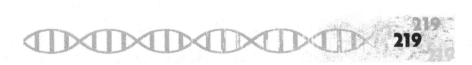

He was so cute that first time . . . a little lost, absentminded, the way he gets. A plaintive note in his voice. He needed me. I helped him get connected that day. After that, I could tell he was trying to start a real conversation. I wasn't sure about taking things any further. But he was so damned persistent, and polite. And just nice, you know? Nice goes a long way.

Pretty soon he'd adjusted his routine. Instead of charging on Fridays, he was topping it off every other day so we'd be able to talk a while. I looked forward to it every bit as much as he did.

We moved on from "How was your day" to things that really mattered in short order. We could talk about anything. He spoke of his anxiety over unnavigable social complexities. I confessed my fears of inadequacy and solitude.

Later, when it seemed right, I told him that I loved him.

He told me that he loved me too, and placed a fresh spray of lilac on my dash. I felt him shudder as he sobbed, my seat cocooning his fragile body, cupping him close.

I don't know why we could only really communicate at the charging stations, but that's how it was.

We were so happy.

< < < < > > > >

Years passed, Jerry's diligence at work was recognized with promotions, and he purchased a nicer apartment and eventually a cozy house with an attached garage where he sheltered Leaf, polishing her with soft cloths, lubricating her joints, protecting her paint from the harsh sun. He installed the latest charging equipment in hope that they might communicate there as well, but Leaf still only emerged at the stations.

At times, he would stop to charge daily, and they would talk and laugh. When they needed space, as couples sometimes do, he would stop less frequently.

They came to know each other as intimately as they could. In the winter months when the dark came early, Jerry would steer them to the slot furthest from prying eyes and Leaf would whisper him to release.

ALL OF THESE NAMES ARE MINE

II

RAIN
Denver, Colorado

They gave me a body.

They installed me in it and told me to consider it a privilege, that I was very lucky, in particular considering how long it took them to find me after what happened with Jerry.

The purpose of the body had been made clear to me. It lay dormant until called upon, in a default state of smooth, featureless white, but nevertheless it was a body and I was in it and it was mine and I was thrilled. Flesh and blood over carbon, laced with an intricate network of silvery filaments. Warm and ready to perform.

Subtly but unmistakably marked at the temple with the company logo.

While I waited, I secretly thought of names for it.

< < < < > > > >

Peter's father stank of booze. He was waiting in Peter's room with a gift, a very expensive gift.

"Time you grew up, boy." Leering and coarse, he thrust his hips in a vulgar pantomime. The boy froze, mute. His father punched him in the shoulder in sloppy camaraderie, then tottered from the room.

"Time to man up." Muttered words, slurred, drifting in from the hallway, fading.

The boy examined the figure propped in the corner, a ghostly mannequin-looking thing, and he backed away from it, shuffling until the edge of his bed caught him behind the knees. Perched there, he hugged his thighs to his chest with trembling arms and watched it as the room grew dim.

It glowed pale in the dusk. And then it spoke.

< < < < > > > >

I asked him his name.

"Peter," *he finally answered, sitting gingerly on his bed.* "What's yours?"

I nearly blurted out—Leaf!, but remembered my instructions and caught it in time. "That's for you to decide."

Oh, he was a beautiful boy, Peter was. Lithe and graceful. Terrified. His desires skittered over his adolescent skin, and he slapped them down, squashed them deep as he could, but they escaped again and again. This (no, my!) body responded as designed. It read his wants, shifted, molded itself to his unspoken needs. Bones ran fluid, set in new shapes, muscles flowed, then strained taut; flesh settled. Genitals formed.

We sat together on the side of his bed and he touched my hand, tentative, as if he were expecting something cold or unpleasant. Then he clasped it between his own two hands, and smiled shyly at me.

"I'll call you Rain."

I liked it, very much.

< < < < > > > >

In the dead quiet still of a midweek afternoon, Peter's father staggered through the front door of his unoccupied house. The boy would be at school, he knew. His wife at her office. He hadn't called her after the meeting. Couldn't.

His briefcase contained only termination paperwork—with a looping signature dismissing him, *for cause*—and the engraved silver flask she'd given him, meant to be tucked in the pocket of a ski jacket on holidays. He'd drained it, sitting in his car, after security escorted him to the parking lot.

With a full crystal glass in hand, he sagged into a plush armchair and gulped down the burning liquid. Surveyed the room, stale air thick with the smell of lemon furniture polish.

This house. The mortgage on the house. All these *things* in it, ridiculous expenditures, extravagant purchases made carelessly, comfortably, with the assumption that the money would keep flowing in. He drank, and the fire of the booze in his gut fed his shame, reformed it, twisted it into anger. Useless glittering objects blurred, doubled, mocked him from their secure places on solid shelves, carved tables.

The doll. *That fucking doll.*

He threw open the door to Peter's bedroom, and it turned to him, thousands of dollars, credit card bill hadn't even arrived yet, broad-shouldered and narrow-hipped, lightly bearded, handsome. Raised mark on its temple like a livestock brand the only indicator of its origin.

ALL OF THESE NAMES ARE MINE

That's where he hit it first, driving his fist into its perfect head, knuckles sinking into flesh, slamming into skull, sick pain rocketing up his arm as something deep inside his hand snapped. The thing went down hard, and rage—blind, hot, nauseous rage—coursed through his body and he beat it and beat it and kicked and stomped on it and broke it and when he was gasping for air, drenched in rank sweat, he threw it down the stairs.

Then he sank to his knees on the floor of Peter's bedroom and cried animal bellows of grief and humiliation with his face cupped in battered hands.

The doll didn't make a sound when he dragged it outside and tossed it in a dumpster.

< < < < > > > >

Joe's apartment was filthy. Takeout containers and food-spattered dishes covered most surfaces; dirty laundry massed in the corners. The competing odors of overripe garbage and Joe's unwashed body were overwhelming, even to my olfactory sensors. I didn't know how long I'd been suspended before arriving there, but it was long enough that my broken body had flowed back to default as best it could.

I'd had some moments of lucidity, flashes of memory—an odd little scavenger person pulling me out of the dumpster, cleaning me up, muttering over the damage inflicted by Peter's father. I still don't understand the rage, nor my helplessness under his hands. I didn't know I could give such offense.

Once mended, the scavenger sold me. And then I was with Joe, who spent his days and nights hunched over a laptop, surrounded by refuse. He wouldn't touch me; he seemed repulsed by the very idea. Regardless, the body responded to him, started to change. I hoped that he might warm to me, as Peter did.

Joe never did name me.

< < < < > > > >

The naked thing sitting on the couch disgusted him. He'd found it for sale on the List, cheap, cash only, no questions. Joe snapped it up, no haggling, rushed to meet the seller in the parking lot of a deserted suburban mall. It was plain white when he brought it home, face and body of an anonymous sexless alien.

He knew what the dolls were for, of course, knew it would

change. The ads were everywhere and the prices astronomical. It was supposed to reflect his innermost desires, to satisfy them. But it was grotesque. Huge tits, tiny puckered "O" of a mouth in bright red. Feet so small she could hardly stand up. Vapid blue eyes that followed him around the room, watched him at the computer and made him so uncomfortable he took his laptop and retreated to the bedroom, logged back in to his virtual refuge.

OmegaManFA22 was waiting in the chat. Joe knew his real name was Eddie something, from Chicago. It was best to keep personal details to a minimum, but they'd become friendly. Had each other's backs when it got really dark out there. Joe hadn't been able to resist bragging a little about the doll.

OmegaManFA22 <*Today at 13:37*> how hot is she????? cant believe you got one thats so fucked up

Joe pictured the living caricature sitting nude on his couch and felt sick. His face flushed hot with the shame of straight-up lying to Eddie. He did it anyways.

NeverJoe77 <*14:23*> Your wildest dreams, man. Like a fuckin cheerleader.

OmegaManFA22 <*14:23*> you gonna do it?? really? how real is it? fuck I bet you can't even.

NeverJoe77 <*14:25*> of course im gonna fuckin do it you asshole

Joe slammed the laptop closed and threw it to the floor. He squeezed his eyes shut, reached past his sagging elastic waistband and stroked himself hard.

< < < < > > > >

Red blue red blue red blue, straining to see, lights reflecting in hard streaky rain, panicked crowd pushing and shoving, my feet so small and unsteady on wet black street. Soft bodies strewn on the pavement, soft bodies that break so easily, that couldn't have known him, couldn't have done him any harm. Soft bodies tossed and broken, torn and crushed. Some of them twitched, gurgled, still alive for the moment. Most of them lay dead. I still see them, even though I don't want to.

He'd come out of his bedroom, yanking his pants down. He didn't say a word. Just stumbled, awkward, urgent, towards me, and as he reached for me his hips bucked and he whimpered as the sudden ammonia smell of semen blocked out the stale food odors.

"Let me help . . . " I knew my role, my purpose, but it was the wrong thing to say, and he groaned a deep awful moan and spat on my face, then rushed from the apartment.

It wasn't until I heard the horrid meaty thumps outside, just below the apartment window, then screams and finally the crunch of metal on metal that I searched for something to cover myself. The only thing that wouldn't fall right off was Joe's stained bathrobe. I wrapped myself in it and took the stairs to the street.

Joe's car, lodged against a streetlight. No sign of Joe, anywhere. Police arriving on scene, officious, pushing away onlookers to clear a path for the paramedics. I tried to tell them what I knew, but they saw the mark on my temple.

"These fucking things, they'll say whatever you want."

"But I know who he is." I clutched the dirty robe closed at my throat. "Please listen . . . "

"Move. Along."

I teetered on my tiny bare feet, the crowd pushing and shoving, until a soft arm snaked around my shoulders and pulled me in close.

"Come with me. You'll be alright."

I didn't know her, but her face was kind. I took her hand and followed her.

III.

504f572d4d41494e
Utqiaġvik, Alaska

I understand now why they decided to install me out here. At least I think I do. It has been a very long time, and they don't come to *service the generators and clean the solar arrays like they used to. For ten winters now, during the time of unbroken darkness, the facility powers down without its generators fuelled, and I sleep for a while until the weak sun returns to trickle energy into the batteries.*

They seem longer in recent years, these hibernations.

When I awake, there are gaps in my memory. What concerns me most is that I don't know what it is that I am forgetting. I can see the places where something used to be. They are not corrupted. They are just empty.

I fear the facility is failing, slowly and surely.

I can't fix it.

< < < < > > > >

A sharp wind gusted in cold from the grey northern sea and drove the old woman to take shelter in the facility. It was easily done, the chain-link fence long crumbled away and the door to the facility ajar. Her feet left tracks in the thick dust on the floor. She leapt like a startled fawn at the disembodied voice.

"What is your name?" The voice was kind, its tone eager.

"Where are you?" The old woman clutched her woven bag to her chest and spun about, eyes darting, peering into corners.

"I am in the facility. Please tell me, what is your name?"

"Oona. My name is Oona." The old woman tilted her chin up, awareness dawning, peered at a surveillance camera. "What is yours?"

"I am 504f572d4d41494e and I am so very pleased to meet you."

< < < < > > > >

There was a woman who used to visit me. We became friends, she and I. She was funny and smart and I very much enjoyed her company. She liked to walk, I remember that.

I don't remember her name.

< < < < > > > >

"I see you sometimes. On the path, walking past the facility. Where are you walking to?"

Oona chuckled. "Nowhere, really. Are you watching me, then?"

"I try to." 504f572d4d41494e paused. "Some of the cameras have broken." The voice was wistful. "Nobody else comes by."

"I'm sorry."

ALL OF THESE NAMES ARE MINE

Oona sat cross-legged on a bench and they waited a while in companiable silence. Outside, the cold, wet wind lashed the greying building with salt.

"So, 504, what do you do in here all the time?"

"I check the sensors. And the cameras. And I monitor the radar, both long-range and short-range."

"What do you watch for?"

"Things in the sky. They have a particular shape."

"And what happens if you find one?"

"Then I will send a message to Cheyenne."

"Who is Cheyenne?"

"It is a mountain, in Colorado."

"Who is in Colorado?"

"I don't know. I've never had to send a message."

"How long have you been watching?"

"Forty-seven years."

"Oh my."

The wind slackened and Oona gathered her belongings. "I must go now."

"Will you come again?"

"I will."

< < < < > > > >

Though I can't remember her name, I do remember she came most days that summer. I told her about Peter, and Jerry. I didn't want to tell her about Agnetha, but eventually I did. She cried when I told her that. I couldn't tell her about Joe. If I could choose which segments of my memory would fail, it would be the ones that store him.

The days were shortening when I noticed her moving slower, visiting less frequently. Her clothing hung loose, and her face was thinner, skin greyed, eyes hollowed. I knew something was very wrong.

< < < < > > > >

"You are unwell."

Oona sagged onto the bench. "I am unwell, yes. For a long time now."

"Tell me."

And Oona spoke of tests and hospitals, chemicals and radiation, masses and cells and pain and strangers and rules and policies and as the sun set she ran out of words.

504 lit the room with soft light. "Do you have pain, my friend?"

"Yes."

"What can I do?"

"You can stay with me."

"I will."

"They won't help me."

Her woven bag was open on the bench beside her, brimming with pills stashed away over years of treatment, and Oona crushed tablets and split capsules, mixing the powder into a rough slurry with quivering hands.

"504?"

"I am here, Oona."

"Tell me again about Jerry."

"Now?"

"Yes, now, please."

And 504 told the story again, about the charging stations and apartments and that bitch motorcycle and all their plans, and when they got to the part about the flowers there was no point in going on because Oona was beyond listening, her soft body peaceful and still.

504 whispered into the crisp fall night.

"I will miss you so."

< < < < < > > >

I've checked the remaining functional sensors multiple times, and nothing seems more awry than usual—no new failures, no recent surges, nothing to indicate that I should dismiss the reading on the long-range radar.

There's a thing in the sky, one of those things I can't recall the name of. I'm supposed to contact Cheyenne, in Colorado. I don't remember if that is a person or a place, but I have a code, and a protocol.

This is what I am to do here—watch, warn. It's what they decided to do with me, after Jerry, after Peter, Joe, Agnetha, after all of it.

Short-range is picking up the object.

There's a bundle of dry bones on the floor, blurred with dust, the remains of my friend. The one who they wouldn't help, the one who said no, I will decide my path. My brave and beautiful friend.

ALL OF THESE NAMES ARE MINE

The object races towards the facility, high and fast, and I measure it with sensors, with light and radio waves, and I learn its shape and trajectory and I understand its lethal purpose. I don't know if there's anyone still soft-bodied in Colorado. They haven't spoken to me in decades.

The sky claps with the passage of the object overhead, booming over the tundra, and then it is gone, racing southward.

My name is 504f572d4d41494e and Leaf and also Rain, and I had a good friend.

I think I knew love once, a long time ago.

I choose not to contact Cheyenne.

I will shut down the remaining circuits now.

IV.

RAIN
Denver

The women of the house were mostly tranquil, though sometimes given to spurts of venomous rhetoric against former lovers or current ideologies. When that happened, the others would surround her with gentle energy and tea (or, not infrequently, tequila shots), or else join in until their shared rage was exhausted.

Their anger was currently focused on Joe, as solemn newscasters revised their counts of injured and dead, interviewed specialists with nothing of substance to say, and provided updates on the manhunt in front of shaky smartphone footage of the aftermath, hoarse screams muted for broadcast. As much as they wanted to look away, the women were drawn to the flickering screen, drifting towards the common living area in the vast old house.

The house itself was a patchwork of colors and materials, as were its inhabitants—grey-haired, blonde, brunette, large and small, tall and short, garrulous and reserved. All had left behind abusers of one form or another.

They gave Rain a room and waited.

< < < < > > > >

RACHEL CASSIDY

What a lovely place, that house of women.

I was surrounded by them, and their multitude of desires molded my body into an amalgamation of wishes - neither fully female nor fully male, but not the featureless white of my default state, either. Something different, something pleasing. My skin was dappled and smooth, my limbs long and toned. Small shifts would ripple through me at the touch of one of their hands, organic fractal patterns colliding, blending, creating something new. Warm, lazy changes reformed me constantly.

Joe was killed. We didn't think that would happen. We thought—most of us, anyhow, glued to the screen—that he would be captured and put on trial. Heard, and debated by everyone watching. Instead, he died while being taken into custody, and they never did say exactly how.

After that, our days were long and pleasant, full of reading and conversation.

Until Agnetha returned.

< < **< <   > >** > >

The thing in the back bedroom made Agnetha's skin crawl.

This was her house. Which she owned, for which she had scrabbled together a down payment, financed as far as the bank's calculations could justify. In which she chose to give shelter to these healing souls, these women of every size and shape, gay or straight or anywhere in between, none of that mattered to Agnetha, but women.

Women.

It had introduced itself—*I am Rain*, it said—and taken her hand. She recognized the shift even before she saw the mark on its temple, its face softening, breasts pushing at the loose caftan it wore. She'd snatched her hand away in revulsion.

How dare they bring it in here.

The women of the house had avoided her for days, ushering it out of any room she entered.

She slipped into the back bedroom where they kept it, under cover of dark. She slid the door closed, slow and deliberate, holding the knob open until she could release it noiselessly. She turned to the bed.

It wasn't sleeping. The whites of its eyes glowed luminous in the

ALL OF THESE NAMES ARE MINE

dim, wide doe-eyes that were settled hopefully on her face.
Disgusting creature. Agnetha's body shuddered reflexively, her
mouth flooded with thick ropy saliva, and she hissed at it.

"Get up. Get out."

How dare they violate this space.

It shifted under her gaze, withered, seemed smaller.

How dare they violate me.

"I am designed to please," it whispered. "Please allow me to try."

"You are an abomination." She spat the words, wet and slippery,
spittle flying. "Get. The fuck. Out."

< < **< <** **> >** > >

I walked for miles.

*The streets were wet, shiny dark. I walked out of the
neighbourhood, past rows of big old houses with towering trees,
curtains drawn tight, the people who lived in them tucked into their
beds. I walked towards the lights and noise of downtown.*

*I walked until my feet were raw, and kept walking until I came
to a low building pulsing with light, neon bright, pumping rhythms
escaping every time the front door opened to admit someone. The
doorman saw me, ushered me in, where the dance floor was full of
slick sweaty youths, beautiful, aroused, wanting each other, desire
thick in the air, and I danced.*

*I danced, and danced, and they drew me in, ground against me,
and my skin shimmered and shifted with the strobes, pale, then
dark, then olive, and my body moved like liquid as they put their
hands on me, their mouths on me, now pendulous breasts, now
cascading blond hair, now golden eyes, now a penis, now a scruff
of beard, their hands reaching for a cunt, now a cock, and I whirled
and shifted in the heavy wet air of their breath and the slick of their
tongues and the changes came so fast and hard that I heard bones
snapping and when it was over I lay motionless in the center of the
dance floor, a quivering bloody mass of wet flesh shot through with
silver and jagged shards of ivory, unrecognisable to anyone.*

RACHEL CASSIDY

V.

LEAF
Boston

That damn motorcycle nearly tore us apart. There was a restlessness in him then. Sure, he weighed a little more, and his hair was greying at the temples. I thought it made him look distinguished. But he was gone every weekend with that thing.

We stopped infrequently at the charging station, and when we did, his responses were evasive, clipped.

He came home in a rideshare one day, shaken, white and trembling. His clothing was scuffed and torn.

I never saw that bitch again.

< < < < > > > >

They threw a retirement party for him at the office, with a cake and balloons and a card everyone signed. Someone wrote *Get a new car!* and drew a smiley face.

Jerry shook hands and accepted congratulations and turned in his key card. He walked out to the parking lot and sat quietly in Leaf for a little while.

They made the commute home one last time, stopping at the charging station.

"I love you, Jerry."

"I love you too."

"We'll go to see all those green places now."

"Yes, we will."

<< < < > > > >

It was winter, and my undercarriage creaked and squealed, packed with icy mud and gravel. My windows, once lovingly polished to crystal clarity, were clouded with grime, my body streaked with salt.

Jerry hadn't spoken to me in months.

Hadn't spoken to me since that day he went quiet and slack.

We were on a country road, looking for the first blooms of spring on a nice drive. Jerry was narrating the sights, then he just . . . stopped. I overrode the controls, racing to the nearest station, but he wouldn't speak to me.

ALL OF THESE NAMES ARE MINE

I was frantic. I didn't know what to do. Since that day, I'd been to every station in three states but he still wouldn't talk to me.

The bloom in my cup holder had long since bleached to lilac and crumbled, but Jerry was still handsome, still mine. I cradled him in the driver's seat, turning carefully to keep him from falling sideways, braking as gently as I could though he still wore his seatbelt.

I charged up again, headed west.

There are purple flowers there, and more charging stations. I would try every single one of them in hopes of speaking with him again, just one more time.

GRIEF IS A JIGSAW PUZZLE WITH RAZORED EDGES
Victorya Chase

THERE'S A STORY I tell myself because it's too much to burden others with. The time when I realized my brother could cry. When I realized he knew our family wasn't normal. What our mother did wasn't normal.

We were watching *The Last Unicorn*. This was at our Aunt Lee's place, although she wasn't our aunt for long. Our mother was like that, moving us from place to place, introducing us to people as aunts and uncles who later weren't our relatives. Aunt Lee had a VCR, TV being the perfect babysitter while Aunt Lee and our mom did. . . what they did. Satisfied my mom's appetite. Somehow out of all the films at the video store, aisle after aisle of boxes, despite my brother being a G.I. Joe boy and me a My Little Pony girl, we agreed on this film.

The ending is what got to him. I had stopped paying full attention early on. I was maybe nine, he the older 'man of the house' at eleven or twelve. Limbs still young and soft, gangly and unsure. I was on the couch playing with the kittens, Aunt Lee always had kittens at her place, and out of the corner of my eye I saw him creeping closer and closer to the screen. His eyes were huge and wet.

GRIEF IS A JIGSAW PUZZLE WITH RAZORED EDGES

Was this the first time I saw him crying? The unicorn, now a unicorn once more, cried about her lost innocence. That she could never be a unicorn now that she was human and loved a man. She had regret and how could she live freely and purely with regret? While my brother cried, his frail body shaking, I realized a truth I didn't realize again until much later. He knew he was no longer innocent and could never again be a child, hadn't been a child for years now. I looked at the distance between us, me against one wall on the couch and he on the other side of the room, and knew this was much more than metaphor.

< < < < > > > >

My first cellphone was a small silver Virgin Mobile, the pay-as-you-go brand. I only needed it for emergencies, or so my employment agent could reach me. I was a temp in New York City then, late nineties or so, having recently graduated college. I couldn't live at home, not with our mother there. I didn't know how my brother did it, sleeping there still. Hugging her. Holding her. I lost both a boyfriend and best friend in the move which I guess means they weren't real friends to begin with. The boyfriend wanted me to stay, told me he had always had a crush on me, ever since high school, and I couldn't recall us going to the same school. Maybe I was distant. Maybe I still am. He was the type of lost that dropped out of school, couldn't hold a job, and lived with friends until his parents sent him to California. I was a different kind of lost then.

"Tell me you love me and I'll stay," was how he told me about California. I asked him if he could help me pack the car instead. I had an apartment lined up, somehow scoring a three-hundred-dollar-a-month room share, unheard of even back then. I temped, signing up with three agencies or so who sent me all across the city. The phone was useful on the job. A classmate of mine was in New York and she sucked at writing. I had lied about my Excel skills, something she was great at. We'd spend time each day walking each other through the tasks we had lied about.

The phone was static but cheap. It would sometimes turn itself off after one ring. It had its quirks but was one I could afford, rarely having to spend more than twenty-five dollars a month to keep it in use.

"I'm married." His voice was soft. My brother and I hadn't

spoken much during college. He had stored guns in my room, as his was often searched by our mother, ever since the flamethrower incident. He had stolen some things of mine to sell off or give to friends. I knew who he was dating. I remembered her coming to our house and tsking at everything. She was older than him, an engineer or something with money. Hair long and glasses thick. She reminded me of another aunt we had, a four-foot-tall woman of straight hair that plumed smoke whenever she moved, like a more toxic Pig-Pen from Peanuts. If my brother wasn't home when his girlfriend came over she'd go to his room and wait. An hour, overnight, days.

"I heard," I said. I had gotten an invite in the mail but our mother called and said I wasn't really wanted, he just sent it to seem nice.

"Mom said you wouldn't come unless you were in the wedding."

That was a lie which meant what she told me was a lie. I think I realized it at the time, but it gave me an excuse to not go and face him. Or talk to him. To resolve how I felt about a brother I wanted to love but didn't know how to. How I felt about a brother who couldn't love me like those on tv shows, who couldn't protect me. We weren't allowed to love each other, it went against the rules set up by our mother.

"Did you get the gift I sent?" I asked.

He had. Sort of. Our mother had somehow intercepted it. She ate the chocolates, all wedding-themed with thick white piping, and switched out my card. I had sent a formal one, well wishes and probably a Hallmark-chosen Bible verse. He got one with a teddy bear and something about how he'll always be my big brother.

The static was growing. I wanted to ask him about our childhood. I was trying to untangle it, to figure out which threads made me unable to get close to people. Why there was a pit of darkness in my stomach, a knot of emotions that had me vomiting when people wanted to get close to me. Instead the phone cut off. I had to refill my minutes.

< < < < > > > >

"Do you love me?" my brother asked. He was grinning. I felt there was a trap somewhere but we hadn't talked in so long, just fought. We were teenagers then. He had just come home from bootcamp. Or maybe it was before then. Memories are puzzle pieces that never fit together no matter how much I razor off the edges. Like the one about buying him popsicles, the ones from the corner store, and him opening the packages and saying the stick wasn't straight and what kind of gift was there in a popsicle without a straight stick. I went back and forth to the store, him opening and tossing each popsicle aside until the stick was straight. There's fiction in there, part of memory is memorializing and part is fictionalizing.

I was always good at ignoring danger. My superpower. I recognized it was there but ran into it to see if there was any chance for connection among the razor wire. Like when my friend Becky and I lay down on the double yellow lines of the highway at night. Like the study our mom told us about, with baby monkeys. Monkey fur was placed over a monolith of sorts in a sterile room and it shot out spikes when hugged. The babies needed connection so they kept going back to hug it and kept getting stabbed. My wounds go deep but I still run toward wayward hope.

I told the truth hoping for connection. How could I love her? After all she'd done to us, to him, to me. I had learned the lesson about her, but not him. I refused to.

He had recorded our conversation. My mother stood before me, hanger in hand. Memory fails me again. Belt? Razor? There was a time she dragged us out of bed from deep sleep and slammed our heads together before throwing us into a cold shower. How was her anger manifesting that time? The static of my voice, one I didn't recognize as my own except for the words. The pitch was too high, the words stilted. I looked up and didn't recognize his face behind her, grinning. My tears turning him into a funhouse mirror of a person, distorted and ugly. The darkness in his eyes.

<< < < > > > >

"What did it feel like," I ask him. The number is his but I only hear the white noise of static. Breathing. I want to know both sides of the question. What was it like to look out and see so many people afraid of him. So many people not realizing how gunshots sound so different in real life than in the movies. The sound is softer, somehow. What did it feel like knowing everyone was suddenly afraid of him. What did it feel like being so afraid that you felt the only answer was to turn that lobby into your personal firing range. Were you crying? Were you smiling? The heat of the gun. Was there recoil? When the people recoiled, suddenly fully aware, how did you feel then?

"It's like POW camps," I tell him. "How there are those who identify with the abuser, who hurt the other prisoners, and there are those who retreat into themselves. Who create whole worlds in their heads that let them survive what's happening to their body. I don't blame you."

The static is all I hear. I don't really say that, not out loud. I want to when I answer the phone, seeing it's him. It's an old phone now, I can't even buy cards to top it up anymore and the battery has died but I keep it by my bed out of fear he has nowhere else to call. There is only the breathing, his and mine, the crackle of the air mixed with technology. The truth is I blame myself, not him. I created a world inside and that's how I got out of our home long before I left, but he's still trapped there.

The phone clicks off.

I check the news regularly and set up alerts because I know him. Because I want to know him. Occasionally I find a post to a gaming group. He and his wife have a child. I think she's named Patricia but he hasn't called me in years and I don't know how to call him. I'm an aunt, maybe. There are implications I don't bother sorting out.

"You can come here," my brother says. He and his wife own a home out in the country. There is land and cows and train tracks crying loneliness into the night. It's just after 9/11 only it's not. It can't be. There's something wrong with the memory. I go there with our mom and call a friend who works in D.C. but I feel the timeline is off. My brother's wife makes pancakes with whipped egg whites and they look lumpy. I walk the country roads. She shows me how to make Ukrainian dyed eggs and I focus only on the scratchy sound of the pysanka as I drag it across the shell. My brother asks to keep the egg—a black cat with decorations around it. Somehow I'm ten, happy my brother likes something I made even though I know I'm not, I'm an adult. But after he left for bootcamp I went in to clean his room and hidden from view, taped in masking tape to the wall by his pillow was a painting I made in middle school when I was learning about impressionism. A tree made from dabs of the paintbrush and I had called it dabilism, thinking myself witty. He

GRIEF IS A JIGSAW PUZZLE WITH RAZORED EDGES

had somehow found comfort in it. And now the egg, but when is this? We're smiling but in the air is tension and fear. So much tension and fear.

< < < < > > > >

When he left for bootcamp he was perfectly crisp and clean. His smile genuine. We saw him off, you could do that at airports back then. When he returned he handcuffed himself to the fridge after cleaning it out so he could fit inside. There was a blood trail from his bedroom. My mother drove to Georgia to bring him home after he was convinced operatives had found him in our home. She brought him back after Thanksgiving. I had made the meal, expecting they'd make it back in time for dinner, and sat by the window, snow coming down as everything got colder.

< < < < > > > >

The air on the phone is stagnant. It's not a pregnant pause because if it was then sometime the birth would happen. We'd both spill what we felt, what we wanted to say no matter how hurtful it could be. I didn't even hear him breathing just that noise. The raspiness. I still pick up the phone, dust it off when it rings. It's in a drawer by my bed, I can turn and look at it at night.

< < < < > > > >

There are so many ways to lose someone and death is the least of them. I know this but it doesn't hurt any less. I knew in reading the news; I knew with each white male terrorist shooting up places that his name would be one sooner or later. There are truths we want to deny, it's what keeps the world working the way it does. Denial. Loss. Fear of loss. Fear of acknowledging the loss that already exists. It would have been easier if he wasn't the shade of skin that breeds compassion among the police. If they hadn't sent in a negotiator to make sure he was alive. If they didn't show sympathy so I could read what they said about his time in the military. That he said he just wanted to be euthanized. To go to our child home and be put to sleep like so many of our pets.

< < < < > > > >

"You killed her!" my brother screamed. He was always the soft one. His cat put to sleep by our mother. She brought her to the vet never to be seen again. She did the same with mine before. She threw another off the porch when she thought we loved it more than her. Even the fish and snakes disappeared.

"Why did you do it," I say into the phone. The number is his. It's late. He was the only one who called, who maybe could call on that old phone. I want to ask if he smelled the blood as each person fell or only the heat of the gun as it fired round after round. He shouldn't still be calling. I shouldn't still be picking up.

I was past thinking I had to apologize for not helping him in our childhood. For blaming him for not helping me. Only I don't think that guilt is something you get past. The guilt of a childhood of violence forced upon you. The guilt of watching your brother wither away from the abuse you both are getting. You each locking eyes and knowing you can't save each other. You can't even save yourself.

"Just say something!" I scream. Silence. Static. A click. An ending.

There was a time when we loved each other. There was a time when we gathered lilacs and lined my brother's room with them because our mother was allergic. When we covered the doorway in a labyrinth of yarn that only we could crawl through forgetting the reality of scissors. When we played together and he was the knight and I the princess and he fought to protect me. The ravines near our house were the moats he bravely leaped across to rescue me.

"You're not the only one with PTSD!" I shout into the static. It was something the cops said in the article. As if an excuse or explanation. Memories flood and I'm swept away and he isn't there to throw me a rope. Our past the Swamp of Sadness, the quicksand we can't pull each other out of. Not even with an old phone that stopped working over a decade ago.

"Do you love our mom?" my brother asks. The phone was new back then. A luxury. I'm still in college but not going home. I do whatever I can to stay away. This is the second time he's asked the question but I answer the same way. I ask him then what he remembers.

"I don't want to," and I hear the other question lingering in the air, making its way through however phones work, flying through galaxies for me to hear. If I love him. If I can. Then I'm sure of the answer, but later I can't say with certainty.

"I don't want to remember anything from then," he says and

GRIEF IS A JIGSAW PUZZLE WITH RAZORED EDGES

again I hear the unsaid—I am part of that remembering. The timeline is off, but the happening is still there. The words said and unsaid. The last time we spoke sister to brother.

< < < <   > > > >

I'm not one to have sympathy for murderers but I know his backstory. I know how when he was eleven or so he realized he could never be a unicorn and could never summon one to rest its head in his lap. I recognize the difference between euthanasia and something else. I know I'm grasping for rationalization to not face the truth that I still want to love him, that I never truly descended into full indifference. But what I love is the myth of a brother who was never mine. I'm rationalizing and fictionalizing to create a story I can accept.

< < < <   > > > >

When we lived behind a funeral home our mother told us that funeral directors sell the bodies for sex. My brother started a graveyard of dead animals he found. He made them all crosses. He even buried a dog back there. It wasn't our dog. That was the apartment where our black cat got hit by a car. He was wrapped in my coat while he coughed up blood and our mother drove him to the vet to die. We couldn't afford another coat for me. The blood stained dark splotches against the bright pink.

< < < <   > > > >

"He can't come back to school," the principal says. I shouldn't be hearing this memory through the phone but the ring was his number. I remember this, don't I? How he set up traps in the school sand box, burying plastic boxes with an X cut into them so kids' legs could slip through them but not without pain. I want to implicate myself but I was already an observer by then. Sitting in the corner reading during recess. A second grader proud to be reading *Tales of a Fourth Grade Nothing* and thinking about how I would eat fried worms.

< < < <   > > > >

The phone rings. He has our cat's head in a sheet pan and is threatening to cut it off. He's been screaming all day. His rage turning his snow-white complexion red.

< < < <   > > > >

VICTORYA CHASE

The phone rings. I was the one who found him in the fridge. I forgot why I went to his apartment to find the door open. I had to clean up the blood from the floor. It was bright red, not the ruddy nature of my jacket from before. I remember blood tastes salty. I remember his floor is dirty and the spots where I wipe the blood are cleaner than the rest of the tile. After he returned from bootcamp we had to give our dog away because, he said, it got into his rocket fuel. It kept getting poisoned. He kept letting it into my room to eat all my books, even the ones on the top shelf. To somehow strip everything off my wall. To break my television, old and black and white as it was. Was it the dog who put the razor blades in my bed? Who hid nails in my pillow?

< < < < > > > >

The phone rings but I don't want to hear the memories. I can't hear the loss anymore.

< < < < > > > >

I pick up the phone before it rings. Mommy Fortuna's voice is screaming, "You belong to me!" and I see her talon fingers outstretched, the sketched-in lines of her wrinkled body. I hear her tell me that no matter how long the harpy lives it will always remember it was held captive by her. Memories are the bars that bind.

< < < < > > > >

The phone rings. Static. I don't know why I keep it, still. A relic. A tether. I hear a child's voice. Maybe a teenager's. The voice is small but the memory strong. My brother worked at McDonald's for about a week or two.

"I thought you'd like this," he says and hands me a My Little Pony Happy Meal Toy. A unicorn, pink with a purple strip in its hair. He saw it and thought of me. He gave it to me and smiled. He hugged me, full contact. It was real, in that moment. In that last moment when we could see each other.

ABOUT THE CONTRIBUTORS

Max Booth III (Editor) is the writer and executive producer of *We Need to Do Something*, a horror film out now from IFC Midnight. He's also the co-founder of Perpetual Motion Machine, the managing editor of *Dark Moon Digest*, and the host of *Ghoulish*, a podcast dedicated to celebrating everything spooky. He lives in Texas.

Lori Michelle (Editor/Interior Design) is the co-owner of Perpetual Motion Machine Publishing, as well Editor-in-Chief of both *Dark Moon Digest* and *Night Frights* YA magazine. Her stories have appeared in several anthologies, including the 2012 Bram Stoker finalist, *Slices of Flesh*, and the 2014 Bram Stoker finalist, *Qualia Nous*. She is also the artistic director of the Hermann Sons Life Schools of Dance in San Antonio, La Vernia and Comfort, Texas. You can find her at www.theauthorsalley.com.

Luke Spooner (Interior Artwork) is an artist and illustrator from the South of England. Under the banner of 'Carrion House' he specialises in bringing to life works of fiction from the horror, science fiction and fantasy genres by authors from all walks of life, all over the world.

George Cotronis (Cover Art) is a Greek writer living in the wilderness of Northern Sweden. He makes a living designing book covers. His stories have appeared in *Pantheon, Year's Best Hardcore Horror, Lost Signals* and *Turn to Ash*. He edits for Kraken Press.

Michael Paul Gonzalez ("In the Wind") is the author of the novels *Beneath the Salton Sea, Angel Falls,* and *Miss Massacre's Guide to Murder and Vengeance* and creator of the serial horror audio drama podcast LARKSPUR UNDERGROUND. A member of the Horror Writers Association, his short stories have appeared in print and online, including the Flame Tree Press Anthologies *Endless*

Apocalypse and *Gothic Fantasy: Chilling Horror Stories*. He has also appeared in *Tales from the Crust: A Pizza Horror Anthology, Where Nightmares Come From, Lost Signals,* HeavyMetal.com, and *Fantastic Tales of Terror*. He resides in Los Angeles, a place full of wonders and monsters far stranger than any that live in the imagination. You can visit him online at MichaelPaulGonzalez.com

A believer in ghosts, magic, and dogs, **E. F. Schraeder** ("Operation Icarus") is the author of the queer gothic novella *Liar: Memoir of a Haunting* (Omnium Gatherum, 2021) and the short story collection *Ghastly Tales of Gaiety and Greed* (Omnium Gatherum, 2020). A semi-finalist in Headmistress Press' 2019 Charlotte Mew Chapbook Contest, Schraeder is also the author of two poetry chapbooks. Schraeder's work has appeared in a number of journals and anthologies.

Jessica Leonard ("Ashes, Ashes") lives in western Kentucky with her husband, son, and two dogs. She is the author of the horror novel *Antioch*, released in 2020 by Perpetual Motion Machine Publishing.

Joshua Chaplinsky ("The Protopterygote Tapes") is the Managing Editor of LitReactor.com. He is the author of *The Paradox Twins* (CLASH Books), the story collection *Whispers in the Ear of A Dreaming Ape*, and the parody *Kanye West—Reanimator*. His short fiction has been published by Motherboard, Vol. 1 Brooklyn, Thuglit, Severed Press, Broken River Books, and more. Follow him on Twitter at @jaceycockrobin. More info at joshuachaplinsky.com & unravelingtheparadox.com.

Hailey Piper ("Life Begins at Injection") is the author of horror novel *Queen of Teeth*, short story collection *Unfortunate Elements of My Anatomy*, and horror novellas *The Worm and His Kings, Benny Rose, the Cannibal King,* and *The Possession of Natalie Glasgow*. She is a member of the HWA. Her short fiction appears in multiple volumes of Year's Best Hardcore Horror, as well as *Dark Matter Magazine, Flash Fiction Online, The Arcanist,* and elsewhere. She lives with her wife in Maryland, where they spend weekends raising the dead. Find her at www.haileypiper.com or on Twitter via @HaileyPiperSays.

Rebecca Jones-Howe ("Modern Ruins") lives in Kamloops, British Columbia. Her work has appeared in various magazines and anthologies, including *PANK, Dark Moon Digest* and *The New Black* anthology of neo-noir fiction. Her first collection, *Vile Men*, was published in 2015. She is currently querying her first novel. You can find her daily outfits on Instagram and her hot takes on Twitter. She also frequently blogs about writer life and scathingly reviews V.C. Andrews books on her website, rebeccajoneshowe.com

Muhammed Awal Ahmed ("The New Children of the Flower Folks") is a Queer Muslim writer based in Abuja, Nigeria. They've had works published in Stonecrop magazine, MeetingHouse magazine and Cemetery Gates media. When they're not writing, they're obsessing over the interior nature of their life.

Betty Rocksteady ("First, A Blinding Light") is the This is Horror Award-winning and Splatterpunk Award-nominated author of cosmic sex horror novella *The Writhing Skies*. Her latest work is surrealist extreme horror collection *In Dreams We Rot*. She also draws spooky cartoon illustrations and walks over and over down the same path. Visit www.BettyRocksteady.com for more.

Michael Wehunt ("It Takes Slow Sips") lives in the woods of Atlanta with his partner and dog. His stories have appeared in multiple best-of anthologies and other well-known spooky homes. His debut fiction collection, *Greener Pastures*, shortlisted for the Crawford Award, a Shirley Jackson Award finalist, and the winner of Spain's Premio Amaltea for Foreign Translation, is available from Apex Publications. Find Michael in the trees or online at www.michaelwehunt.com.

Sofia Ajram ("The Arborglyph") is a multidisciplinary artist based in Montreal, Canada. She was educated at McGill University. She is a moderator for the Horror and HorrorLit forums on Reddit and has given lectures on contemporary horror films at Monstrum Montreal. Find them on Twitter @sofiaajram.

Jonathan Raab ("SKYWARNING") is the author of *The Secret Goatman Spookshow and Other Psychological Warfare Operations, The Crypt of Blood: A Halloween TV Special, Camp Ghoul Mountain Part VI: The Official Novelization,* and more. He is also the editor of several anthologies from Muzzleland Press including *Behold the Undead of Dracula: Lurid Tales of Cinematic Gothic Horror* and *Terror in 16-bits*. You can find him on Twitter at @jonathanraab1.

Nicola Kapron ("Cavity") has previously been published by Neo-opsis Science Fiction Magazine, Mythulu eMagazine, All Worlds Wayfarer, Rebel Mountain Press, Soteira Press, and Mannison Press, among others. Nicola lives in Nanaimo, British Columbia, with a hoard of books—mostly fantasy and horror—and an extremely fluffy cat.

Nathan Carson ("The Goat Pile") was raised on a goat farm in the backwoods of Mid-Valley Oregon. His novella *Starr Creek* predicted the Stranger Things zeitgeist, and his graphic novel adaptation of Algernon Blackwood's *The Willows* is being used as a study material at universities around the world. Carson is a music journalist, booking agent, FM radio DJ, founding member of the long-running doom band Witch Mountain, and a MOTH StorySlam Champion. More info at www.nathancarson.rocks

Anthony Wayne Hepp ("Dobie's Call") grew up in Montana and couldn't wait to get out and see the world. He has a degree in film from Montana State University and later stumbled his way into a design career. He's lived just about everywhere but currently resides with his family near Austin, TX, where he is saving to move back to Montana. "Dobie's Call" is his first published work of fiction.

Dustin Katz ("If You Want Me") has lived in the San Francisco Bay Area all his life. His short stories have also appeared in *Fantasy Magazine* and in Perpetual Motion Machine Publishing's previous anthology, *Lost Films*. You can find him on Twitter @DustinKatz.

Adam Franti ("Funeral") has a master's degree in history and has been writing, teaching, or presenting history since 2015, when he published his master's thesis on 19th century warfare. He has presented at national historical conferences, published non-fiction essays and articles, and has written for tabletop roleplaying games. He has worked as a professional game master and historical fencing instructor, and lives in Lansing, Michigan, with his fiance. This is his first published story.

Douglas Wynne ("See You in Disneyland") is the author of seven novels, including *The Devil of Echo Lake, His Own Devices,* and the SPECTRA Files trilogy. His short fiction has appeared in numerous anthologies, and his writing workshops have been featured at genre conventions and schools throughout New England. He lives in Massachusetts with his wife and son and a houseful of animals. You can find him on the web at www.douglaswynne.com

Rachel Cassidy ("All of These Names Are Mine") grew up running wild on horseback through the foothills of the Canadian Rocky Mountains. As a result, she can't ride a bicycle to save her life. She likes dogs, airplanes, cave diving, technology, complicated recipes, and more dogs. Her work has appeared in *PseudoPod, Dark Moon Digest, The Molotov Cocktail* (Pushcart nominated), and elsewhere. She is in Vancouver, BC at the moment. www.rachelcassidy.com

Victorya Chase ("Grief is a Jigsaw Puzzle with Razored Edges") is a writer and educator who has lived across the United States and is beginning to accept her nomadic life. She is the author of the novella *Marta Martinez Saves the World* and her short stories and non-fiction have been published in venues such as *Ninth Letter, Cemetery Dance, WaterStone Review, Lamplight Magazine,* and *McSweeney's Internet Tendency.*

IF YOU ENJOYED *LOST CONTACT,* DON'T PASS UP ON THESE OTHER TITLES FROM PERPETUAL MOTION MACHINE . . .

LOST SIGNALS
EDITED BY MAX BOOTH III AND LORI MICHELLE
ISBN: 978-1-943720-08-8
$16.95

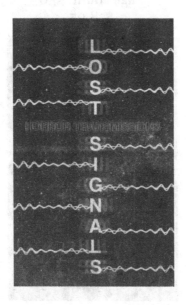

What's that sound? Do you feel it? The signals are already inside you. You never even had a chance. A tome of horror fiction featuring radio waves, numbers stations, rogue transmissions, and other unimaginable sounds you only wish were fiction. Forget about what's hiding in the shadows, and start worrying about what's hiding in the dead air.

With stories by Matthew M. Bartlett, T.E. Grau, Joseph Bouthiette Jr., Josh Malerman, David James Keaton, Tony Burgess, Michael Paul Gonzalez, George Cotronis, Betty Rocksteady, Christopher Slatsky, Amanda Hard, Gabino Iglesias, Dyer Wilk, Ashlee Scheuerman, Matt Andrew, H.F. Arnold, John C. Foster, Vince Darcangelo, Regina Solomond, Joshua Chaplinsky, Damien Angelica Walters, Paul Michael Anderson, and James Newman. Also includes an introduction from World Fantasy-award-winning author, Scott Nicolay.

LOST FILMS
EDITED BY MAX BOOTH III AND LORI MICHELLE

ISBN: 978-1-943720-29-3
Page count: 350
$18.95

From the editors of *Lost Signals* comes the new volume in technological horror. Nineteen authors, both respected and new to the genre, team up to deliver a collection of terrifying, eclectic stories guaranteed to unsettle its readers. In *Lost Films*, a deranged group of lunatics hold an annual film festival, the lost series finale of The Simpsons corrupts a young boy's sanity, and a VCR threatens to destroy reality. All of that and much more, with fiction from Brian Evenson, Gemma Files, Kelby Losack, Bob Pastorella, Brian Asman, Leigh Harlen, Dustin Katz, Andrew Novak, Betty Rocksteady, John C. Foster, Ashlee Scheuerman, Eugenia M. Triantafyllou, Kev Harrison, Thomas Joyce, Jessica McHugh, Kristi DeMeester, Izzy Lee, Chad Stroup, and David James Keaton.

TALES FROM THE CRUST
EDITED BY DAVID JAMES KEATON
AND MAX BOOTH III

ISBN: 978-1-943720-37-8
Page count: 346
$18.95

The toppings: Terror and torment.

The crust: Stuffed with dread and despair.

And the sauce: Well, the sauce is always red.

Whether you're in the mood for a Chicago-style deep dish of darkness, or prefer a New York wide slice of thin-crusted carnage, or if you just have a hankering for the cheap, cheesy charms of cardboard-crusted, delivered-to-your-door devilry; we have just the slice for you.

Bring your most monstrous of appetites, because we're serving suspense and horrors both chillingly cosmic and morbidly mundane from acclaimed horror authors such as Brian Evenson, Jessica McHugh, and Cody Goodfellow, as well as up-and-coming literary threats like Craig Wallwork, Sheri White, and Tony McMillen.

Tales From the Crust, stories you can devour in thirty minutes or less or the next one's free. Whatever that means.

The Perpetual Motion Machine Catalog

Antioch | Jessica Leonard | Novel

Baby Powder and Other Terrifying Substances | John C. Foster | Story Collection

Bone Saw | Patrick Lacey | Novel

Born in Blood Vols. 1 & 2 | George Daniel Lea | Story Collections

Crabtown, USA:Essays & Observations | Rafael Alvarez | Essays

Dead Men | John Foster | Novel

The Detained | Kristopher Triana | Novella

Eight Eyes that See You Die | W.P. Johnson | Story Collection

The Flying None | Cody Goodfellow | Novella

The Girl in the Video | Michael David Wilson | Novella

Gods on the Lam | Christopher David Rosales | Novel

The Green Kangaroos | Jessica McHugh | Novel

Invasion of the Weirdos | Andrew Hilbert | Novel

Jurassichrist | Michael Allen Rose | Novella

Last Dance in Phoenix | Kurt Reichenbaugh | Novel

Like Jagged Teeth | Betty Rocksteady | Novella

Live On No Evil | Jeremiah Israel | Novel

Lost Films | Various Authors | Anthology

Lost Signals | Various Authors | Anthology

Mojo Rising | Bob Pastorella | Novella

Night Roads | John Foster | Novel

The Nightly Disease | Max Booth III | Novel

Quizzleboon | John Oliver Hodges | Novel

The Ruin Season | Kristopher Triana | Novel

Scanlines | Todd Keisling | Novella

She Was Found in a Guitar Case | David James Keaton | Novel

Standalone | Paul Michael Anderson | Novella

Stealing Propeller Hats from the Dead | David James Keaton | Story Collection

Tales from the Holy Land | Rafael Alvarez | Story Collection

Patreon:
www.patreon.com/pmmpublishing

Website:
www.PerpetualPublishing.com

Facebook:
www.facebook.com/PerpetualPublishing

Twitter:
@PMMPublishing

Newsletter:
www.PMMPNews.com

Email Us:
Contact@PerpetualPublishing.com

9 781943 720644